Tina Biswas was born in 1978 and read Politics, Philosophy and Economics at New College, Oxford. She lives in London.

Dancing with the Two-Headed Tigress

Tina Biswas

BLACK SWAN

DANCING WITH THE TWO-HEADED TIGRESS
A BLACK SWAN BOOK : 9780552773232

Originally published in Great Britain by Doubleday,
a division of Transworld Publishers

PRINTING HISTORY
Doubleday edition published 2006
Black Swan edition published 2007

3 5 7 9 10 8 6 4 2

Copyright © Tina Biswas 2006

The right of Tina Biswas to be identified as the author of
this work has been asserted in accordance with sections 77
and 78 of the Copyright Designs and Patents Act 1988.

Set in 11/15pt Melior by
Falcon Oast Graphic Art Ltd.

Black Swan Books are published by Transworld Publishers,
61–63 Uxbridge Road, London W5 5SA,
a division of The Random House Group Ltd.

Addresses for Random House Group Ltd companies outside the
UK can be found at: www.randomhouse.co.uk
The Random House Group Ltd Reg. No. 954009.

Printed and bound in Great Britain by
Cox & Wyman Ltd, Reading, Berkshire.

The Random House Group Limited makes every effort to ensure
that the papers used in its books are made from trees that have
been legally sourced from well-managed and credibly certified
forests. Our paper procurement policy can be found at:
www.randomhouse.co.uk/paper.htm.

Dedicated to my mother, whose faith in me is unswerving and unending, even when I don't deserve it.

'I was about half in love with her by the time we sat down. That's the thing about girls. Every time they do something pretty . . . you fall half in love with them, and then you never know where the hell you are.'

Catcher in the Rye, J D Salinger

CHAPTER ONE

The Majumdars

Darshini Majumdar was running late again. She scanned the platform and wondered whether she should go backwards to go forwards. She walked down the stairs, but before she had to make a decision about which train to take, the lop-sided crowd parted like the Red Sea, allowing her to board before her turn. She was on her way to meet Tuhina, her mother, for breakfast in the City. Tuhina left the house at seven and drove into work, but Darshini was not one for unnecessarily early starts. She sat down – even on the packed eight-thirty commuter Tube there was a seat with her name written on it – and took a deep breath. The sweet stench of a London summer morning filled her nose: early sweat, shower-gel, sunscreen, smokers' breath. She enjoyed travelling by Tube, mechanical moles making their way in the dark; there was something life-affirming about it. And it was a good opportunity to people-watch.

Opposite Darshini sat a middle-aged Indian woman in a sari, a rare sight at this time of day. Her belly hung over the obscenely embroidered material, and her chalky face, with raccoon rings around the eyes, was punctuated by a feathery moustache. As the woman got off at Stockwell, Darshini caught sight of her rear – a tyred back and an oily bun – and her mouth involuntarily turned down with distaste. She wondered whether she would succumb to the same fate. If she turned out like her mother, she thought, then no. But deciding not to take any chances, she pulled out a small mirror and a pair of tweezers from her pencil case. She believed that one should never rest on one's beauty laurels, and started to pluck daintily at the invisible hairs under her perfectly arched eyebrows. She considered it a good investment of time to indulge in some 'plucking-fucking', as her mother had once amusingly and inadvertently called it. Eyebrows frame the face, she had read somewhere. And what a face it was.

A perfect fragile heart, with wide, wide hazel-brown eyes, a small straight nose with nostrils that flared elegantly when angry, and a Cupid's bow of a mouth, her beauty brought wistful stares from both boys and girls, but also despair to her father, Prakash, whose part-time job it was to ward off phone calls from prospective suitors. It wasn't an easy task: that level of pulchritude brings with it persistence. Darshini knew deep down her father would have been happier with a son.

Putting her tweezers back inside her pencil case, Darshini quickly checked her watch – her mother disliked tardiness – then applied some lip balm with the tip of her little finger. Tilting her face upward, she coolly assessed her image and, pleased with what she saw, placed her cosmetic condiments back in her bag and zipped it shut. The man sitting opposite gazed at her appreciatively but Darshini didn't notice.

Walking to the café where she was to meet her mother, Darshini glanced at her watch again, and although she was in good time, she quickened her pace. By the time she arrived, her mother was already seated at a table on the pavement, scanning the menu. She was wearing sunglasses and most of her face was concealed by the menu, but Darshini spotted her straight away by the way she had her legs crossed, her elegantly pointed foot tapping rhythmically, slightly impatient.

Darshini sat down and looked round for a waiter to fetch a menu. Before she could find one, Tuhina took her sunglasses off, handed her menu to Darshini and said with a broad smile, 'Here – I've already decided.'

As Darshini pondered whether to have her eggs poached or scrambled, a handsome young man, fairish and freckled, approached them, and without so much as a glance at Darshini greeted Tuhina with a smooth and confident wave.

'So, I thought the meeting went well, don't you?' he asked. Now his eyes flickered towards Darshini, who was playing with her fingernails.

'Yes, I think so,' said Tuhina slowly, crossing her arms and leaning back in her chair. The young man's eyes were now fixed on Darshini, but still she didn't look up.

'I'm just getting a coffee,' he continued eagerly, awkwardly. 'Need the caffeine after such an early start!'

'Good,' Tuhina retorted, amused.

Seph shifted his weight, and looked at Darshini again. Tuhina sucked in her cheeks to stop herself from laughing. Then, unfolding her arms, she leaned forward and coughed loudly. Darshini looked up at her mother and raised her eyebrows quizzically.

'Darshini,' said Tuhina slowly, 'this is my colleague Seph, and Seph,' she continued, turning her body to face him, 'this is my daughter Darshini.'

Seph immediately puffed out his chest, took his hands out of his pockets and adjusted his tie, then put his hand out to greet her.

'Hi!' he said with enthusiasm.

'Hi,' she said without, giving his hand a quick, perfunctory shake.

'Well, I'll see you at the office,' Tuhina said to Seph firmly.

As Seph walked away, he remembered that he hadn't bought himself a coffee. Looking behind him to check that Tuhina wasn't watching, he furtively brought his hand up to his face as if to stifle a yawn, and inhaled deeply. Where Darshini's wrist had rubbed against his fingertips, he could smell the heady scent of tuberose. For the rest of the day, he didn't wash his hands.

The first time Seph had seen the photograph of Darshini on his manager Tuhina's office wall he had been immediately mesmerized. The photo had been taken when Darshini was three and a half years old, in her mother's arms on the beach, wearing a red gingham-checked swimsuit with a double frill around the hips. Mother and daughter were gazing into each other's eyes. It was the first thing everyone looked at when they walked into Tuhina's room. The rest of her office was bare, functional; on her desk was an in-tray, an out-tray, a pot containing 3 biros – blue, black and red, a fountain pen for signing important documents, a highlighter and a ruler (Tuhina didn't like wobbly lines). Her briefcase was kept out of sight under the desk. In the corner was a small flipchart on a stand; the paper was always free of scribbling.

At work, Tuhina was well liked; actually, not so much well liked as well respected. And that was the way she wanted it. She wanted people to notice her work and not her. Her uniform consisted of a plain dark suit, with a neutral shirt, a pair of dark shoes with a medium heel (stilettos were too queen bitch, she had concluded, wear flats and you were a walkover), pearls, and natural make-up which played up her beauty without drawing attention to it. Elegant, of course, but nothing to comment on. She didn't say more than was necessary, apart from the obvious courtesies – 'hello', 'goodbye', 'please' and 'thank you', but she always made herself very clear. Not that she was a party-pooper. She attended all social events, drank enough but not too much, and was witty and amusing without ever over-stepping the mark. Once, at her department's Christmas party a couple of years into her career, one of the vice presidents had grabbed Tuhina's bottom. Not a mistaken brush of the palm, not even a light tentative squeeze, but a full-fat grasp. Everyone saw, and an uneasy atmosphere prevailed as they wondered what she was going to do. She simply smiled, not a sexy smile or a coy smile, but an unreadable smile, and said 'Excuse me.' What she did not do was slap him around the face and throw her drink at him (which most people there thought she was entitled to do). Nor did she run to the loos and cry about it. And she most certainly did not stand next to the coffee machine on Monday morning and tell all the girls how she'd been harassed, and what a sad wanker he was, who probably wasn't getting any at home. In fact, she never mentioned it. That was the kind of woman she was. Which meant that the other women, despite using words such as 'great' and 'brilliant' to describe her, never went to her with boyfriend problems or asked to borrow her lipstick. Tuhina simply wasn't frivolous enough to have a wine spritzer with at lunch. She didn't even keep any hand-cream or a surreptitious nail-file in the top drawer of her desk, underneath the paperclips. Her secretary, Penelope, who was still a girl even though she was thirty-eight, called her 'Mrs Majumdar', even though Tuhina hadn't asked to be addressed that way.

Seph felt he belonged in that photograph. Every day, for three years, he had looked at it and constructed a personality around the image. He thought that she would stand with her hands on her hips when arguing. He thought that she would pay special attention to drying in between her toes. He thought that she would always be running late. Now he had to find out for sure.

* * *

At home, Prakash wondered where Darshini was. He had made her a bacon sandwich and taken it to her room, but there was no sign of her. He sat down on her bed, placing the plate beside him, and looked around. There was a photo of Darshini and her mother on her bedside table. There wasn't one of Darshini and him. He had always bristled slightly at this. On the shelf above her books was an assortment of candles, in various stages of burn-out. He had told her that she shouldn't light candles in her room, especially near paper, but she had taken no notice. He half hoped that a fire *did* start, just so he could be proved right, and then felt guilty for even thinking this. Chomping on the sandwich, he looked at Darshini's desk. There were ticket stubs and programmes from concerts, the theatre, the cinema. She never asked his permission to go to any of these, she always asked her mother. He didn't understand why – he would have said 'yes', too.

Nor did he have any influence over his wife. It had become a source of embarrassment, especially in front of those friends who had gone out of their way to marry white women, and had still retained more control over their spouses than he had. Tuhina also had a fancier, better-paid job than him; as an investment banker, she made his earnings look like pocket-money. Oh, the shame of it, the shame! But

16

he was living in England now, and had to believe in equality between men and women, so he kept his mouth shut and thought only to himself: 'What exactly is equal about my wife earning four times as much as me? You tell me, what!'

And that wasn't the end of it: not only were they too much for him on an individual basis, but as a single entity, motheranddaughter, they were terrifying. He felt that they did nothing more than humour him; he might be King of the Castle, but only because they allowed him to be. Often, when sitting opposite them at the dinner table, he imagined himself as a shabby lion facing a sleek two-headed tigress. And it made him deeply insecure. Although he was confident that his wife was faithful, and his daughter was devoted and loving, he always felt as though some divine joker had played an elaborate trick on him. One day he would wake up with a homely wife who could only speak broken English, and a dim-witted daughter with a lazy eye. Yet he always found his nightmare strangely calming; the struggle was over.

His own mother, Arundhuti, had been a bit of a go-getter, and his father had coped admirably, so, he wondered, why couldn't he? He had read a little psychology as a medical student, which had given him enough self-awareness to examine himself, but not enough to develop any kind of understanding.

Too much inner monologue, not enough action, he thought to himself: his whole damned life story in one clichéd sentence.

To comfort himself, he fantasized about moving back to India, where he considered life to be simpler, less complicated. And then he thought of all the grand holidays he had taken in foreign climes (he always picked hot, sunny, languid countries where the people were brown and impressed by his money and the fact that he was a doctor, although he would of course never admit to this). He preferred to be a big fish in a small pond.

His favourite time for fantasizing was while he was commuting. Despite being within walking distance of his surgery, he always took his car, and what should have been a fifteen-minute trip became a traffic-soaked forty-five. But it was his car and his space, and, unlike the streets, he didn't have to share it with thousands of others. Where in Calcutta he had been happy to pack himself on to an over-crowded bus and feel the warmth and sweat of other bodies, in London he would put on his cassette of Rabindra Sangeet and sing along with feeling and heart, dreaming about leaving the greyness for good. If he had looked out of his window (although this may have constituted dangerous driving), he would have seen the Nigerian women in batik-printed gowns, the Bangladeshi men with well-engineered moustaches, the Australian students wearing baggy shorts. But Prakash had forgotten how to look.

As though to highlight more rudely the differences between father and daughter, Darshini loved London and London loved her right back. It welcomed the exotic beauty into its smoky arms and kissed her full on the mouth with its neon lips.

From an early age, Darshini had bypassed all the usual trials and tribulations that mark a person's life, from petty toddler squabbles over toys to early teenage crushes on the wrong boy. She had managed to live in close enough proximity of such events to have experience of them, but always as a spectator rather than a participant.

When she was about ten, she imagined she might have been given a vaccine that made her immune to suffering. Not that she never fell over and scraped her knee, or never felt the palm of her father's hand when she had misbehaved – she wasn't immune to that kind of pain – but she never felt the hurt which colours and restricts our future thoughts and actions. This immunity made her neither smug nor conceited, it just put a 'so?' on the end of all her sentences. Not a moody teenager's 'so', but a light, airy 'so' which implied that anything could happen and life was full of possibilities. Experience did not cling to her like damp clothing waiting to be peeled off; she came to everything with fresh eyes. Which is a blessing and a curse.

Her attitude towards life was as carefree as her attitude to death. Every morning as Darshini boarded the Tube for school, she contemplated exactly how easy it would be to cross the yellow line that divided safety and danger, and place herself on the train track. Not be pushed or accidentally fall, but just happen to take that one extra step. Just one more click of a size five stiletto. And every time she crossed a road, she thought about how it would only take the slightest of misjudgements to end up on the bonnet of a black taxi, its cabbie for once silenced. The randomness of life pleased her; she often threw a coin to make decisions: heads – do it, tails – don't. This way, she could take the decision entirely out of her own hands – if that car turns left, I'll go out tonight, if it turns right, I won't. Everything does *not* happen for a reason, some things just happen. And that's that.

Something that had recently happened to Darshini was a boyfriend – Seph. He was her first one. First serious one. Although, in such matters, first nearly always equals serious, at least at the time. Prakash had claimed he was unable to attend one of Tuhina's work functions on the premise that he needed to watch the cricket highlights, although in truth it was because he found such events rather over-whelming, full of peacock-men displaying their designer feathers. So Darshini had been asked instead. Nor was Tuhina too upset about having to take her daughter. She enjoyed showing off such a beautiful possession to her colleagues; she felt it added to her status.

The aim of the function was to encourage the staff to reacquaint themselves with each other; the human resources department believed that in the age of faceless and voiceless email, the benefits of personal contact, however vague they might be, were being lost. And by inviting employees 'and guest', they were breaking down the walls between work life and home life; it was important to keep people happy – it encouraged them to work harder. So by running to a budget of twenty-five pounds per head – two and a half glasses of cava, eight bite-size savoury and two dessert canapés each – the company showed how much it cared for its staff.

Darshini didn't like cava. She looked around for the waiter with the glasses of orange juice. And whilst she was looking around, she found herself, as usual, being looked at, in much the same way as a painting or sculpture; a thing to be admired but also to be coveted. Several of her mother's colleagues who shouldn't have been looking at her in *that* way were looking at her in *precisely* that way. Not that they were to blame. There is a certain type of beauty that implies sexual precociousness.

The interested man, Seph (christened Joseph) O'Shea had been wondering anxiously when he would see her again. Now he smelled her for the second time. She had walked past, leaving him in her Queen-of-the-Night-scented wake, and he felt his mouth salivate, as if he had smelled his mother's cooking – pork chops marinated in cider with baked parsnips. He turned around and saw her standing next to Tuhina, her hand tightly wrapped around the crook of her mother's elbow. He watched her all evening but spoke not one word, even when he was reintroduced. He thought she already knew. Even so, at the end of the night he stood behind her, and very carefully, like a put-pocket, slipped a piece of paper into her coat.

The next morning, Darshini emptied out her pockets, which she did every morning, and threw the piece of paper in the bin. She thought it was a receipt, and she never read or saved them. So she turned down his first invitation without even knowing it.

Seph was used to asking and being given. So a week later, he asked a girl in the Human Resources department, who was unusually willing to do him favours, if she could perhaps pass on Tuhina's contact details. She didn't know why, and she didn't have enough inquisitiveness to ask. She wrote down the home phone number on a Post-it, which she had rubbed her perfumed wrist against. She was rewarded with a tall latte and a banana and date muffin in the local coffee shop, with its whistling espresso machines and wobbly custard pastries. He knew it would be enough.

It was a sticky evening, much more languorous than it should have been for spring; the pungent odour of the river drifted into the City and stuck to the heavy air. Scallop-edged crimson clouds nestled around the dome of St Paul's. Seph walked solemnly through the streets, deep in thought, trying to formulate what he was going to say. The well-trodden path of alleyways and cobble-stoned courtyards offered him no answer. The fumes from the passing cars did not choke him with inspiration. Once home, he stood in front of his bathroom mirror and looked at himself intensely. His symmetrical features distorted into a face that didn't belong to him. Perhaps it was the face of his father, whom he had never known. Then he thought of Darshini's face and went to pick up his phone. After three rings, he heard a 'hello', then another, then a 'hell-ow-oo'. It was the same kind of hello Tuhina used when a colleague had missed an obvious point. He hung up.

Seph considered himself neither religious nor

superstitious. He made a point of not going to church, even for Midnight Mass back at home on Christmas Eve, when his mother wept and pleaded with him to attend. He would sit at home and watch TV on Channel Four, and try to ignore the red candles, decorated with holly, on the window sill, reflecting their light on to the screen. And the next afternoon, when his pseudo-family, made up of an assortment of neighbours and hobos his mother had picked up at the pub, were all sitting around the dining table, heads bowed whilst saying Grace, he would sit bolt upright and remain silent. But he still left a slice of plum pudding and a glass of whisky out for Father Christmas.

After the phone call that night, he took out of a shoe box, kept on the top shelf of his wardrobe, a gold locket engraved with an image of Saint Joseph, the patron saint of families, and put it under his pillow. It had been blessed by the local priest, Father Thomas, and his mother had asked him to wear it around his neck. He had refused.

'I won't wear it,' he had said.

'Why not?'

'Because I don't believe in God.'

'Don't say that; you don't mean it.'

'I do, too!'

'Well, wear it for *me*, then.'

'Why?'

'Because it will make me happy.' Ciara had paused. 'Do it for your mother. Please, son.'

A sulk, but no response. So she went on, 'I've had it blessed by Father. It'll protect you.'

'It's just a piece of metal,' Seph had retorted, but he took the locket reluctantly anyway, and put it on. Ciara had smiled at him, pleased and satisfied, but Seph had not smiled back.

Before he had gone to bed that night, he had looked in the mirror at the gold around his neck, winking with ridicule. He had half-heartedly tugged on the chain a few times, willing it to break, but it held on tight to his neck. The very day he left home, he removed it.

But now, he slept with the charm under his pillow for a week. And then he tried again.

Darshini often picked up the phone directory and at random pulled out a number to call. Her longest call so far had been about twenty minutes, which she considered quite an achievement; whose, she wasn't sure. She had just been talking to a Mrs Misra, who was miserable because her children no longer visited her. She had tried to keep Darshini on the line for as long as possible, grateful to hear another human voice. One of her daughters, she told her, had become a punk, cutting off her lustrous raven hair and transforming it into a pink Mohican. The other was such a 'high-fly' that she no longer had time to call home. Her husband had run off with another woman, possibly white, possibly black – which, she didn't confirm – but definitely not brown.

By the woman's tone of voice, a whimpering, nasal whine, Darshini was not surprised by any of this. She made her excuses and put the phone down mid-flow. She jotted down her findings in her A4 scrapbook, page thirty-six. Each page had a name, a telephone number, an address, the length of the con-versation, a summary, and various doodles and other miscellaneous items – an American dollar bill for the Government Issue Tom, who stayed in England after marrying Mary, who had worked at the local munitions factory in the East End; a news-paper clipping of a review of a restaurant that was owned by Mrs Angelucci's darling son, Angelo; a piece of gold thread for Zamina, who had been married wearing the most beautiful red dress em-bellished with golden yarn, and now sat at home every day, waiting for her drunken husband to return.

Darshini was scribbling a picture of a face with zigzag hair when the phone rang. She listened with interest, then took a coin out of the top drawer of the bureau and flipped it. Her belly flipped with it. She replied to the question, and then went up to her bedroom, pulled out a new scrapbook, and stuck the ten-pence piece to the first page.

* * *

Saint Joseph had served Seph well – precisely a week and two hours later, he was sitting across from both a curious three-and-a-half-year-old and the most striking and mysterious girl he had ever met, in a suitably fashionable and expensive restaurant in the City. They sat on the terrace for cocktails; he hoped she was impressed by the view. The sommelier greeted him by name; she didn't seem to notice. He picked a bottle of 1996 Puligny-Montrachet from Domaine Leflaive; she toyed with her glass. He pre-ordered chocolate soufflés which weren't on the carte; she didn't look up from her menu.

He was chasing after a ragwort parachute sailing in the wind on a fresh summer's day. It was invigorating. He imagined flying kites with her. He felt strangely paternal, although not enough to keep him from wondering a) how long it would take for her to sleep with him, and b) would she marry him.

For the former: one month. As far as Darshini was concerned, it was entirely whimsical. It could have been three days, two weeks, a year; she had heard a song on the radio with the phrase 'one month' in it, and so the decision was made.

About a week before the one-month deadline, Darshini made a list of all the things she especially liked about Seph. The way he cocked his head to the side and said with an Irish lilt, 'What's the craic?' even though she didn't know what the craic was. How he knitted his fingers together and frowned when he was concentrating on what she was saying. The sly long-eyelashed wink to let her know how sexy she was looking. And then she made a note of the parts of him that she particularly appreciated. The freckles on his nose, the soft skin of his eyelids, the smooth muscular shoulders, the lean torso with its geometric pattern, the muscular quadriceps which made a graceful arch to his narrow hips, the slight stubble that glinted gold in the light, behind his ears – the part that smelled the most of him – where she liked to press her face . . . she particularly appreciated *everything* and made a note to herself that she should show her pleasure by kissing everything she appreciated particularly.

At first, he was bemused. A girl had never kissed his thighs (all the way from the knee to the hip) before. But soon bemusement gave way to a rather more luscious feeling, and he relaxed. Everywhere she kissed felt as though a butterfly had landed there. When she finally stopped, he opened his eyes, and looked down at his body. It was covered in lipstick marks; a deep maroon at his knees where she had started, fading to a light pink near his shoulders where she had finished. He looked at the heart-shaped marks covering his skin and felt both vulnerable and powerful.

Afterwards, he lay wrapped around her like a lazy boa constrictor. He didn't notice, until after she'd left, the patch of blood shining from his white sheet. And he felt vulnerable and powerful again.

On the way home, sitting on a Saturday Tube crowded with shoppers (Seph had offered to drive her, but she had declined), still clothed in an emerald backless dress and golden sandals, and looking like an Abyssinian lovebird in a cage full of sparrows, Darshini felt something too, deep in the recesses of her belly, but she didn't know what it was.

Tuhina didn't need to see the sheet to know what had happened. She didn't even need to see the Mona Lisa smile on Darshini's face. And she didn't need to ask who the co-conspirator was. She just knew. It was a special and sometimes unwanted talent of hers, knowing what had happened without being told. When another bank won a deal her team had been pitching for, she knew; no letter needed. When Bodthmaish the cat had been run over in a road accident, she knew; no identification of the furry body needed. When she fell pregnant with Darshini, she knew; no test needed. And when her mother left her father, she knew, even before a stoic but sobbing Ma came into her room to gather up Tuhina and her belongings.

*　*　*

Tuhina's mother, Joya, had left her husband Vimal and her son Sachi when Tuhina was four years old. Husband had said to wife, 'You can take the girl, but you're not taking my son!' Good, Joya had thought, *good*; I don't want Sachi, who's lazy and slow and ambitionless and clumsy. I want only *my* beautiful Tuhina. Tuhina, although five years younger than Sachi, had known, as soon as she had slipped through her mother's legs, in the golden age of filmi, that she had a good-for-nothing brother. And as she came to be familiar with him, this was only confirmed. He never let her play with his luridly coloured plastic dog-on-wheels which he pulled along with a scabby rope, never read to her from his copy of Sukumar Ray's *Shomogro Shishu Shaitya*; never let her listen to the forty-five of Hemanta Kumar's 'Kachhé Rabé, Kachhé Rabé' on the old wind-up gramophone, never heard anything she had to say, all because she was a girl and therefore beneath consideration.

Joya's mother-in-law, Ushma, had felt the same about Tuhina. The first time Ushma went to visit her, Tuhina, lying on her back in her wooden cot and following the blades of the ceiling fan as it hummed, had felt her mother's unease. Joya's stomach had held a bubble of worry instead of a baby.

Ever since Joya had insisted that she would not live with her in-laws, but set up her own house with her husband, Ushma had turned against her. But Ushma's anger was a silent one, which could not be confronted; its fire burned without wood or air. For Joya's husband Vimal, the choice had been between wife and mother. And since the birth of his son, he had become even more of a carcass of a husband. He behaved as if Joya was the cat and he was the cream. His mother Ushma had revelled in Vimal's dismissal of his wife. She felt vindicated. So when she heard of Tuhina's birth, her face curdled: another bad seed had been planted.

Tuhina had been well aware of her grandmother's animosity towards her. When Ushma bent over the cot and dutifully squeezed Tuhina's chin between turmeric-stained thumb and forefinger, the white fingerprint impressions she left on her jaw were marks of loathing. But when Ushma squeezed her grandson Sachi's chin, the marks glowed with adoration.

On top of that, Ushma had refused to eat in Joya's house on account of some vague stomach problem, the cause of which was purposefully unspecified. She had sat down on the daybed, whilst both son and grandson begged her to eat, carefully eyeing up the tempting food and poignantly refusing it. The plump raisins in the mung dhal sank with defeat.

Joya hadn't eaten either. Tuhina had felt her mother's hunger all night.

So, by the age of four, Tuhina was more than pleased to be starting a new life without her brother Sachi. Although her clairvoyant talent still meant that his colourless life story was unavoidable for her; despite the distance and lack of contact, it was as though she still lived in the same house as him. She knew when he received his first (and last) job offer; no telegram needed. She knew when he was getting married; no wedding invitation required. And she knew when he died.

CHAPTER TWO

The Sharmas

Mousumi Sharma sat cross-legged on the sofa, an empty bowl, which had minutes ago been filled to the brim with channa dhal, balanced precariously in the triangular space created by her fleshy thighs. She grimaced as she watched a programme about wannabe singing stars, patted her fulsome chest and gave a little theatrical cough. I, she thought, can sing better than any of those screechers. Pulling one of her pigtail plaits, which her mother Rekha had tied extra tight that morning, over her shoulder, she squeezed off the brown elastic band and separated the wound hair into waves. Now she looked as good, if not better, than that girl on the screen who was screaming Lata Mungeshkar's 'Terabina' into her hand-held microphone.

Turning down the sound on the TV, she cocked

her head towards the kitchen, and heard her mother zealously frying the spices, which spat oil back at her in protest. Satisfied, she turned the TV up to a much higher volume, and tiptoed to the bedroom. Standing in front of the mirror, she shook her shoulders and arms, as if she were an athlete limbering up for a race, and then she stepped back, lifted the hairbrush from the dressing table, and held it to her wide-open lips.

But just as she was about to sing the first note, she heard the door slam, and seconds later her father Sachi shout, 'Why the damn television is on so loud? And where are my slippers?'

Mousumi panicked and dropped the hairbrush. She fell to her knees and looked under the bed for her father's slippers. Somehow they had been pushed to the middle – she could not reach them without crawling further under the frame. Lying flat on her stomach, she wiggled her way under the bed, her flesh being squashed one way, then the other. Stretching out for the slippers, her hair became entangled in the springs. Slowly, she tried to move her hand towards her head to free herself, but there wasn't enough room to manoeuvre. Anxious that her father was still waiting, her face became hotter and hotter. To release her locks, she jerked her head downward with some force, ripping her hair from her head. Tears came to her eyes. Shuffling backwards, she straightened herself up, quickly wiped her eyes with the back of her free hand, and walked into the hallway, where her father was still standing, his arms crossed, tapping his foot like a conductor's baton.

'Why it took you so long?' he asked. 'Getting lazy in your old age?'

Mousumi dared not answer back. Instead she kneeled by his feet, and carefully placed them in the slippers. As she was doing so, Sachi pulled at her broken, fluffy hair, and said dismissively, 'And what you call this? You call this fashion?'

Mousumi wanted to scream.

Sachi didn't beat his wife often. And besides, it wasn't so much a beating as a disciplining. It was out of love and a desire for her to see the wrong of her ways. Sometimes she didn't grind the mustard seeds finely enough when cooking his hilsa fish, or she didn't scrub the collars of his shirts with enough gusto. Although it wasn't really this which angered him. More, it was her refusal to accept that she had done anything wrong. Wrong! There was always a moral element to his criticism. She hadn't simply failed to perform a job to his standards, she had failed as a wife, and in so doing not only let him down, but also herself. The beatings would redeem her. But they were not frequent and barely left a mark. They had become a ritual of life, and there was little to be gained by dwelling on such a subject. And besides, they were happy.

Sachi worked as a medical representative for a big pharmaceutical company. He was therefore never short of a supply of shiny new pens, which he delighted in handing out to poorer relatives and friends, especially children. He would open his briefcase, with the combination lock, and from among the samples of headache tablets and medicines for indigestion he pulled the pens, each sponsored by some new cure for an old malaise. The highest-ranked pens were the ones for clinical depression with their yellow smiley face on the pocket clip; the least popular were for piles, with red lettering and go-faster stripes. Which pen they received was entirely the luck of the draw. Uncle Sachi would hand over the pen to the child with a big smile and, just before letting go, would say, 'An aid to your education.' Then he would reluctantly accept a cup of tea – No, no, don't go to any trouble for old Uncle Sachi – while gazing over his beneficiaries and putting at his dirty black tobacco cigarettes, which made the children cough and splutter and run to their mother.

Sometimes, if he visited his extended family later in the evening, he swapped his tea for a glass or three of whisky. He imagined himself quite the gentleman as he reclined on a bed, propping himself up on one elbow whilst gulping his drink. He was a Western Man, dressed in a polo shirt tucked into chinos, with his shiny new pens attached to his shirt pocket. His calloused feet, gnarled by years of wearing sandals, dangled off the end of the bed. Years of no exercise had created a barrel shape, with his polo shirt straining at the seams. After a drink and a smoke, he heaved himself into a sitting position, shuffled his heat-swollen feet into his dusty outdoor slippers, and bade his farewell. On occasion, just as he was about to leave, he would press a few hundred-rupee notes into the hand of his brother or one of his in-laws, and when they demurred, he would wave aside their protests with one hand and gaze skyward with a small smile. He rather enjoyed dispensing advice and money, and his worse-off kin, realizing this, invented imaginary problems from leaky taps to unruly children in order to give him a chance to preside over their woes. On finding a solution, he would nod sagely and then hand over the money. And, as if by magic, the leaky taps and unruly children began to behave, and Sachi could bask in the glow of his advice, which only served to make him even more generous.

On his return journey, he often stopped to eat a mishti paan – he had a sweet tooth which he indulged at any opportunity – and in the taxi on the way home (which he took to avoid getting out of breath) he would spit the betel juice out through the window on to the dirty Calcuttan roads.

When he arrived home, Mousumi would lay the table and watch him sipping whisky from the corner of her eye. Sachi earned enough money to eat goat every three days, king prawns once a week (always a Saturday), and basmati rice not just on special occasions. On Fridays, he sat after dinner, inhaling from a filthy cigarette, with his huge belly full of whisky, rich spicy goat, basmati rice, laddoos, whisky, rice pudding and whisky. He would have liked to have listened to music, but since he had stopped Mousumi's sitar lessons on the pretence that he didn't like music, he had to relax by watching the news.

In truth, when Mousumi had shown more talent for music than was strictly necessary, and even that wasn't much, her father had quickly put a stop to the lessons. No daughter of his was going to be a musician. He wanted his daughter to do well, but not *too* well. No singing, and certainly no dancing. Not too much academic work lest it lessen her feminine appeal. Men did not like to marry women more intelligent than themselves. 'Not just a pretty face' was not a compliment. A friend had once used that phrase about Mousumi in a disapproving voice, and he had learned. He had to make sure that his friends knew he was no soft touch with his family, and he duly informed them of the cancelled lessons. Mousumi's one and only string had been taken from her bow. She felt bereft. So instead of singing, she watched other people sing on the television, and ate. Sa, Re, Ga, Ma, Pa, Dha, Ni, Sa was replaced by the spicy crunch of Bombay Mix and the graceful slide of salty lassi.

At work, Sachi was well respected; actually, not so much well respected as well liked. His lack of real ambition, and tendency to expound his theories on a wide range of subjects, from nuclear weapons to single malts, of which he knew little, meant that his promotion had been limited to one upward move to District Manager early on in his career. His complacency meant that District Manager remained a source of pride, and the pinnacle of his achievements at work. Neither was he particularly conscientious. Since 1974, he had refused to keep himself up to date with advances in medical science, believing it to be static. Any new product formulated by his employer he regarded not with interest but self-satisfaction: the company could easily fool those doctors, but he knew it was just new packaging. That is, if he ever bothered to read the packaging. On one now famous occasion, he had inadvertently handed over a tube of toothpaste rather than haemorrhoid cream. Dr Chilka's patients' bottoms never felt quite so fresh and tingly again. But this attitude became a chronic ailment: his lack of observation meant that he failed to pick up the signs that his own body was giving him.

Even as a child, Sachi had failed to inspire in people the tenderness and affection normally shown to the young, if only because of their miniature scale and presumed innocence. Not that he was disliked; he just wasn't cute. Or sweet, as a mother might say as she pinched his chubby cheeks. He was a part-time bully; mean to those weaker than him and unable to defend themselves, but obsequious to those whom he considered to be better than him. When he made the school football team, he carried the captain's kit to the changing room and cleaned his boots, but refused to make one pass to the boy he thought shouldn't have been picked in the first place. He didn't want to improve his position, he just wanted to keep it. The pecking order provided him with stability, and fitted in with his idea that everyone has their own immovable place in the world. Nothing disturbed or infuriated him more than someone with ideas above their station. How dare they change his place in the line-up!

Like his belly, his mind was solid and didn't wander – Sachi was not one for existential angst.

Although over-analysis is tedious and without benefit, the ability to question ourselves is also what separates us from animals, but Sachi had neither the inclination nor the capacity. He never asked himself whether he was a good father or a good husband, or even if he was a good employee – even the fact that he rarely received a pay rise above the inflationary increase didn't spur him on to ask this question. He just assumed he *was* – he was the defendant, the judge and the jury. What was more important for him was to seem than to be. Impression quashed Intent under Its hollow foot. Everyone's actions were judged on how they reflected upon him. Even his family's; no, *especially* his family's.

Sachi's wife was only that: his wife. What little personality she had had been drained away by years of preparing her husband's meals and ironing his trousers. She was a pleasant, rounded woman, dark, with glinting eyes and a sweet smile. Any conversation she made consisted mainly of 'How are you?' and 'Everything is going well.' For the first eighteen years of her life she had obeyed every order that had fallen from her father's mouth; now she placed herself at the disposal of her husband. Or did she place herself? No; she belonged to that generation of women which was always placed and defined in relation to someone else – a mother, a wife, a daughter.

In the beginning, she would crouch in the doorway of the sitting room, with her sari draped over her head, listening intently to her husband and his friends speak of Marxist politics, the state of Calcutta's sewerage system, various health problems from boils to creaky knees, and over-zealous bosses. And she had something to say. She knew that diluted vinegar would calm the redness of Mr Chatterjee's boils, that warm mustard oil rubbed into Mr Bhowmik's knees would help stop the creaking, and that if the socialist party was ever overthrown, Calcutta would have a brand-new sewerage system. But her words seemed to get jarred in the doorframe, and any that managed to escape, and were heard (not listened to) by the men, seemed to be misunderstood as yet another offer of a cup of cha and more thin arrowroot biscuits. And before long, her words lingered between her brown lips before they were sucked back in and swallowed down with a drink of water from her stainless-steel beaker. Gradually, the words moved further back into her mouth until she could swallow them with the aid of her saliva only. Those words filled her up, puffing out her ankles so that the bones disappeared under her remedies for colds; the chubby rings of flesh around her neck held the key to many a marital lock; and her padded hips . . . Actually, she just had fat hips, but the words were heavy, and there was a year-on-year increase in her weight, so that by her late thirties she had taken on a potol-like appearance (much like her husband), and when washing the pots had to squat with a wide stance, like a sumo wrestler, with her belly resting on her thighs to prevent her from toppling over. This wide stance spilled over to all of her movements: she would walk along parallel lines, because if she placed one foot in front of the other her heavy thighs rubbed against each other and the skin there chafed, aided by the voluminous layers of petticoat and synthetic sari, so that not even a liberal sprinkling of Ponds talcum powder could prevent it. Her toes were also splayed, with the gap between the big and second toes being especially prominent, widened by her continuous usage of flip-flops. The bridge of her foot was flat and spread out, as if built to give her a solid base, and when she placed her chubby fingers on her hips, with her sari tucked up through her legs and into the back of her petticoat, her rickshaw-puller calves on display, she looked more the wife of a fisherman than of a semi-successful medical representative from the big city.

Not that this was unattractive to all men; some like their women sturdy. And one such man was Sachi's manager, Mr Ray. Mr Ray had one eye (the other lost in an unfortunate fishing accident) and it was definitely for the ladies. So when Sachi invited him round for dinner, he was quite taken with his hostess. Sachi tried to banish Rekha to the kitchen, but Mr Ray patted her plump knee and said to him jovially, 'No, no, let her stay. I'm sure she's been working hard in the kitchen all day; she deserves a break!' and even Sachi knew that you don't invite your boss round for dinner to contradict him. So he smiled and let her stay.

Not that he could stop challenging Rekha. Anything she said, he had to correct or go one better. When she said, 'You see, the reason why I'm having such difficulty explaining myself is because Mercury is retrograde in my sign at the moment. That's why when I asked the tailor to let out my shalwar kameez pants, he misunderstood and took them in, and now I can't even pull them past my knees!', Sachi sniffed and incorrectly corrected her, 'It's not Mercury that controls communication, it's Saturn!', adding, 'And it wasn't the tailor's fault, you're just fat.' And at this he turned to Mr Ray and said conspiratorially, 'When you become engaged to them, they're always slim-slim; then you marry them and they get fat-fat.'

But instead of agreeing with Sachi, Mr Ray looked nonplussed, and stated definitively, 'Your wife is lovely. *Lovely*. And such a hostess! You're a lucky man.'

Sachi bristled with anger. And when Rekha

ventured, 'I've recently started watching tennis on TV when I get time. They hit the ball with such power, no? And run around the court, here, there, everywhere!', Sachi interjected, 'What you know about tennis? You think it's one-nil, two-nil? You know fifteen-*love*, thirty-fifteen, forty-all is called *deuce*!'

But Mr Ray was not the least interested in Sachi's ramblings. Despite being a womanizer, he genuinely liked women and their company, and when dinner was to be served, he got up to help Rekha. Sachi's eyes widened in horror and his mouth dried.

'I'm so sorry!' he choked.

'Sorry about what?' Mr Ray asked, confused.

'You don't have to help!' Sachi answered.

'But I want to,' Mr Ray replied with a smile, and then followed Rekha into the kitchen. Sachi sank back into his chair; he felt powerless.

Dinner was a quiet affair. Sachi had lost his appetite, and could only nod at anything Mr Ray had to say. Rekha, noticing that Sachi wasn't eating (and he only ever lost his appetite when he was furious), lost her own appetite and her voice, too.

After Mr Ray had left, Rekha tried to hide in the kitchen, cowering in the corner as she cleaned the dishes. She could feel Sachi standing in the door-way, staring at her. Then she heard his voice, the one he used for telling her off.

'You think you're cleverer than me, do you?' he spluttered. She wasn't sure whether to answer back – sometimes it made things better, sometimes it made things worse. He continued, 'You like to make me look silly in front of my boss?'

'No,' she whispered.

'What did you say?' he asked. 'I didn't hear you.'

Raising her voice a fraction, she said again, 'No.'

'Hmmm,' Sachi mumbled. 'Hmmm,' as if he were thinking, although he knew exactly what he was going to do.

The beating didn't last long. They never did. Although it's said that quality matters more than quantity, and the black bruise on Rekha's left arm was first class. And just to make his point, Sachi said to her afterwards, having regained his composure, 'You're nothing without me. Do you think someone like Mr Ray would ever be interested in someone like you? No, I'm the only idiot who was stupid enough to take you on! You should stop thinking so much of yourself!'

Mousumi had tried to watch the evening's proceedings from the bedroom; she had been especially curious to see what Mr Ray looked like. She had stood by the door, looking through the small gap between door and frame. She hadn't managed to see much, but she had heard everything. When she had heard her mother talking too much, she had known there was going to be trouble. Her face drooped with disappointment and also frustration: why hadn't her mother learned to keep her mouth shut, just like she had? And when her father had followed her mother into the kitchen at the end of the night, she had quietly closed the door and slumped against it, her face expressionless; she didn't need to hear any more.

But although Sachi tried to prevent Rekha from becoming too much for her own good, he couldn't stop her from fantasizing. In her dreams, she had fair, pinkish-tinted skin, with dark-brown hair and almond eyes, like all the Kashmiri heroines. Her crimson-toed, slim feet wore jewelled sandals and her slim bony ankles were emphasized by gold anklets. And those brown eyes, gold-flecked, with their dreamy melancholy stare, enticed all the men in the kingdom, until she blinked too hard and her small dark eyes looked straight back at her in all her fat-hippedness.

But Rekha was not the only one to look in the full-length mirror, with its ornately carved chipped frame, and be confronted by someone else. Sachi himself, despite the self-satisfied pats on his well-fed belly and the gaze of benediction when handing out alms and advice, saw himself in an altogether different light. With luxuriant, wavy black hair, a rosebud-pink mouth and smooth pale skin, he liked to think that his mellifluous voice, accompanied only by tabla and sitar, could charm even the most cold-hearted of maidens.

And so the two of them lay there together in the dark of their bedroom, with the curtain flapping lightly in the cool breeze against the rusty iron rods of the window, an ancient upturned cockroach under their bed, her foot, for a moment soft and slim, rubbing his hairy calves; and his balding pate, for those few minutes, a head of thick and shiny hair. They would lie there with their fantasies, not of each other but of themselves. And from their excessive stillness, as if any movement might destroy their alter egos for ever, Mousumi, lying on the mattress beside her parents' bed, could hear her mother's desire for gold-flecked brown eyes, and she felt her own hips and fingers transforming with her own words and wishes.

But Sachi, despite his hirsute fantasies, was in all other respects practical: he wanted to eat well, sleep well, and marry his daughter off well. To do this, he had to turn his dark-skinned child into a desirable wife. So he started to feed her, as if she were a goose destined to become foie gras. Resistance was futile.

Although Sachi considered himself a Western Man, he most certainly did not want a Western Wife or a Western Daughter. It might have been the done thing in some parts of Bombay society with its film stars and movie moguls, but it was not acceptable for a university-educated professional man. Through friends who had relatives in England, and some even in America (those who had done especially well), he had heard about the trials and tribulations that accompanied Western Women. Once, even his sister's husband, Prakash, who lived in London, had muttered something on the phone about women not knowing their place. So, to prevent his daughter from being brainwashed into this fate, he would not allow her to read any English magazines, or even any magazines which had film stars or models (he knew what *model* was the polite word for) in their pages. English-speaking television programmes were also banned, as were English-speaking films, although Sachi himself sometimes visited the cinema on his own in the afternoon, joining an audience composed of middle-aged men sitting on their own, and teenage boys sitting in groups, to watch those naughty Western Women being naughty.

At school, Mousumi felt a great sense of loneliness when all her classmates gathered in the corridors to discuss the latest shenanigans of Bollywood stars, and the most fashionable design of shalwar kameez. She tried to join in with the conversation, but not being the most confident of people, she was easily silenced by a superior look from one of the girls who had dyed hair and a chauffeur. She didn't even fit in with the brown-nosers, who would do their homework in advance and tucked their shirts in properly – for them, she didn't have enough dedication or ambition to become a full-blown sycophant. Out of school, she did not fare any better. Her saris were not stylish enough: they were the wrong print, the wrong material, and she wore them too high around her waist. All the skirts that her mother had bought for her were pleated and long, and as more weight continued to attach itself to her, they flared out from her hips and looked like a tent. Her blouses were also ill-fitting, straining across her fat bosom and often held together by a safety pin. When she wore sandals, they were flat and had a buckle across the ankle; all the other girls would wear high-heeled strapless sandals with painted toenails. And worst of all was her hair. Thick, black and *natural*. Some days, even oiled with Cantheridine. She tried to stop her mother from massaging it with the highly fragrant oil but Rekha could not understand why and persisted – it was a guarantee that Mousumi's hair would not fall out in later life. The next day, Mousumi would spend her break at school in the washrooms, looking at herself, a shiny fat person with shiny fat hair.

Despite her weight, she often felt as light as air, as

if she would float into the sky with nothing to hold her down. She felt she had no substance; if someone asked her about herself (which they rarely did) she had nothing to say. Life seemed to avoid her. She was a hermit crab looking for a shell. The only time she was truly happy was when she stood alone in front of the dressing-table mirror, an imaginary audience in front of her, singing hit after hit to her heart's content, trying to carry out the dance moves she had choreographed in her head, but which her body was not supple enough to realize. The only time she was truly happy was when she was not being herself.

Her misery was undetected by her father, who congratulated himself on raising such wonderful wife material. What would a father understand about the importance of high-heeled shoes and ammoniaed hair?

But her saviour was to come in the unlikely figure of Hariprasad Varma. He was a wealthy shop-owner, with a string of sweet shops and newsagents, and an unusual predilection.

When his beloved father had died, Hariprasad had been left with a broken heart and a large in-heritance. But he believed that money was worth nothing without paternal love and affection. Whatever he did with the lakh lakh taka would have to honour his father. And then it came to him: he would open a sweet shop. Since he could remember, every day at half past six in the evening his father had taken him (even as a grown man) to the local one, where they eyed up the delicacies on display before picking a selection. Hariprasad always felt sorry for the pieces of glacé cherry barfi that were never picked and sat shoulder by creamy shoulder in the aluminium tray. But he soon forgot about them when he saw the panthuas – a tribe of deep-brown spongy spheres, each protecting a cardamom seed; the orange-skinned laddoos with their hats of grated pistachios; and his favourite – the rasogollas – balls of sweet cheese swimming in a sea of rose-scented syrup.

So came his first shop, Hari's Mishti. It was different from the other grotty sweet stores in the neighbourhood. It was painted turquoise on the outside, and pink within. The trays holding the sweets were gold-plated. The girls serving the customers were all plump and pretty, and wore cerise lipstick and white hibiscus flowers in their hair. For all the Europeans and Americans in Calcutta, the store became rather a novelty. At first, they entered purely out of curiosity; not having Indian tastebuds, they found the mishti too sugary. But their eyes couldn't resist the shiny trays piled with sweetmeats decorated with gold and silver leaf, and soon their mouths followed. One Californian woman, whose husband was in India on oil business, installed herself in The Grand, and from there walked every day to Hari's to buy the softest shandesh. She was a large woman, standing at least two and a half head and shoulders above the natives, with broad muscular shoulders and swollen biceps, but she insisted on fitting in with the locals by wearing saris, which came up too short on her legs, and blouses which strained over her athletic back. Combined with her white-blond hair and Los Angelino tan, she cut a figure both comic and captivating; once Hariprasad had seen her, he could not have forgotten her.

One day she had said to him, '*Hairy*, as in Princess Diana's youngest?' and he had nodded. 'Well, honey, I gotta tell you, that's spelt H-A-R-R-Y!' And from that point, Hari's became Harry's.

Through mitosis, Harry's single cell soon split and multiplied into a thriving body of stores, and then through evolution, they developed a newsagent arm. All across Calcutta, billboards proclaimed 'Pick up a newspaper and a naru at Harry's.' His shops were a hit with everyone, from Americans buying a day-old copy of the *New York Times* and a bag of nimki (the closest they could get to pretzels) to schoolgirls flicking through celebrity magazines and buying the smallest piece of Harry's Special Low-Fat Rhabree.

Of all the young women who frequented his original shop, which Hari still presided over, after school each day, huddling round magazines and riffling through the packets of lozenges and gum, it was Mousumi who caught his attention, or rather held it. There was something about her disposition, a quiet nervousness or maybe timidity, which attracted him to her. She had none of the superficial over-confidence of the other girls, and stood away from the crowd. She looked like a dreamer, and Hariprasad liked dreamers – he was one himself. But what he liked more was the lush pocket of fat under her chin, the puffy belly, the meaty arms and the bloated breasts. Fat sumptuous flesh; just the thought of it made him expand with desire. And she was less likely to run away than the others. So came the approach.

CHAPTER THREE

A Compliment a Day

'**N**o.'

There; he'd said it. He wasn't very good at saying it, but this time he had managed. His back, he felt, deserved a pat. And as no one else was offering, he would have to do it himself. But before he could reach over his shoulder, he was interrupted by a rather stern voice.

'But Dr Majumdar . . .' The *dar* seemed to float on without the rest of its body.

'Yes, Rose Mary?' he enunciated carefully.

Rosemary wondered whether to correct his pronunciation, but then thought better of it, as he had been calling her the wrong name for the last ten years. And he was in one of his moods. 'Well, she's not all there, is she?'

'All where?' he asked. He said this in his clever voice, the wry, slow one he used when he had an imaginary audience.

Rosemary tapped at her temple with her fore-finger. 'Up here ... she's not quite ... with it. I really do think you should make a home visit. Plus, if she comes to the surgery she wees everywhere, and then I have to clean it up.'

This last piece of information had the effect of a hypnotist's double-clap. He had forgotten about the woman's incontinence.

'Hmmm,' he said, buying himself some time. 'Hmmm.' He wondered how he could capitulate, without entirely negating his magisterial 'No.' And then he said, 'Well, we mustn't have that, must we?' using thoughtfulness to disguise his lack of willpower.

'No,' said Rosemary firmly. 'We mustn't!' She turned on her heel and walked out of the room.

Tail drooping, Prakash picked up his car keys from his desk, and reluctantly set off to make the home visit.

Recently, Prakash had been thinking about living, dying, the purpose of life – all of the Big Themes. And he had come to the temporary conclusion that on his deathbed he would want to look back and feel that he had lived his life the way he thought fit. Not the way other people wanted him to. Hence the very, very short story of 'No.' But his problem was too much heart. Too much heart had led him to take on a patient whom no other doctor would treat, and too much heart was now leading him all the way across London to Bow, where the mad, incontinent woman lived in a high-rise, with lifts that smelled of piss, and where condom wrappers and silver foil from cigarette packets were discarded on the stairwell.

Tuhina, sitting on a plane miles away, could see Prakash's face as he made his way to see his patient. She rolled her eyes, and exhaled deeply. Tuhina didn't think Prakash had too much heart; she thought he didn't have enough backbone. When she had first met him, she hadn't realized how malleable he was. In a rare misjudgement of character, she had mistaken his willingness to go along with what others said as consideration. But after years and years of his indecision about everything, from which restaurant to eat at, to which school to send their daughter to, and his constant refrain of 'What do you think we should do?', she had realized that his generosity came not from self-lessness but from fear.

Being the eighth son, like Krishna, Prakash's birth had been auspicious, and was celebrated with much delight. He was also considered a miracle, as his mother had been sterilized fifteen years before, and had then had the chutzpah to fall pregnant at the

57

grand old age of fifty. So he was born bearing the weight of expectation which comes with good fortune. And even before the moment his gummy mouth clamped on to his mother's milk-filled breast, his future had been decided for him. He had no say; from his beginning, as a red-skinned baby, with curly black hair and a flat African nose, he had been emasculated, like an Action Man doll with nothing but a smooth plastic curve underneath his trousers.

How would he speak of his childhood? It would be dishonest to say that it was at all unhappy. His parents doted on him, he had many friends, he wanted for nothing, and he did well at school. In that sense, he was to be envied. So what was the problem? The problem was that he was decision impotent; nothing he did was of his own volition. He was smothered by a pillow stuffed with everyone else's actions and purposes.

Although not at all aggressive by nature, there was one occasion when Prakash had nearly been involved in a fight, a proper one, with proper punches and proper kicking. It started when Anil Jennings, an Anglo in his maths class, had made a comment about his best friend Shanti's mother and her virtue or lack of. Prakash felt pangs of excitement in his stomach as the two boys squared up to each other in the playground, surrounded by their respective supporters, all rubbing their hands, getting ready to join the battle. Jennings was quite a big fellow, and when he caught Shanti with a thumping left hook, Prakash knew it was time to get into the ring. He knew he was going to get hurt, but he didn't care. He would wear his battle scars proudly. But just as he was hopping from foot to foot, and cracking his knuckles, a voice rose from the back of the crowd like a rain cloud threatening to destroy the day's play.

'What's going on here, then?' said the voice. The crowd moved apart to let the voice in. It was one of Prakash's older brothers. He was a teacher at the school and didn't make any allowances for Prakash.

'Break it up, boys,' he said sternly, giving Prakash a quick but intense stare. 'Sir's just around the corner and you'll be in detention if you're not careful.'

The fire turned into a pile of glowing ashes as the boys dispersed, sulking and muttering macho never-to-be-fulfilled threats under their breath. Prakash scowled silently.

'Why d'you have a heavy arse?' his brother asked dismissively.

'I don't,' Prakash retorted, his pouting lower lip contradicting him. He had missed his moment to be a hero. Through no fault of his own, he felt as if he was a coward who had purposely avoided being conscripted into the army.

So for all his trying, he was always an outsider on the inside. Once, his gang had all been playing a game of dares: the challenge was to go into a local mishti shop dressed only in socks and shoes, and buy a carton of panthuas, which they thought bore a resemblance to brown-skinned testicles. They all thought it a hilarious scheme. Prakash was up for it. This was his chance to prove that he was no scaredy-cat, and was as game as anyone else. His embarrassment and public humiliation would be his crown. But he turned out to be only a pretender to the throne: just as he was about to whip off his short pants, who should come round the corner but his grandmother. The other boys said hello to her courteously, and when she said to Prakash, 'Well, let's go home, then!' he could do nothing but follow her. Not that any of the other boys blamed him; they would have done exactly the same thing. But for Prakash, it was yet another defeat and once again he resented himself for his docility. He felt like a cat without claws.

Driving down the dual carriageway, a featureless grey central reservation separating the characterless shops on either side of the road, Prakash pulled up into the smooth expanse of concrete in front of the block of flats. A group of kids who were standing in the corner, some with bikes and others with skateboards, turned around to eye up his car. It was a mystic blue S500 Mercedes with five-spoke alloy wheels and dark sand leather upholstery – a feature he was especially proud of, because he had chosen it. Tuhina had chosen the model, and Darshini had chosen the colour. Although he wouldn't admit that he liked driving a flashy car, Prakash did like driving a flashy car. He told his friends that it was Tuhina's idea, and that he had simply gone along with it to make her happy, but secretly he believed that such a car not so much fitted but rather added to his status. They had two other cars: an SUV which they used at weekends, and a sports car, which Tuhina drove to work in the City. Prakash was also proud of being a three-car family, and not any three cars, but very nice three cars – although he didn't like to brag about it, of course.

The kids were still looking at the car. Shouldn't they be in school, Prakash wondered, looking at his watch, although he already knew roughly what time it was. He felt a little bit nervous. Groups of children intimidated him. And they didn't look like very well-brought-up children who would respect him because he was a doctor. This place wasn't like home. He shifted around in his seat, wiping away a little sweat from his brow with his handkerchief, which was attached to his inside suit pocket by a piece of thread and a safety-pin, like his mother had

61

taught him. Prakash found something reassuring about his handkerchief.

Slowly, he opened the car door and inched himself out. He walked around the car, all the time glancing at the group, pulled his briefcase out of the boot, pushing down the boot-door with theatrical strength, then started to walk towards the entrance of the flats. The kids switched their attention from the car to him. Prakash walked purposefully, with his head down. Then he heard a voice, casual, cocky:

'That's a really nice car you have there, Mister.' The 'Mister' seemed both genuine and sardonic.

Prakash lifted his head to see a young man on his bike, one foot on the ground, the other on a pedal, nodding his head in acknowledgement. Prakash nodded back cautiously, and gave the young man a small smile.

Mrs Winterson was batty. That's what was written in her medical notes. It was Prakash's professional opinion. Although from time to time he did wonder whether her battiness was somewhat cultivated. For a start, he could find no physical reason for her incontinence. Nor any chemical reason for her madness. But he had referred her to a psychiatrist, only to receive a report back with 'I found this patient to be lucid and sound of mind.' But Prakash wouldn't give up on her. He knocked on the door gingerly, pressing his ear up against it. There was no reply, so he knocked again, a bit louder.

'Fuck off, you little bastards!' screamed Mrs Winterson. Prakash jerked his head back in surprise. A moment later, he bent down and opened the letterbox.

'Mrs Winterson!' he called tentatively through the gap. 'It's Dr Majumdar – you called me, remember?'

There was the sound of shuffling and then the screech of a disturbed cat.

'Is that you, Dr Mojder?' Mrs Winterson asked.

'Yes, Mrs Winterson,' Prakash said, 'it's Dr Mojder.'

The door opened. Mrs Winterson, sixty-seven years of age and too voluptuous of body, engulfed the doorway, wearing a transparent nightie with nothing underneath it.

'That's a pretty outfit,' Prakash said. He thought he should say something nice.

After a half-hour check-up during which, once again, nothing about Mrs Winterson's health was discovered apart from the fact that she was perfectly OK, Prakash got up to leave. He was feeling a bit better. But as soon as the lift door closed, nervous tension gripped him again. The inside of the lift smelled stale, metallic. The grubby lighting flickered, whilst the cogs and pulleys wheezed and grunted. He chastised himself for taking the lift instead of the stairs. For Prakash, the grass was frequently and very convincingly greener on the other side.

While the lift slowly went down, he started to worry about the car. First of all, he should have parked it elsewhere, somewhere safer, and walked the rest of the distance. Actually, the damn car shouldn't have been bought in the first place – it was just showing off, wasn't it? – because that sort of car attracted all the wrong kind of attention (and when he was in a good mood, all the right kind). In fact, his whole lifestyle was a bit ostentatious, and flamboyance was just another form of moral degeneracy!

By the time the lift had lowered to the ground floor, he had convinced himself that everything about his life was wrong. Wrong! Prakash's logic knew no boundaries.

Outside again, he saw the kids still standing exactly as they had been when he went inside. They looked more menacing to him now – their lips contorted into disdainful sneers, their shoulders slumped with contempt. He was convinced they had damaged his car in some way – punctured a tyre, perhaps, or scratched the paintwork. Something to punish him for having such a nice car.

As he approached, he furtively gave it the once

over – it seemed fine – and then clambered in, threw his briefcase down on the passenger seat, switched on the ignition and put his foot down. But just when he thought it was all over, the car stalled. He tried to start it again without taking it out of gear, and without his foot on the clutch. The car made an annoyed sound. He put it in reverse and it jolted backwards. Would he never be able to get out of this hell?

He looked out of his window: the kids were laughing and laughing. Or maybe they were saying something to him; he couldn't tell and he daren't lower the window. They looked like little devil spirits, grinning maniacally. He wanted to roll down the window and confidently shout at them, 'Go to school, you little sods!' He wanted to get out of the car, walk over to them and say, 'You won't be laughing when I tell your headmaster that you've been truanting! Then you'll be in trouble!' But he was too scared; he felt like they were the adults and he was the child.

At last, he managed to pull himself together and drive away. He knew he should never have made the home visit; he hadn't wanted to, but he had been forced into it, and look what had happened. It was all Rose Mary's fault. He knew that if Tuhina had been in the same situation, the bastard children wouldn't have even laughed in the first place, because she wouldn't have stalled the car. He miserably wondered what she would think if she could have seen him.

Tuhina did see what happened. She wasn't surprised in the slightest. The only surprise to her was that Prakash had managed not to crash the car in a fit of panic. For that, at least, she was grateful.

By the time Tuhina arrived at Heathrow, it was dark. She liked the night. Especially the city at night. She had asked her taxi-driver to take her from the airport to work, to pick up some mythical paperwork, and then home to Clapham Common, just so that she could be driven over Waterloo Bridge. As she admired the magical lights, she hummed 'Twinkle, twinkle, little star' to herself. When Darshini had refused to go to sleep as a baby, Tuhina had often bundled her into the car, driven here and got out to walk back and forth over the bridge, with Darshini's soft little head resting on her shoulder, gently and rhythmically patting her back and humming lullabies, and despite the noise from the traffic and the bright lights, Darshini would fall asleep. This memory cheered her up after her exasperation at Prakash's humiliation that afternoon. Tuhina turned her body so that she could look out of the rear window, and watched as the grand buildings grew smaller. They were buildings with gravitas; buildings with history and knowledge and meaning.

She especially liked the square stone one with the multitude of windows and the clock at the top. She didn't know what it was called. I must find out the name of that building, she thought. She thought that every time she crossed the bridge. It was a comforting routine. She was pleased to be going home again. And she was looking forward to kicking off her shoes, having a bath using her full-size glass bottle of bath oil, not the miniature plastic type issued by hotels, and eating a home-cooked dinner, of lamb which fell off the bone and melting potatoes, with Darshini and Prakash.

Prakash's evening surgery had been a rather humdrum affair after his tumultuous afternoon. But instead of being relieved, he was bored. He found it difficult to hit upon the happy medium, with its rested and refreshed complexion and serene smile. I never seem to get it quite right, he mused, and this made him feel quite emotional. Then the fact that he felt emotional, and was a man, and therefore shouldn't be emotional, made him feel anxious. Then the anxiety made him feel helpless. Then his helplessness made him feel even more emotional. Which made him angry. He went to the pantry and looked at the shelves stacked with various bottles of pills and capsules and powders and liquids. Although there was a problem, the problem was a nebulous mess, which didn't indicate a specific treatment, and so he prescribed himself a bottle of red wine, which he thought would help him forget there was a problem at all.

The scrawny chicken legs were not behaving as they should have been. Prakash, two glasses down, violently cursed (under his breath – he didn't like swearing out loud) the halal butcher in Bow who had insisted that the chicken was free-range and organic.

'You're sure?' Prakash had asked, squinting at the saggy skin.

'Sir, yes, of course, sir! I no lie to you!' And as Prakash didn't like upsetting people, he didn't feel that he could not buy the chicken without offending the man. If only he hadn't had to visit Mrs Winterson at lunchtime, he could have popped home to the local butcher, where there were framed certificates on the wall and the employees wore sturdy health-and-safety shoes, not plastic flip-flops. And now the chicken was refusing to brown, instead remaining a rather dull pink colour. And Tuhina would be home in half an hour. Rose Mary had a lot to answer for.

Darshini's belly was rumbling a little. A nice little rumble though, just loud enough to let her know she was hungry. She could smell the comforting aroma of melting butter emanating from the kitchen. Her dad could always be relied upon to concoct some mouth-watering dish; she wandered through to the kitchen to watch him cook. She didn't like cooking herself, but she enjoyed watching. She leaned casually on the counter and asked, 'What are we having for dinner tonight?'

'Chicken,' he replied as he extracted a bouquet garni from its bottom. At last it seemed to be cooking.

'Smells really yummy,' she said, sniffing the air. This cheered Prakash up. *A compliment a day keeps the doctor away* was his favourite maxim. He had made it up himself.

'Thank you,' he said, feeling slightly woozy from the wine. He wasn't used to drinking that much. He believed his tolerance level was higher than it actually was and never seemed to learn. He liked to think of himself as someone who could drink a lot without adverse effect. As if imperviousness to alcohol marked him out as someone of standing.

By the time they sat down for dinner, Prakash's head was beginning to spin slightly, and his blinks became longer and longer. He could just about follow the conversation, but the sentences which were as ordered as synchronized swimmers in his head seemed to have forgotten their routine by the time they came out of his mouth. There was a large stain on his shirt where he had missed his mouth and spilt the red wine sauce. Tuhina thought about mentioning it, but then bit her tongue: Prakash reacted badly when he was asked to use a napkin. On one occasion, when he had been asked, he had retorted, 'I'm not child, you know! You can't tell me what to do!'

Tuhina had been bemused by his response; she had only asked out of consideration for the help who did the laundry. But as she hadn't wanted to start an argument, she had merely taken a deep breath. But this particular stain was really beginning to irritate her. She tried not to look at it, but as it was directly in front of her it was unavoidable. From the crimson nucleus spread a dirty oil-slick, making Prakash's shirt transparent.

Tuhina looked at Darshini to see if she had noticed; they usually noticed the same sort of thing: the salt bloom on a glass caused by a dishwasher (Tuhina insisted all crockery and cutlery was washed by hand. And rinsed, too. Rinsing was as important as washing), the lightest speckles of dandruff on a dark collar, a heel mark on an otherwise pristine floor. She had, and was looking at it with some interest.

'Dad,' she asked, munching on a carrot, 'do you know you've spilt something on your shirt?'

'Hmmm?' Prakash asked dazedly.

'There. On your shirt,' Darshini said, pointing to the mark.

'Ohhh,' said Prakash, waving his fork around dismissively, 'noothing,' proceeding to peer down at the red-wine sauce on his chest and then rub it in and spread it out with some vigour. 'Noothing at aall!'

'Great, Dad!' Darshini said sarcastically. 'That stain, along with the Great Wall of China, can now be seen from outer space!' She was especially irritated as the shirt had been a Father's Day gift from her, and she had spent a lot of time choosing it. Now he was just behaving like a boor. Boors didn't deserve fancy shirts.

'Youuushutup,' Prakash slurred.

'Don't tell her to shut up,' Tuhina snapped, pulling her shoulders back.

'I talk to youuu?' Prakash asked angrily, narrowing his eyes at Tuhina and pointing at her with his index finger. Tuhina ignored him.

'Darling,' she said, turning to Darshini, who was sitting at the head of the table, 'has your father been taking those sleeping pills again?'

Prakash knew he was being insulted but he couldn't formulate a response.

'Just booze, I think,' Darshini replied, shrugging casually and picking a fibre from a fine bean out of her teeth.

Come on, Prakash chastised himself. *Come on; think of something to say back.* Then in his clever voice, which he had made use of only that morning, and stroking his chin as if he were a sleuth, he said to Tuhina, 'Why you aasking her? Hmmm? Why not aask mee?'

Tuhina finally allowed herself to roll her eyes. 'Oh Good Lord, Prakash, I really do think it's time for you to go to bed,' she said, and with that she excused herself from the table, taking her plate with her.

'Nice one, Dad,' Darshini said, following suit.

Prakash was too drunk to sulk, but his mouth drooped downward, and he pressed his fork into his mashed potato over and over again. He tried to lift some to his mouth, but it dropped into his lap. Then he tried to scrape it up from his trousers and it fell on to the floor. In the kitchen, he could hear Tuhina asking Darshini what flavour ice-cream she wanted – vanilla, chocolate or pistachio. He fancied some ice-cream, too, but he felt sheepish, although he couldn't work out why, and couldn't face going into the kitchen. So he sat on his own at the table, and sat, and sat, and sat.

It was only when he heard the television in the kitchen being turned off, and the light switch flicked, that he moved. Tiptoeing to the fridge, he opened the freezer section and took out the tub of vanilla ice-cream. He helped himself to three generous scoops, his hand gripping the spoon tightly and digging it with force into the tub. He slumped at the kitchen counter and shovelled the ice-cream into his mouth, dripping it down his shirt. It had been a horrible day. Rose Mary had caused all the trouble. Not that he would dare tell her that.

When Prakash finally went to bed that night, Tuhina was already asleep. It was usually the other way around. He carefully tiptoed about, trying not to make any noise. Having put his pyjamas on, he sat on the edge of the bed and looked at his sleeping wife. *Why is she so beautiful?* he thought sadly. He wanted to stroke her face and kiss her temple, but knew he would only irritate her if he woke her up. He hadn't kissed her properly in years. Any time he tried to show her affection, she would brush him off and find herself something else to do.

Tuhina wasn't really asleep, but she didn't want Prakash to disturb her and then have to go to the trouble of fending him off. She thought his advances were clumsy, irritating, like an enthusiastic puppy pawing her and barking incessantly. When he tried to kiss her, she felt nothing but exasperation. He was so desperate for her attention that whenever he touched her, her skin prickled and she wanted to bat his hand away as if she were shooing away a buzzing fly. Occasionally he would, not registering her annoyance, become insistent, and then she would resort to sleeping in the spare room, on the pretext that his snoring was keeping her awake. She wished he would learn to leave her alone.

CHAPTER FOUR

Death of a Belly

Rekha sat in the waiting room of the Accident and Emergency department of the Calcutta Medical College and Hospital on College Street, with her Proper Indian Widow's grief on display – wailing, crying, hysteria. A nurse tried to comfort her by stroking her hair and muttering comforting aahs, but just when Rekha's cries had reduced to a hunched-shouldered shallow-breathed sniffle, a deep well of pain built up again in her belly and overflowed out of her eyes and nose and mouth in streams of salty water.

And where was her daughter whilst all of this was going on? Mousumi was joyfully ensconced in the storage space of Hariprasad's newsagent, a room plastered with posters of curvaceous women in wet saris and stacked with bars of chocolate that had a light coating of white powder on them when

75

opened, reading every page of *Bollywood Stars*, poring over the photographs of the actors and actresses striking mail-order-catalogue poses. One day, she thought, one day I too will be in one of these magazines. And then those girls with dyed hair and chauffeurs will pay me some attention! Then *they* will want to be like *me*, and have my hair and my shoes and my fancy shalwar kameez.

Of course, this was just a variant on the school-reunion scenario, which is the solace of all misfits and unpopulars: walking into a crowd of once condescending tormentors, now a shocked (but not *too* shocked) appreciative assembly of onlookers.

Hariprasad watched her carefully as she swirled an aniseed lozenge around in her mouth and turned the pages of the magazine; his eyes lit up with feverish anticipation as she absent-mindedly pushed the sweet into the side of her chubby cheek, creating a phallic bulge. Fortunately, he had a photographic memory, and could wait until later to satisfy himself.

Ensnaring Mousumi had been simple enough; Hariprasad believed it far easier to catch a hippo than a cheetah. All he had done was ask her to try out a new type of sweet that had recently come on the market – Creamy Kisses – and she was his. As soon as she popped the sphere of melting caramel in a coat of chocolate into her mouth, and chewed on

76

it thoughtfully, his loins stirred. And to butter her up further, he presented her with a magazine, pulled it open and suggested that he thought she looked just like a certain film star who was advertising the sweet. If Mousumi had ever been the recipient of any male attention apart from that of her father, she would have realized the comic-book nature of the seduction. But lacking knowledge of the danger of menfolk, she satisfied Hariprasad's yearnings without even knowing it.

When Mousumi arrived back at home early in the evening, just as the light was dimming, and the symphony of the streets fading, with a small paper packet of liquorice sweets wedged between the pages of a volume of poetry, she was in for a surprise. Normally, as soon as her mother heard the key in the door, she called out, 'Sumi, is that you?' (there was no chance of it being anyone else), but this time there was no familiar voice.

'Ma?' she called out, standing in the hall. No answer. Furtively, she rooted around in her school bag, pulled out a sweet and popped it in her mouth. After a couple of minutes of chewing, she called again, 'Ma?' Still no answer.

Mousumi was worried: her mother was always at home when she returned from school. But suddenly her senses were heightened, so that the muggy air made her skin prickle and the hairs on her body stood to attention. She carefully lowered her bag to the floor without making a sound and breathed as quietly as she could – iin-oouut. She looked around her to see if anything had been stolen, but the only items that could be taken from the hall were a dusty pair of sandals and a broken umbrella. All her speculations about whether *this* film star was really going out with *that* cricketer flew out of her head and were replaced by the here and now. Any minute, she might come face to face with a thief, and then what would she do? She could go to the kitchen to get the goat-chopping knife, but what if he was in the kitchen? Then another thought struck her: what if her mother had tripped and fallen and was now lying unconscious on the bedroom floor, or what if (and this is where those magazines had their influence) her mother was having an affair and had lost track of time, or what if . . . Mousumi felt overwhelmed by possibilities. She padded silently into the bedroom, bracing herself for whatever she was about to encounter. But there was nothing. The bed was made, the wardrobe and dressing table were undisturbed.

What to do? Neither of her parents had cell phones (for flashy Bombay businessmen only, her father said), so there was no way of contacting them. Her armpits and brow slightly more sweaty than usual, she went to the kitchen and fried herself a pile of poppadums, which she served up with a generous dollop of mango chutney. She sat on her parents' bed, her lap cradling the plate, her back resting against a side-pillow, watching a syndicated Agony Aunt programme called, sinisterly enough, *Tell Aunty Everything*, and presented by a woman named Chi-chi Chakraborty whose solution to most problems seemed to be to show more cleavage.

At a quarter to two that afternoon, Sachi had heaved himself out of a rickety rickshaw, tipped the rough-footed wallah generously, and entered the waiting area of Dr Ajoy Banerjee, one of his best customers. Filling a Styrofoam cup with water from the cooler, he sat down in a plastic chair, still wheezing a little. Since that morning, his chest had been feeling slightly tight, with darting pains travelling through it every so often. But he often felt his chest tense up after smoking a cigarette or few, and he thought nothing of it. With his briefcase by his side, he rested his eyes as the doctor tended to his last patient. A clenching pain in his sternum had caused him to wake up early in the morning, and he had been sick; now he felt tired. He had been sick again at ten, just after visiting Dr Chilka, but again, he thought nothing of it: rich food can do that to you, and he had eaten an extra generous (even by his standards) portion of guur-laden rice-pudding the night before.

As he was led into the consulting room by the young receptionist, whose bottom quivered enticingly with every step, Sachi wondered whether he could possibly take the rest of the afternoon off. He hitched up his trousers as he sat down and took up the receptionist's offer of a cup of tea – two sugars and milk.

Opening the briefcase with the combination lock (combination 000–000), he pulled out his company's newest drug: Cordistympan, an ACE inhibitor. Sachi thought it would be of great use to Dr Banerjee, whose patient list was monopolized by paunchy men with little hair and lots of money. Just as he was about to straighten up, he felt a massive pain in his heart, as though a serrated-edged knife had first pierced it and then been twisted. He tried to gulp for air. His hands, still holding the blood-red packet of tablets, involuntarily shot to his chest. He managed to rise to his knees, then collapsed on to his side.

Dr Banerjee, who had been noisily rummaging around in his drawers for some soap, had his back to Sachi, and only turned around when he heard the giant thud. The next thing he heard was the smash of crockery, as the receptionist, on seeing the passed-out man on the floor, dropped the cup and saucer. 'Don't just stand there!' Dr Banerjee barked. 'Call an ambulance!'

Sachi made it to the hospital, but there was nothing they could do. Time of death: two seventeen. Cause of death: adult cardiopulmonary failure.

If Sachi Sharma was semi-successful, his half-brother Anil, younger by ten years, was quarter-successful. Anil wasn't unemployed, he had just taken extremely premature retirement, and could therefore be found at home at any time of the day. At the age of thirty-four he had set up his own business, using cheap child labour to embroider clothes worn by women who were too glamorous to have children. When a large textiles company bought him out the next year, he made a killing. But he was a fool; instead of investing the substantial sum, he squandered it on dancing girls and Scotch. He married a young woman whose beauty disappeared faster than his money, and had three averagely disobedient children.

When Dr Banerjee pressed the calling-bell of their once beautiful but now dilapidated apartment in Bagbazaar, they were all busy snoozing their way through an afternoon siesta, having eaten a considerable pile of rice and fish and dhal for their lunch. Dr Banerjee rang on the bell again. And again. Eventually the younger daughter came to the door in a scruffy dress, rubbing her eyes with hands that looked as if they could do with a good wash.

'Monisha,' Dr Banerjee said in his uncle voice used for talking to small children, 'is your daddy in?'

Monisha shook her head unconvincingly. There was silence, then a 'Ssshhh!' in the background.

'Are you sure?' he cajoled.

She looked furtive.

'Why don't I just come in and check?' Dr Banerjee said quietly, pushing her gently backwards to allow himself into the hall. He padded softly to the room where the 'Ssshhh' had come from and opened the door. Anil, his wife and the other two children turned to look at Monisha, but were instead confronted by the rather different figure of Dr Banerjee.

'Doctor-babu,' said a startled Anil, 'if I'd known it was you –', but Doctor-babu didn't have any time for his lazy excuses. He looked around the room: the last time he had visited it had been shabby, now it was shabbier still. Two single beds, covered by sheets with a faded floral print, formed an L-shaped seating area in the right corner. Between them was a jute mat where the dirty dishes from their meal were still laid out. There was an empty bookcase in the other corner. On top of it stood a brightly patterned china vase with an obvious crack in it. The paint on the walls flaked in patches like eczema.

'Anil,' Dr Banerjee started solemnly, 'I have some very bad news for you.' At this, Anil signalled the children to be absolutely silent by sharply putting his bony index finger to his lined lips. The children immediately froze, as if the music had stopped in the middle of a game of Musical Chairs. 'I'm afraid your brother's not well,' said Dr Banerjee, somewhat understating the case.

'What's wrong with him?' asked a worried Suleka. An ill Sachi would mean no more evening trips where he pressed a few hundred-rupee notes into her hand.

'I'm afraid he died of a heart attack this afternoon.'

Everyone and everything was silent, until a stray dog started barking outside, interrupting the trance.

'Does Rekha know?' Anil asked.

'No, I'm going to tell her now. As his only brother, you know that *you* will have to carry out the rituals, because Sachi doesn't have a son,' Dr Banerjee said with emphasis. 'And,' he continued, 'Sachi's sister lives far away in London.'

Anil had never met his half-sister Tuhina.

'Yes, of course,' Anil replied, looking at the ground. His lower lip trembled and his left eye twitched uncontrollably. He had never had this much responsibility.

Rekha took the news as well as could be expected, and insisted on going to the hospital to see her husband's body. In her rush, she did not leave a note to let Mousumi know where she was. She returned to the house five hours later to find Mousumi still on the bed, demolishing another pile of poppadums, this time accompanied by lime pickle.

'Ma, where have you been?' Mousumi asked, exasperated. 'You didn't even call!'

Rekha started crying again. Mousumi put her cleared plate down on the floor and went over to her mother, who was standing at the foot of the bed. 'Ma?' she asked, gently shaking her shoulders. 'Ma, what's wrong?'

When Rekha finally stopped crying, she looked at Mousumi with watery eyes and tear-smudged cheeks and said, 'Your father's died,' and then promptly burst into tears again.

There was no time for quiet contemplation that night, as a supernaturally calm Mousumi informed relative after relative of the news. They poured through the door in a torrent of tears and swept into the sitting room, where Rekha sat on the bed oblivious to anything but her sorrow. The men and the women separated into groups; the men stood stoically smoking cigarettes and wondering out loud whether Sachi had made a will, and the women congregated in the kitchen making cups and cups of cha, *aah*ing and *ish*ing over the tragedy, and taking it in turns to crush Mousumi to their plump bosoms.

Sachi's body was brought home and placed on a jute mat in the sitting room. Everyone fell silent and the men quickly stubbed their cigarettes out. Mousumi noticed the way Anil was shaking and felt sorry for him. But a few of the men and even more of the women were not so forgiving. They suggested – under their jarda-scented breath, of course – that he had been drinking. But this casual empiricism had for once led to the wrong conclusion; Anil was simply nervous, and as he had *not* had a drink to steady his nerves, he was trembling like a scantily clad beggar caught out in the monsoon rain. Even though his wealth had long since evaporated, many of the assembled had not forgiven him for not sharing his good fortune with them readily enough, and were secretly pleased when his life fell into disrepair. Mousumi noticed how they focused on Anil and barely looked at her father. She felt invisible, as if she was no longer important. She understood that even now, they were looking for Anil to fail in some way. She wanted to scream at them to remember the reason why they were all assembled. She wanted to tell them that even now, when they should have been humbled by Almighty Death, they were still full of petty politics and jealousy. And she felt bitterness rise up from her stomach to her throat as she realized that they fervently believed themselves to be good and God-fearing people. But she knew she couldn't and wouldn't say anything – her father would not have approved – so she hung back, her arms hanging loosely, her head down.

To Mousumi, Sachi's belly seemed to be bloated to an even greater size than normal. His head faced south. There had been several moments' discussion about which way was south – in the end, Ram, one of Mousumi's cousins, pointed to his trainers, which had a compass embedded in one tongue and a digital clock in the other, and the matter was settled. Anil poured a few spoons of Ganga water over Sachi's closed mouth and repeated 'Nama Shivaya' three times into his right ear. Sachi's toes were tied together, and then his thumbs were tied and rested on his chest, so it looked as though he was doing a Namaskar. When his body was covered up to his neck with a white cloth, Rekha started to sob again: a thin white veil now had enough strength to contain a colourful, vibrant, pig-headed man, a belly full of enjoyment. Anil, still shaking, fumbled around in his pockets for a lighter. One of his smoker cousins waited for a few cruel moments before producing a box of matches; the oil lamp and candle near Sachi's head were lit with a flustered hand. Outside, a fire made of charcoal, wood and camphor burned in the dark dusty street. It was getting late and some of the younger children had fallen asleep in their mothers' arms, while a tape of the Bhagavad Gita played gently in the background.

In the very early morning, even before the large black crows had taken their seats on the electricity wires, Sachi was bathed with care and tenderness, like the first time he was bathed as a baby. There followed a heated debate about what he should be dressed in: as a Western Man, his favourite outfit was a maroon polo shirt and beige chinos, but the priest found these rather inappropriate, although Anil was insistent that his brother would rather be sent to heaven in a pair of trousers than a dhoti. In the end, a smart Punjabi pyjama set was decided to be the best compromise: trousers, but Indian trousers. Sachi's forehead, forever free from worry, was decorated with sandalwood paste. Anil then bathed himself, and remained in his wet clothes. He placed betel leaf and nut on his brother's right side. His hands stopped shaking.

Along with the men, only Rekha and Mousumi accompanied Sachi to the crematorium. The casket was carried from the vehicle to the platform, legs pointing south (no discussion this time). Starting at Sachi's hardened feet, Anil walked around the body anti-clockwise three times, followed by Rekha, Mousumi and a few of the closer nephews. On completion of each circle, a few grains of rice and deep-orange marigold flowers were placed at

Sachi's shrivelled mouth, the blooming, vibrant petals in contrast to the muddy brown lips. After the last prayers had been recited, Anil carried an earthen pot of water on his left shoulder, and again walked anti-clockwise around Sachi three times. Behind him, Mousumi followed carrying a sharp iron rod. On reaching the head for the first time, she knocked a hole in the bottom of the pot; on the second time, a hole in the centre; on the third and final time, in the top. Mousumi splashed the Ganga water on to her dead father with the back of her left hand. Then Anil dropped the pot, and the rest of the holy water washed over the floor, separating the living from the dead. Mousumi was free of her father for ever.

What does one do if one is a widow left to take care of a family (albeit a family of two)? In Rekha's case, the answer was obvious: find an official husband for Mousumi and an unofficial companion for herself. There was no cold calculation or gold-digging motive here, just simple logic: she could not contemplate existence without a man (how would she fill her days if not cooking and cleaning?), especially when she did not yet have any grandchildren to devote her time to. And Rekha knew of no other way of spending her time. She had no friends with whom to have a long lunch and a gossip. She had no hobbies, no drawing class or flower arranging. It didn't occur to her that she now had the time to go to the cinema or the theatre, or to spend a leisurely afternoon on the grass in front of Victoria Memorial Hall reading books and magazines, or feeding the skittish chipmunks at the zoo, or having her nails painted and her arms massaged at the beauty parlour, because she had never done those things. She had only ever done things for others, not for herself.

And neither did she know what to do with Mousumi. Sachi had been in charge of her. He had decided everything, from what subjects she should read, to what type of clothes she should wear. From what time she had to be home by, to how much she should eat, to what television programmes she was allowed to watch. Rekha's role as mother had been confined to plaiting and oiling Mousumi's hair, telling her about the monthly machinations of the female body, and carefully ironing the pleats of her school skirt. Mousumi, Rekha thought, needed a husband, who could take responsibility for her. But Rekha also knew that Mousumi had only just turned seventeen, and by modern professional standards this was a little too young to get married. Rekha didn't want to betray her own modest village background by marrying Mousumi off to the first coconut-seller who came along. And

Anil would be of no help to her. So, what to do?

After a few days of deliberation, she penned a letter to Tuhina (instead of a phone call, which she believed would not convey the right degree of importance).

Sachi had barely mentioned his sister, but when he did talk about her to friends he was trying to impress, he would say of her, 'She has top, top job in London. Obviously luck plays its part, but also clever girl.' Tapping his head, he would continue, 'Got something up here,' and then add graciously 'Husband a very good man, too.'

And as Sachi rarely gave compliments, Rekha thought that Tuhina must be a very clever woman indeed. Certainly clever enough to know what to do with Mousumi. So she wrote:

Dearest Tuhina,

Even though deep in grief over the death of my beloved husband (your brother also), I felt that I should write to you so you do not think you are alone at this difficult time.

I know it must be very hard for you not being able to attend your own flesh-and-blood's funeral, but of course it was all so sudden and un-expected. I am still in deep shock and I will never be able to understand why God has made us all suffer this, but we must accept what has been written on our foreheads and carry on living as best as we can.

As you can imagine, this is an especially difficult time for Mousumi, who is not even a woman yet. I really do not know what to do with her and I thought you could offer some wise words. In this modern world, finding a husband is a very difficult job, especially without the efforts of a father. So I am really feeling the pressure, a widow with a teenage daughter, and society's eyes on me. I thought, then, that maybe Mousumi could perhaps stay with you in England for, say, six months to a year, which wouldn't be too disruptive to her studies. She will have the chance to improve her English (and here, young men from good families like their wives to speak English well) and generally smarten up in the ways of the world. A little Western Touch brings added attraction, as you know.

I know this is a very large request, but I am sure that you will understand my position. As you know, your brother has always been very proud of you and you had a special place in his heart. I know that even in heaven, he will be watching over you.

Please write back or call with any advice you have. And give my love to Darshini and Prakash Da.

Rekha.

Mousumi came back home an hour and a half past curfew time. Now that her father was no longer around, there was no one to tell her off. Her mother didn't even ask where she had been. She turned on the television and watched a programme her father wouldn't have allowed. She sat on the sofa, relaxed, no longer tense and waiting for the slammed door which had always signified Sachi's arrival. Her mother called from the kitchen that dinner was ready. Mousumi answered back that she would eat in the sitting room; her father had always insisted that they eat at the dinner table. She felt calm.

Tuhina was expecting the letter. She arranged herself on the chaise, steeled with a bottle of Chablis. She could hear Prakash sauntering around in the kitchen, happily mixing spices in his brand-new blender, and Darshini watching television in the den; she had the sitting room to herself.

Putting the piece of paper down for a moment, she looked around the room and breathed it in. This was her room: everything in it had been chosen and arranged by her. The heavy raw silk pistachio drapes clung lazily to the huge sash windows. The teak floor looked slightly dull but distinguished from use. A taupe cashmere blanket sat politely on the Queen Anne chair in the corner, next to a bookcase in which the hardback books were arranged alphabetically by author. The fresh flowers – creamy peonies and marbled pink roses – that were delivered every Saturday morning rested in a large Murano speckled beige glass vase on the marble fireplace. Tuhina smiled. Then her face settled back to its normal expression of repose, and she sliced open the airmail and read its contents. Then she put it down, took a sip of wine, casually rolled her thorny-lashed eyes upwards, and said 'Shit.'

CHAPTER FIVE

The Roving Eye

Rekha pulled out of the armoire a battered old suitcase, in which she had packed her own belongings when she had moved away from home to live with Sachi. Her own mother had also used it when travelling from East Pakistan to India during Partition. It was a historical suitcase filled with anguish and sadness and hope. When Rekha pushed the lid open, the smell of dry-cleaned saris, sandalwood soap and attar rose from it, filling her nose with nostalgia and her eyes with tears. She had lost her husband and now she was losing her daughter, too. By choice. It was almost too much for her to bear; maybe there was some way that she could tell Tuhina she had changed her mind. But the flimsy business-class ticket, worth more than Rekha could comprehend, was sitting in Sachi's combination-lock briefcase, which Rekha had occupied with her own few pieces of paper, and there was no way back. To comfort herself, she thought, But it is a return ticket, a *return* ticket, although the anguish was so heavy it nearly flattened her under its weight.

Meanwhile, Hariprasad stacked the confectionery in his store room, running a hand repetitively through his thick, slick hair, and wondered where Mousumi had gone. She never missed visiting him on a school day, but it was now Wednesday and he had not seen her all week. He had prepared, with his own hands, some extra-soft shandesh for her, the kind that would crumble down her chin, leaving a greasy snail-trail around her mouth, but now it was turning rancid. He would have to find her. And perhaps take her a gift. And on his way, he decided, he would visit Mrs Chatterjee, one of his oldest and dearest friends, to whom he had been devoted since he was a young boy. He wondered what to take her, and decided on flowers; Mrs Chatterjee always appreciated beauty.

It was Mrs Chatterjee's servant who opened the door, and Hariprasad lingered behind him, waiting to be led through to the drawing room. But as soon as the fragrance of roses and magnolias wafted through the flat, Mrs Chatterjee called out, 'Hariprasad, is that you!' and he immediately pushed past the servant and hurried to her.

*　*　*

When Hariprasad was six, his father had told him
the story of Lord Ram, who had sought the blessing
of the Goddess Durga before his final battle against
Ravan. Durga had demanded one hundred blue
lotuses from him but Ram was only able to collect
ninety-nine. Instead of the hundredth lotus, Ram
cut out one of his own blue eyes and offered it to
Durga, along with the flowers. She was so taken by
this show of intense devotion that she appeared
before him, conferring her blessing on him; Ram
won the battle. In that way, Hariprasad learned the
power of devotion.

Mrs Chatterjee lived on the top floor of a flat on
Camac Street. She lived with a general servant
(cooking included), and spent most of her time
reminiscing about the times when her husband was
still around and she had one servant to oil her hair
and massage her feet, one to press her saris with
rose water, one to dust her trinkets and mahogany
furniture, one to cook her lau-chingree, and one to
chauffeur her from friends' houses to the Chinese
beauty parlour.

Mrs Chatterjee's apartment had changed little in
over twenty years. It was kept as it had been in her
golden years of carmine nail varnish and Darjeeling
sipped from delicate china cups painted with
decorative elephants. The velvet on the daybed had

faded in parts to a pale pistachio; the intricately patterned Persian rug had grown threadbare around the edges; the side-pillows had lost their firmness – the place was in a state of elegant decay. Mrs Chatterjee herself was fading gently. When Mrs Chatterjee's husband had left her (he never asked for a divorce), her heart had stopped momentarily, and when it started again the pulse was faint and sleepy. Once she had lost Love she had decided never to look for it again; her Love was irreplaceable.

In Hariprasad, however, she found the cotton softness of comfort. As time went on, she met with the world less and instead asked of it through him. He kept her up-to-date with what was going on: deaths of presidents, births of pop stars, the price of rice, party politics. He understood her need to retire from the world's gaze, to peer at it through the thinnest muslin sieve; acknowledgement existed without words – his acceptance was without intrusive whys and why nots.

When she was younger, she used to love to sit in her rocking-chair, on the little balcony off the sitting room, and watch the children play cricket in the street below. She did not have children of her own, and saw them as delightful curiosities, with their bright eyes and gleaming teeth. Often, after watching them play, she would call to them and ask them to join her for a glass of lassi and some refreshments. One of those young boys had been Hariprasad, nick-named Lhati on account of his skinniness. The first time the stainless-steel dishes, laden with biscuits, salty snacks and mishti, had been put on the table, Hariprasad headed straight for them, while the other kids looked at each other with embarrassed grins and had to be coaxed. Mrs Chatterjee had wished she had the same metabolism as him – she was rather plump, although it was an elegant plump-ness. He had been her favourite. She had been given someone to nurture, and even though he was now an adult, her heart still stored that same maternal love for him; he gave her unoccupied life some filling.

Mr Chatterjee was a Very Important Person and therefore a Very Busy Man. His gait was that of a man whom others waited for: despite being five feet and two inches tall, he walked like a giant, his shoulders straightened, his neck tilted slightly back-wards so that he could peer down his nose, and when he walked, each step was slow and deliberate, as if he were giving the ground beneath him the privilege of caressing his feet. Mr Chatterjee (known as Chatterbox by his minions because of his verbosity) was the Defence Minister for India. Although a more appropriate title would have been

Attack Minister. In common with many men of his stature, he compensated for his height by being super-belligerent. His grand, stately walk was in total contrast to the rapid-fire arguments that shot from his twitching mouth. He openly advocated annexing back Bangladesh and forcing yet another religious conversion amongst its people. He even advocated not allowing Muslims into the Indian Forces, since they would always be Muslim first and Indian second, which would undo the army in any war against Bangladesh.

It was therefore somewhat surprising when a rumour started doing the rounds that Mr Chatterjee was having an affair with a Muslim courtesan. What was not surprising was that Mr Chatterjee was having an affair – he was party to an unusual living arrangement. Despite the fact that his job required him to live in Delhi, Mrs Chatterjee had steadfastly refused to up sticks. She wanted to live in Calcutta where she had grown up and that was that. She liked wandering around the Marble Palace and feeding the dandy peacocks, who had had their hey-day but strutted around their cages like old queens. She enjoyed walking down College Street, with its hundreds of bookshops, and buying books, especially in the English language, that she occasionally read but which more importantly decorated her bookcases beautifully. On grimy close days, she walked along the banks of Mother Gonga and waited for the cool breeze to soothe her prickled skin. She celebrated Calcutta's birthday on the twenty-eighth of August with golda-chingree.

The Delhi wives thought her choice unseemly. They speculated in their salons bedecked with imported Italian furniture that *should* Mr Chatterjee decide to take a, coughcough, companion, well, he could hardly be blamed. A man has certain needs, they said matter-of-factly, whilst sipping cha from diplomatic-gifted china teacups. But their seemingly idle gossip had been a disguised mantra: if they said it enough, surely it would happen. Who did Mrs Chatterjee think she was? So when the rumour broke, they made the right sounds, whilst suppressing their satisfied smiles and keeping their gold-encrusted fingers crossed.

At first the rumour was dismissed by Mr Chatterjee's aides as propaganda put out by the opposition, but soon even they began to wonder if there was actually some truth in it – he was bellicose sporadically instead of continuously, and he often appeared baffled when asked a question, as though his mind was on other matters. After a month of dithering, they decided that someone should follow him. They were ashamed, but the eyes don't lie. So one evening, after a fiery meeting with the chancellor, who demanded to know exactly what Mr Chatterjee's department was doing with the money it had been allocated, his driver Ravi followed him. First, to a fruit stall where Mr Chatterjee felt up a blushing mango. Then to a sweet shop, from which he emerged carrying a white box tied with cerise raffia. His step changed from that of a self-important middle-aged warthog to that of an eager puppy – Ravi began to find it difficult to keep up with him as he bounced along the street, dodging businessmen and tourists. At last he came to a stop next to a young rickshaw wallah who looked incongruously healthy and well-kept, dressed in running shorts and a T-shirt. Ravi hid behind the rickshaw and listened to the conversation.

'Do you know who I am?' Mr Chatterjee enquired suspiciously, with a bristly eyebrow raised.

'No,' answered the man, hesitantly, in case that was the wrong answer.

'Well, let's go then!' Mr Chatterjee said, and then whispered an address, which Ravi could not hear. Ravi had no other choice but to scamper after the rickshaw. He weaved between beeping Ambassadors, circumnavigated holy cows, and dodged past braking scooters, sweating and panting all the way.

Selina Rashid was a broken ballerina. Despite having been born to a beshya who bore children like a stray mongrel bitch, and therefore into a life of bloated, underfed bellies, she dreamed of a time when every tree had its own gardener. For from a scabby ashen body had come a clean-complexioned, leaf-faced girl whose beauty was enough to transcend her beginnings. It had not been enough to make any man forget them, however. Her shrill but sweet singing voice and rhythmic hips had won her many admirers, but their appreciation never stopped there. They rose hastily from her bed in the morning and the sweet nothings of the night before left a sour ringing in her ears.

Until Mr Chatterjee. He, a man of too many words, had been silenced when confronted with her exquisiteness. She was worth putting in a frame. She was also a Muslim – but now repulsion gave way to curiosity and head gave way to loins. And after a few months, loins gave way to heart.

Sex makes men secretive but love makes them careless: they were spotted in the courtyard of the Jama Masjid at sunset, holding hands and gazing above the minarets which were piercing the sky; schoolchildren on an outing at Lodi Gardens saw them walking down the palm-lined avenue, giggled, and then told their teacher, who in turn told them not to be such little gundas; a colleague of Mr Chatterjee's even saw them wandering through Sarojini market and averted his eyes.

As he made his way to Selina's abode that evening, Mr Chatterjee was so intoxicated with passion that he didn't notice his driver stumbling behind him. Ravi watched them through the iron-barred window of a ground-floor flat in an alleyway off Chandni Chowk, the sweat dribbling into his stinging eyes, the smell of garlic mutton from the street vendors itching his nose. The low sun had cast a diffused light on the street, hiding its imperfections and bathing it in a hazy glow.

Inside, Selina Rashid sat on a low chair, her face lit by the lone evening beam struggling through the window. Ravi looked at her face, her head thrown back so he could see her profile, and immediately understood. Then he looked further down her body, which was veiled by the dusky blue light, and saw Mr Chatterjee kneeling between her legs, kissing the inside of her knees. He felt ashamed and excited. Mr Chatterjee edged up her legs. Further and further. And further. Ravi's breath became shallower; he moved away from the window to clutch at the smoky air and then, with one final gulp, fainted into a flower cart. He came round minutes later surrounded by hibiscus flowers, with two yellow tongues tickling his nose. The rumour was true.

The children had waited below Mrs Chatterjee's window for fifteen minutes after their game of throw-the-ball had finished, but there was no sign of her. Eventually Hariprasad was elected to go up to her flat and find out what the matter was. Five minutes later, he appeared on the balcony like a sombre general addressing his troops, and indicated that the others should go home.

Mrs Chatterjee's face was so puffy from crying that she thought she might scare the children, but when Hariprasad turned up on the doorstep, she allowed him in, and then clutched him to her chest for comfort. He did not know what had happened, but pressed to her torso he could hear sorrow in the hollow of her lungs. After half an hour of being crumpled against a tear-soaked sari, Hariprasad was told. He didn't grasp much. What he did understand was that Mrs Chatterjee had been deserted. But *he* was devoted to her and was determined to demonstrate that.

Perfidia was an arrogant Persian cat. She sneered at the stray street-dogs and was courteous when offered a stroking hand, but was not so agreeable as never to extend a claw. She lived in the flat next door to Mrs Chatterjee and would often stretch out on the grey stone of the communal hall area after sunning herself on the balcony. Once, Hariprasad had gone to run his fingers through the warmed fur and had been rewarded with a thin red line bordered by jagged skin, and a piercing blue-eyed glare.

On his way home that evening, Hariprasad took the cat with him; Perfidia screeched and scratched but not enough to overcome Hariprasad's dedication. He took her to a 'doctor' who treated both humans and animals. The doctor was surprised by the request, but he was to be paid well, and besides, it was a cat, not a human. The makeshift operating theatre with its blood-flecked instruments had been witness to worse. The stumpy beggar-children in the vicinity, with their pimps hovering in the background, bore testimony to that.

Despite the trauma, Perfidia lived; she was too proud to die just because she had lost one, albeit eye-catching, eye. That night, Hariprasad took her home and hid her in his room. He took some goat milk, which was already thickening, from the cool stone ledge in the kitchen and moistened his skinny fingertips with them, then rubbed them over Perfidia's mouth. She licked her lips sleepily. He stroked her fur gently. She didn't scratch.

The next morning, Hari crept out of the house before his mother came to wake him, and took Perfidia back home. He replaced her on the sun-heated concrete floor to recover. She stretched, confused, but happy to be back. In his pocket, wrapped in a blood-stained handkerchief, was his token of devotion.

Mrs Chatterjee was too confused to be shocked. She took the roving eye and put it in a preserving jar in which she normally stored chanachur. And then used it as a bookend for her non-fiction books. Hariprasad's ardour sat on the shelf for years cuddled up to Stuart's *The Achievement of Personality: in the light of Psychology and Religion*, until one day the tome collapsed on to the jar and the eye could see no longer.

Mousumi could not eat. Her belly felt full of air; when two pieces of fish managed to get past the gate of her throat, they wouldn't settle and felt as though they were floating around in the uncluttered cavity. She soon released them again.

Meanwhile, Rekha did nothing but eat. She filled the gaping hole in her middle with ghee-laden luchis and aloo-dom, and syrup-soaked sweet samosas, trying to clog up the hole that was letting out all of her strength and energy. She swallowed a rasagulla whole, to plug it up, but she still felt sapped and weary. Still, she had to keep preparing for Mousumi's departure.

They visited their local tailor, which had English clothes patterns from the seventies. Rekha did not want Mousumi turning up in England inappropriately dressed. She wondered whether Sachi would approve of the bell-bottomed trousers, and cropped tops with fluted sleeves. He had been a Western Man, after all.

Mousumi tried to stand still as an undernourished and over-enthusiastic apprentice took her measurements. He stood so close that she could smell his hormone-soaked shirt. His hands jittered as the tape measure stretched across her bosom. She looked down at his head and was disgusted by the pearls of perspiration clinging to his hair like frogspawn. He crouched down and pulled the tape tightly around her hips; she felt the fleshy walls of her inner thighs flatten against each other. She was embarrassed, but she didn't know why. And she felt like an actress in rehearsal who wasn't yet prepared for an audience.

When the apprentice had finished writing down the measurements on creased, salted paper which had held monkey-nuts that morning, he handed it to the tailor, who raised his eyebrows slightly when he came to the hip measurement. Three pairs of trousers, three chemises and two skirts were ordered. And at Rekha's insistence, to mollify her late husband, they were to be decorated with embroidery and joree.

A week later, dressed in one of her new outfits, Mousumi was paraded around to friends and relatives as she said her goodbyes. They turned her into a human pinata, as they pressed little good-luck tokens into her hands, tenderly forced shandesh into her mouth, filled her pockets with a miniature wood statue of Ganesh, a prayer written on the back of a colourful tinsel-framed postcard adorned with the image of Sri Ramakrishna, and rupee coins full of fortune and worth nothing.

Mousumi didn't want to go to London. She might not have liked many people in Calcutta, or more accurately they might not have liked her, but at least she knew what to expect. She had armed herself to deal with superior looks and girls laughing at her. She had learned to cope with her father's tyranny. But now she was facing the unknown. Her tummy ached with anxiety and her palms sweated with fear, but she didn't tell her mother that she didn't want to go. She desperately wanted to be brave.

Tuhina also had a funny feeling in her stomach. It was something warmer than apprehension but colder than anxiety. She couldn't quite locate it – she stored away her memories and their attendant feelings as neatly as a Peter-Pan-bloused librarian files her books. Some folders – Maternal Pride; Anger (subfolder: Others' Incompetence); Amazement (subfolder: Wildlife Programmes) – were full to bursting point and had been visited recently; others, including the one which this feeling belonged to, were cool to the touch and dampening at the edges. She closed her eyes and wandered through the aisles of her mind.

When Darshini heard of Mousumi's pending arrival, she went to her bedroom and flipped a coin: I'll like her, I'll like her not. I'll like her not.

Prakash responded with more contemplation. The last time they had had an Indian in the house was ten years ago, when his brother and sister-in-law had visited. They had brought with them the smell. A smell so powerful that it had affronted his nose and made him long for sour phuchka and ghal-muri from Dalhousie, on the walk home from watching cricket at Eden Gardens with his friends on a summery evening. He wondered whether Mousumi would feel at home, and how she would deal with the weather and the two-headed tigress.

They all went to the airport. The journey there was silent. Mousumi walked through the Arrivals doors wearing a pink satin blouse and skirt suit, with the flight blanket wrapped around her as a shawl, white buckle-up shoes, and an expression both nervous and vacant. Having never flown before, she had not popped her ears, and now she felt as if she was underwater: she could see everything, but even people standing next to her sounded meters away. She carried a single suitcase. Her hand was gripping the handle so tightly that the knuckles had turned white. She looked around, noting the difference between the airport she had departed from and the one she had arrived at. This one was bigger, cleaner, newer; there were more lights, more signs, more people, but they were spaced out and not crammed up together in a seething brown mass. Everyone and everything moved faster. She felt insignificant.

Tuhina recognized her straight away, even though she had not seen a photo of Mousumi since she was six. But she did not say anything. She simply watched as Mousumi looked from side to side, becoming increasingly disconcerted, standing in the way of floppy-haired gap-year students wearing wooden beads and cheesecloth shirts, and hunched-over grandmas wearing socks with their sandals. Prakash and Darshini shared a nervous smile; how were they to know her?

Finally Mousumi looked in their direction, and recognized Tuhina from the photo her mother had given her – a wedding photo where Tuhina's face was obscured by heavy powder and whips of kohl shrouded her eyes, the only photo of Tuhina Rekha had owned. The relief brought tears to her eyes. She dragged her suitcase over to Prakash and went to greet him by touching his feet. Prakash quickly moved before she could give him pranam, and said jovially, 'No rubbish like that over here!', but when

Mousumi went to touch her aunt's feet, Tuhina allowed her to, and when Mousumi's plump brown fingers touched the silky light skin, the feeling travelled through Tuhina's whole body like a bushfire.

CHAPTER SIX

The Bucket

Mousumi sat on her new bed and gazed out of her window, which overlooked the leafy, sedate street. The road, she noticed, was clean – no litter or stray dogs or stray dogs' shit – unlike home. The hedges were well kept, the cars parked on the street were shiny and new without broken wing-mirrors, the windows of the houses were clean and didn't have any bars to keep thieves out.

She had never had her own bedroom before. She bounced on the mattress a little, which creaked under her weight, and pushed down with her hands. The divan was thick and springy, unlike the flat mattress she slept on at home. And instead of a cotton top sheet, there was a cloud-weight sage-green satin quilt. At the bottom of the bed lay a neatly folded cashmere blanket, and at the top, a harem of dusky cushions. She imagined it was the type of bed that a Rajasthani princess would sleep on or maybe a Bollywood film star. She took her long hair out of its plait and ran her fingers through it. Then she lay on the bed, spread her waved hair over the cushions and waited for her prince.

After an hour's nap, she was woken by Prakash's voice. He was speaking to her in Bengali; in unfamiliar surroundings, the sound of her mother tongue soothed her into waking.

'Mousumi, are you sleeping?'

She stirred.

'Sorry, sorry, sleep, sleep. I just thought you might be hungry – are you hungry? I can make you an omelette.'

Mousumi's belly rumbled – she hadn't eaten for several hours.

She watched him carefully as he cooked, trying to hide her surprise – Sachi had never once set foot in the kitchen. She remembered how he had shown an acquaintance around the apartment one day, indicating the kitchen with a dismissive hand gesture and saying grandly, 'Women's things – I don't go in there!' His guest had smiled politely.

Prakash chopped the green chillies until they looked like a pile of freshly cut grass, much finer than Rekha did, equipped with her swollen fingers and blunt knife. And he cut the onions without crying; Rekha would blubber over them, sniffing and weeping, and pulling up the anchol of her sari to dab at her eyes.

They ate out in the garden, just the two of them. Tuhina had gone back to work after dropping them off at home, and Darshini had gone out. Prakash had said nothing. He thought it rude that she was going out so soon after Mousumi had arrived, but he couldn't muster the authority to tell his daughter to stay. Although he had very firmly but politely told Darshini that she was to take Mousumi out later in the week for a sightseeing tour of London – Darshini had shrugged lightly and said 'Whatever.' Rage had built up at his temples like seagulls crowding on a cliff top, but then subsided. He didn't want Mousumi to think they weren't a happy family. She might tell her mother, and then everyone back home would gossip over cups of tea and biscuits.

Whilst Prakash washed the dishes, Mousumi took a turn round the large garden, with its romantic climbing roses which sprawled seductively over a set of fine metal arches, and a pond containing the smallest orange fish she had ever seen. Instead of dry and brittle earth, the soil in the flowerbeds was moist and crumbly like a chocolate brownie. The flowers were prim and elegant, organized into groups of matching colours, like lunching ladies. The shrubs didn't have a hair out of place. There was no room for dissent.

When she walked back into the kitchen, she saw Darshini leaning over the sink, drinking a glass of water, her angular shoulder-length hair glinting under the lights. Mousumi touched her own oiled witch's hair self-consciously, trying to coil it into a bun. Darshini turned her head to look at her and then turned straight back.

'Did you a good evening?' Mousumi asked. She had picked up a few phrases from American daytime soaps (which she had sneakily watched when her father wasn't in the house) and from Sachi's occasional English conversations on the phone, when he was trying to impress.

'It's have.'

Mousumi looked nervous; her hands became clammy and minute beads of sweat formed on her wide nose.

'It's "Did you *have* a good evening?" And yes, I did. Thank you for asking.' Darshini's condescension was vicious; her civility was a sleek silver case containing a poison pill. From the sitting room, where Prakash was reading the newspaper, he could hear the conversation. Again, the seagulls started to gather at his temples, but this time they squawked loudly and flapped their wings.

Seph was perpetually unpacking. His flat had an air of grand emptiness about it. Comfort made him feel

115

smothered; mantelpieces crowded with faux-antique-framed family photographs tightened his chest, just-so-placed cushions prickled him. Yet he was naturally extravagant – he threw away used wine glasses instead of washing them and had all of his laundry cleaned outside, even his socks. His home was like a sharp, cold winter's day – pale and refreshing.

Since his teens, Seph had attracted neglected women. Whilst his friends were cavorting with girls of their own age, having sloppy sex in their parents' sitting rooms, inhaling too lightly on a cigarette and talking too loudly about their conquests, Seph was familiarizing himself with women twice his age. He did not find it either exciting or unusual. In fact, he thought there was something desperate and sad about it; after sleeping with them, he felt the same way he did after watching re-runs of *The Black and White Minstrel Show*. He always told these women that he loved them, not because he did, but out of a sense of necessity and duty.

He left his home in Cushendall with the desperation of a wild animal caught in a trap, chewing off its own leg to escape. But in London he found his allure stronger than ever. Like ants to a melting toffee stuck on a dirty pavement, women who needed to be reassured, loved, cherished, swarmed over him. They went into his flat and tried to make their imprint on the place, but he resisted. They left items behind – a toothbrush, a hairband – only to find the next time they came that they had been placed in a carrier bag, ready to be taken away. Seph was trying to escape again.

When he had seen that photo of Darshini on his manager's wall, he saw someone who didn't need reassurance, and he felt relieved. And each day he saw that photo, he felt lighter. When he lay next to her for the first time, his stomach wasn't gurgling with pity. And when she didn't leave anything behind, he wished that she had.

Originally from California, the Darlingtonia californica, or Cobra Lily as she is more commonly known, is one of the most prized of carnivorous plants. The Cobra Lily was given her name because of the unusual pitchers that curve upwards, along with her rounded head and two fang-like projections jutting from what could be her mouth. The Cobra Lily originates in areas where cool running water permeates the ground and the plant is therefore not very tolerant of high temperatures. Cobras are considered challenging to grow and much is dependent on where the plant is kept.

'I thought it would look nice in your flat,' said Darshini casually as she walked in. 'Do you like it?'

She placed it on the window ledge. Her tone implied curiosity, not care.

'Er, yeah,' replied Seph, a little quickly. Then, after a pause, 'What is it?'

'It's a Cobra Lily.'

'Well, er, thanks a million.'

They went out to eat – Darshini insisted on walking to a Korean restaurant on Marlborough Street and they lost their way. A few taxis, proclaiming their availability with strips of yellow light, were ignored.

'We could get a cab,' Seph ventured.

'It's a nice night,' she replied, by way of an answer.

For as long as she could remember, Darshini had enjoyed getting lost. Since September 1522, when Pigafetta and the crew of the *Victoria* arrived back in Spain, having circumnavigated the globe, there was proof that falling off the earth was an impossibility; wherever you started from, there was always a way back. She didn't understand other people's fear of the unknown.

As Darshini made her way through the unfamiliar streets, Seph kept up with her, but his steps were more tentative, his gaze more furtive. The lack of rhythm in his step put Darshini off her own stride. She stopped dead, and turned to face him.

'Are you scared?' she asked matter-of-factly.

'Of what?' he said, glancing from side to side.

118

'Don't be. You won't enjoy it then,' she said gently, so as not to dent him, and continued strolling.

In London, darkness comes slowly in summer. Every shade of the sun coats buildings, roads, parks and people until they melt very suddenly into a deep translucent grey, as if embraced by a squirrel's tail, at about nine, perhaps half past. From then, everything is lit fleetingly by street lights, neon signs on XXX shops, glaring car headlamps.

Having trailed through backstreets with derelict warehouses brightened by suggestive graffiti, and wandered down tree-lined avenues filled with the smoky perfume of cars and buses and scooters, they finally emerged in Soho, where the smell of burgers frying in their own fat whetted their appetites. They were exhausted and exhilarated and forgot about the Korean restaurant, instead settling for street-vendor sausages, fat and hot in their tight shiny skins, topped with fried onions, caramelized to a sticky burnt-sienna around the edges.

'Do you want to come back to mine?' Seph asked, wiping his mouth with the greasy hot-dog wrapper.

'I can't; my dad said I have to take my cousin out tomorrow morning.'

The phrase 'my dad said' reminded Seph how young she was and he waited for the pang of guilt, the dry mouth, but nothing came. Her age had become a fact without sensation.

'Your cousin?' he asked, hoping for some more detail.

'Yeah,' she replied, not giving him any.

'Well, come over on Saturday morning then. We'll spend the day together.' He didn't raise his voice at the end; he wanted to see how she would respond to direction.

'OK, see you then.'

She pressed herself up against him so hard that he could feel her hipbones digging into him, kissed him firmly on the lips, smiled and walked away before he had a chance to say anything else.

On his way home he tried to count how many words he had said that evening. Definitely less than fifty. Was fifty words per evening an acceptable level? he thought. He had never been short on words before: charming words, funny words, encouraging words, words-that-got-women-into-bed words. Now he was reduced to functional words only – yes, no, Saturday morning. He ran his tongue along the roof of his mouth and along the walls of his cheeks, as if to feel whether any words were stuck there.

When he arrived home, he went straight to the Cobra Lily. She looked impatient, as if she was waiting to be fed. Seph didn't know how to take care of her. He looked around for an instruction leaflet, but Darshini hadn't left one.

* * *

By the time Mousumi made it downstairs to the kitchen the next morning, Tuhina and Prakash had already gone to work. Darshini was ready to go, dressed in a pair of low-cut tight jeans and a floral-patterned lace and silk camisole that Mousumi thought looked more suited to bedtime. She sat at the table and toyed with a glass of orange juice, moving her head slowly from side to side to stretch her elegant neck. Her gleaming hair swung from side to side. Mousumi was still in her nightdress, her hair an unbrushed thatch.

'You ready to go, then?' Darshini asked, raising her eyebrows slowly and running her tongue along her top teeth.

Mousumi wasn't sure what Darshini had asked her, but her expression made her feel nervous, and she crossed her arms in front of her; her flimsy gown felt transparent under Darshini's direct gaze.

'Go up – change?' she asked, pointing to the ceiling, then tugging on her nightie.

'Good idea,' answered Darshini, twisting a strand of hair around her finger and cocking her head again.

They took the Tube to Baker Street and boarded an open-top bus. Darshini bought the tickets from a young Indian man, and he smiled at Mousumi in recognition. Mousumi grinned back – he was the first person apart from Prakash who had smiled at her since she had arrived in London.

Mousumi had never seen a double-decker bus before and was pleased when Darshini climbed the stairs to sit on the top deck, right at the front. Mousumi watched carefully as more passengers boarded. A group of ten geriatrics in matching blue T-shirts printed with SUNSET RETIREMENT HOME creaked up the stairs, and fussed over where they should sit. A young man, equipped with a nappy bag, and a portable cot, struggled on to the top deck, followed by a woman carrying a gurgling, farting baby wearing a pink sun hat.

As the bus started on its way, Darshini pulled a magazine out of her bag, and idly began to leaf through it. Mousumi surreptitiously glanced at the pages but Darshini caught her and closed the magazine, indicating that Mousumi should put her headphones on. Mousumi quickly did so, but she couldn't hear anything. She looked around, confused. Darshini leaned down, picked up the end of her cousin's headphones and plugged them into the socket.

'Thank you,' Mousumi said.

Darshini nodded in acknowledgement.

But still Mousumi couldn't understand what was going on: the language was completely unintelligible to her. Again, she looked confused. Darshini noticed and peered over at the small panel displaying flags.

'You're listening to it in Japanese,' she said, unmoved. 'You need English.' She tapped a button. 'All OK now?'

Mousumi listened for a moment and nodded, even though she could still barely understand what the guide was saying. So she stopped trying, and just looked out in front of her instead. But she didn't find any of the buildings impressive – they were dull and grey and boring compared to the fancy palaces in India with their intricately carved facades and their beautifully decorated domes. But she didn't want Darshini to think she wasn't enjoying herself, so every so often she gave her a quick smile and Darshini gave her one back.

Stopping off at Leicester Square, Mousumi's attention was caught by the rows of caricaturists and portrait painters. What brilliant artists they are, she thought, delighted. Darshini noticed her watching them, and asked, 'Do you want one done?'

'Hmm?' asked Mousumi.

Darshini pointed at one of the portraitists, and then pointed at Mousumi and raised her eyebrows.

'Me?' beamed Mousumi, astonished and excited that she might have her picture painted. 'Me?'

'Yeah, sure,' Darshini replied nonchalantly.

Mousumi sat down nervously on the wobbly stool. It was still warm from the last person to have sat on it, and she shifted around uncomfortably.

'Sit still, love,' directed the man.

Mousumi stopped moving. She wanted her picture to be perfect. Shaking her hair over her shoulders, she tilted her chin up, stretched out her bulky legs and placed her hands, one on top of the other, on her knees. She breathed as lightly as she could.

Ten minutes later, the man took one more glance at her, nodded, and then said, satisfied, 'All done.'

Mousumi jumped up enthusiastically from her seat and went to take a look at her portrait. As soon as she saw it, her face fell. The person looking back at her had huge bulging breasts, wild frizzy hair, padded knees, dimpled fingers, a double chin, a large bulbous nose, piggy black eyes. It was grotesque.

'Like it?' Darshini asked, paying the man. 'It's quite good, I think.'

'Yes, please,' said Mousumi. She didn't know what else to say.

After that, Mousumi lost her energy, and even when Darshini took her to Selfridges food hall she didn't perk up much. As they munched on a hot beef sandwich (Darshini didn't tell her what kind of meat it was and Mousumi didn't ask), Darshini asked, 'So, you want to go to Madame Tussauds?'

Mousumi shook her head.

'Well, what about the London Eye?'

Mousumi didn't respond, so Darshini drew a large circle on her napkin, and two stick people walking towards it. Mousumi glanced at the drawing and shrugged.

'Well, what about Buckingham Palace, then? You know, where the Queen lives.'

Mousumi wanted to go home and curl up in bed.

'Tired,' she said hopefully.

'Oh,' Darshini said. 'OK. I guess we can go home then.'

As soon as they got home, Mousumi went to her bedroom. And stayed there. When Prakash got home that night, he asked Darshini, who was sitting in the den, 'So, did you have a good time? Where's Mousumi? What did you do?'

Darshini looked at her father and said, very clearly, 'No, we didn't have a good time. We didn't do anything because she was tired and grumpy, so next time, why don't you take her out yourself?' She got up from the sofa and brushed past Prakash, adding, 'And for your information, she's in bed and has been since half two this afternoon!'

Prakash was lost for words.

Mrs Chatterjee sat down on her bed. Ever since Mr Chatterjee had left, she slept only on the right-hand side of it. The left side was decorated with needle-point cushions and silk bolsters. Since her husband's departure, Mrs Chatterjee spent a lot of time in bed, trying to sleep, willing herself to dream of happier times. She would close the wooden-slatted shutters and sink into the mattress, her palms pressed into her belly, thinking about the child that she would now never have, thinking of his name, his voice, his tiny hand wrapped around her little finger, his hot milky baby smell. Next she would fantasize that her husband would come back to her, and tell her that he had made a mistake: he had always loved her, and always would. But occasionally her own thoughts would become too much for her, and she would rise from her bed and throw open the shutters to let the outside world back in. Then she would pick up the newspaper and read about other people's lives so that she could escape from her own.

Since her little accident, Perfidia had become rather lazy, and instead of using the litter tray in one of the pantries, she would go to the loo whenever and wherever it pleased her. Her owners didn't have it in their hearts to tell her off – she was disabled, after all, and allowances had to be made for her condition.

One particular afternoon, Perfidia was feeling especially lazy. Taking respite from the midday sun, she sat on Mrs Chatterjee's doormat on top of *The Times of India*, which was delivered every morning and had been dropped on the mat with especial excitement that morning. And then she did her business. The brown sludge seeped through the paper, the top pages disintegrating on contact with the putrid goo. Perfidia shuffled away and found herself another less pungent place to slumber.

At two that afternoon, after an unsatisfactory session of daydreaming, Mrs Chatterjee went to fetch the newspaper. As she opened the front door, the smell of the turd, which had been baking in the heat, hit her. At first she turned her nose up and sniffed the air, wondering from where the smell came. It was only when she looked down that she realized what had happened. 'Ish!' she said to herself as she pulled her sari up to make sure that the hem didn't touch the edge of the newspaper. She squatted down to rest on her haunches, keeping her back straight, her nostrils pinched together between thumb and forefinger, and looked down her nose to see if she could make out at least the headline, but it was no good. All she could see was a smudged JEE and a faded ERNM. She rose to her feet carefully, then called to her servant to clean the mess up. And to hurry up with it! The servant ran to the door and gathered up the mess. Up so close and personal, he could just make out the headline, and had he not been illiterate he would have seen that it read CHATTE JEE OUST D FROM GOVERNM NT.

* * *

There were three bathrooms in the house, one for each floor. Until Mousumi arrived, Darshini had had the use of the top bathroom all to herself. Now, she had to share it. She wasn't used to sharing. She liked the idea of it, but wasn't quite sure how to. She wondered whether she should clear a little shelf space for Mousumi, but then she saw the contents of her wash-bag – and decided they didn't warrant it; they weren't smart enough to be on display. She realized that wasn't very sisterly of her, but sentiment, she thought, should not get in the way of good taste. Although in the end she conceded to her conscience and cleared a little room on the ledge behind the door.

It was the bucket, and to a lesser degree the jug in it, which aggravated her. It appeared in the third week of Mousumi's stay. The uncouth object was squatting in her original French bateau bath, which had been restored to a deep rose pink, with gilt ball-and-claw feet. The intruder was fluorescent yellow, plastic. Darshini picked it up by the handle, holding it at arm's length as if it was a pair of soiled knickers, and walked into Mousumi's bedroom, knocking on the door but not waiting for a response.

'Is this yours?' she asked, her tone thoughtful.

Mousumi turned around, surprised. She was naked, her damp hair tangled against her back, her

128

body still dripping. She struggled to contain herself in the small towel; if she covered her breasts, her pubic area showed and vice versa.

Sensing her discomfort, Darshini settled down on the bed. As Mousumi tried to dress, Darshini, as objectively as an art critic, dissected the picture in front of her. The feet were ugly for a start. Peasant's feet. Not Greek like hers, or Roman like Seph's. OK ankles, but could do with being finer-boned. Fat calves. Fat knees with darkened skin – perhaps try lemon juice. Loose, unrefined thighs. Darshini leaned back on her elbows, delicate, soft, and extended a ballet dancer's leg. Pubic hair, hmmm, unruly, like spider's legs, not enough shape; topiary needs trimming. She wondered whether to suggest it.

Mousumi had by now managed to pull some clothes out of her drawers, and was struggling to get into her undergarments. She dropped her towel as she fought with a pair of panties. Belly: too much of it. Far too much of it. Breasts: pendulous, like a cow's udders. Tiny pimple nipples (no good for sucking), amorphous areolae. Rounded shoulders, surprisingly sharp collarbones.

Mousumi still hadn't answered her question.

'So, *is* this yours?' Darshini asked again, knocking the bucket over with a pointed foot. Mousumi looked at it and nodded. A little frown appeared between Darshini's eyebrows. 'Well, what's it for?'

Mousumi walked over to the bucket, tipped it back to standing position and started miming, filling the jug with non-existent water from the bucket and then tipping it over her head.

'Yeah,' said Darshini, dismissing the little sketch with a wave of her hand. 'You don't have to do that in England. You can use the shower. I'll show you.'

Furtively, Mousumi followed her to the bathroom. 'Look,' Darshini said, rolling her sleeves up, 'H for hot, and C for cold.' Mousumi nodded. 'Clockwise, on. Anti-clockwise, off.' She demonstrated by turning the water on and wetting her forearms under the tap. 'Now this,' she said as if she was a magician revealing her trick, 'is the lever that turns the shower on!' She pulled the knob and water sprayed down from the showerhead, splashing her top. 'Look!' she said, admiring the jet of water as if it was snow on Christmas Day. She smiled.

'Thank you,' said Mousumi. 'But I like bucket. OK?' She wobbled her head from side to side.

No, it was not bloody OK, thought Darshini. It was a downright affront to her sensibilities. 'Yeah, fine,' she deadpanned. 'Suit yourself.'

At school, Darshini had been exempt from games. It wasn't that she wasn't any good, she just couldn't understand the point of them. During her first game of hockey, when a terrier of a girl had raced towards her for the tackle, Darshini had simply moved away from the ball and let her have it. When her teacher asked her why she hadn't tried to keep possession, she had replied that the other girl wanted the ball, and she didn't. Her teacher looked thoughtful. 'Don't you want to win?' she had asked finally. 'No,' Darshini shrugged.

Her teacher believed that the problem was that she was afraid of being hit by a hockey stick. She thought that Darshini might be better at something less aggressive. With her physique, she was a natural middle-distance runner. In training, she had consistently come up with times that beat the school's record. But in her first competition, some-thing amazing happened: on the last hundred-metre straight, Darshini was well ahead of the competition when, two strides away from finishing, she stopped dead, allowing the girl behind her to cross first, before casually walking over the white painted line. Later on, her teacher again asked her why. Darshini answered that in the changing room the other girl had said she was desperate to win. 'And you're *not* desperate to win?' her teacher had queried incredu-lously. Equally incredulous, Darshini replied with a dismissive stare, 'No.'

The teacher wrote a letter to Tuhina and Prakash asking them to come in for a chat. They duly turned up and were informed of the problem. 'Well, I don't suppose it's too much of a crisis as long as she doesn't want to be a sportswoman,' Tuhina had said wryly. The teacher's suggestion that perhaps the problem was the lack of siblings was met with polite laughter, although when they arrived back home Prakash had asked Darshini whether she would like a brother or a sister. 'No,' she had answered, without looking away from the television screen. The matter was never brought up again.

The only games that Darshini liked were ones that she could play on her own. Patience had been a favourite, as had the Rubik's Cube. But she cheated. If she didn't turn over a red five to follow a black six, she would gently lift the corner of each face-down card before she found one. When she couldn't twist the Rubik's Cube into six walls, each face with a different colour, she would peel the stickers off and rearrange them. And then one day she flipped a coin and stopped playing games altogether.

So on Saturday morning, when Seph called Darshini and suggested they go for a game of tennis, he was turned down. He didn't know why; there was no face in front of him to read for clues, no tell-tale tone of voice in the simple 'No, thank you.' His belly felt hollow. 'But you still want to hang out?' he asked tentatively. 'Sure,' she replied, 'I'll be round in an hour.' Seph put the phone down. His palm was white from clenching the receiver. Relief is the most concrete of emotions.

As Darshini walked down the stairs, she could smell the coffee brewing and bacon frying – Prakash made a fry-up once a month on a Saturday morning, as well as offering Tuhina a double whisky (single malt) on Friday nights, and eating a boiled egg with soldiers on Wednesday morning (he *would* eat that every morning but he had to keep his cholesterol down. Lead by example, and all that). She could hear the fizz as eggs were cracked into the heated oil, and the whine of metal against metal as Prakash pulled out the grill tray to turn the sausages. She felt the saliva build in her mouth. As she walked into the kitchen, she saw Tuhina sitting by the breakfast bar, reading the newspapers. They exchanged a brief greeting. Tuhina didn't like talking first thing in the morning. Nor did she like any kind of noise, music or television, so as Darshini switched on the TV she turned the volume down to watch Jerry silently hitting Tom over the head with a frying-pan.

Mousumi walked into the kitchen just as Prakash was putting the plates on the table. Prakash smiled at her and said, 'Good morning, Mou.' He was pleased with the diminutive; he had come up with it himself. Darshini looked up from the television and offered a vague nod. Tuhina kept reading the newspaper.

Mousumi sat down and looked at the crowded plate before her. So far, she had only taken toast (or a version of – bagels, crumpets, Scotch pancakes) or cereal for breakfast. She recognized only the two fried eggs and two pieces of toast. The unfamiliar bacon, unadorned by garlic or ginger or spices, made her belly churn, but she didn't want to offend anyone, so she cut a piece and gingerly put it in her mouth. Seconds later she retched. Tuhina looked up from the newspaper. Prakash immediately took the plate away.

Mousumi caught her breath and said, 'Sorry, Kaku. The smell hurts,' with an apologetic smile.

Prakash nodded. He had felt the same way when he first came over to England. The odour of roasting meat had made him feel sick. Once, an English friend of his had invited him to his family's house one weekend for a Sunday roast, and Prakash had spent the whole meal excusing himself to go to the bathroom. 'How many times does the poor bugger have to pray?' he had heard his friend's mother say as he left the dining room.

Darshini wasn't as sympathetic.

'What are you? A Muslim?' she said, raising her eyebrows sardonically.

'Shut up,' Prakash snapped. Darshini looked at Prakash with what looked like amusement but was actually bemusement. She picked up a sausage and then pushed the plate away. She kissed her mum on the forehead, and walked out of the room.

'Where is she going?' Prakash asked Tuhina.

'To see Seph, I think.'

Prakash wanted to ask exactly what the relationship was between Seph and Darshini, but he didn't want to reveal that he didn't know what his own daughter was up to. He had once read an article of Tuhina's on game theory. It was even more difficult in practice.

'Oh,' he said as neutrally as possible, and then turned to Mousumi, and asked brightly, 'What about some cereal and toast, then?'

'I hate her,' Darshini said to Seph. He was brushing her hair into a ponytail, so she shook her head free of him to turn around and see his reaction.

'It took me ages to do that!' he said in mock annoyance as the strands fell from his hands.

'I really do,' she said emphatically.

'Why?'

'She's just awful.' She fixed him with her cat's eyes.

'I can imagine,' he said with feeling, then started to brush her hair again.

Darshini turned around again, pleased. They always took each other's side, and not just to please each other but because they meant it. 'I don't like him', 'Neither do I'; 'I think that was weird', 'Same here'.

Despite being nearly ten years older than Darshini, Seph often felt younger. But when he had been with those other women, he had felt older than them despite being younger. It was because Darshini didn't make what he categorized as *female requests*. She'd say 'Kill that spider,' or 'My feet hurt – carry me home,' but not 'How do you feel about me?', or 'Why don't you *ever* listen to what I'm saying?' Those were the questions which made him feel old, weary, as if an annoying child was tugging on his sleeve, demanding his attention. What Seph should have done was to say something, anything, to make them shut up – there are standard answers to standard questions. But they took his aloofness as a sign of sensitivity and clucked over him even more. So, despite not wanting their over-eager affections, he became used to being indulged, until the point where he would purposefully withdraw, just so they would chase after him to win back his attention. But after the delightful little cruelty would come the guilt. He would capitulate by lavishing them with what he called *princess gifts* – hand-tied bunches of birds-of-paradise and ginger flowers wrapped in royal-purple crepe paper, Italian handmade stilettos (which he would occasionally ask them to keep on in bed), antique seed-pearl and diamond earrings ('I thought they'd look pretty on you'); he knew that women, despite any superficial protestations ('Love doesn't cost a thing,' etcetera), never turned down extravagance – it made them feel precious.

Rekha looked at the clock on the bedside table. It was three in the afternoon and she still hadn't got out of bed. She hadn't left the flat since returning from the airport. She drew the curtains and sank back down in her mattress. She simply couldn't work out what to do with herself. She had even lost her appetite. When the midday sun became too powerful for the curtain to contain, she pulled the sheet up over her head and retreated into a world that was filled only with her, and the smell of an unwashed body – salty and sour and sweet. And not the smell of laziness either, but the smell of grief. The phone rang intermittently; Rekha knew that her relatives would be concerned, but she didn't want sympathy. She wanted to wrap her suffering around her, like a layer of clingfilm that had grown saggy from overuse.

A week after taking Mousumi to the airport, there was loud knocking on the door. Rekha tried to ignore it, but the sound was urgent, insistent, and would not go away. She crawled from her bed, her sorrow trailing behind her. Her skin had slackened like a baby Shar-Pei's and her hair was as matted as a shadhu's. She looked like the crazy beggar-woman who squatted under the bridge, caked with patties of cow dung, who cursed through a gummy mouth at anyone who didn't throw a few coins into the hammock of her filthy sari.

She eventually opened the door to find a palm-tree-shaped man standing outside, brandishing a turquoise paper box of mishti tied with pink ribbon. They were from Harry's. Her favourite.

Hariprasad was a romantic pragmatist. When Mousumi had stopped visiting his shop, he had asked one of her classmates what her home address was; his excuse was that he had promised to post a magazine. Having no reason to doubt him, she told him, and to thank her he allowed her to take her pick of the sweets. After much thoughtful sighing she picked a packet of guava-flavoured lollipops. Mousumi's privacy had been sold for twenty-three rupees.

And so he turned up on her doorstep, with a turquoise box of his milkiest shandesh, tied with pink ribbon, and a magazine, determined to woo her back. But when the door opened he was confronted by something similar but not the same, a larger size in a series of Russian matryoshka dolls. The hair may have been matt not gloss, and the skin a little darker, but the vital attributes were there: the rounded limbs, the swollen breasts, the wavy belly. Hariprasad smiled, gave a little bow whilst bringing his hands together in a namaste, and invited himself inside. He explained who he was and asked whether he might give the magazine and shandesh to Mousumi in person. At which point Rekha burst into tears, her chest heaving and wheezing, and her lips quivering. Hariprasad did not know what had happened, but instinctively, and quite inappropriately, went to put his arms around her. The damp stench of sorrow took him back to a time when he was still in short pants and played cricket in the street outside Mrs Chatterjee's apartment. Another deserted woman; he could smell it.

When Rekha finally stopped blubbering, she told Hariprasad exactly what had happened. He was momentarily heartbroken, then he took a closer look at Rekha herself – the delightfully protruding tummy, the soft rounded shoulders, the tight skin around her chubby fingers, and best of all, the ballooned breasts, and thought nonchalantly, 'Why not?', as if he were deciding whether to eat another bag of puffed wheat sprinkled with palm sugar. After all, he needed to devote himself to someone whilst Mousumi was away. And although Rekha was older, she certainly didn't seem wiser, so how difficult could it be to weaken her plump boneless knees?

Well, slightly more effort than he had expected, as it turned out, but Hariprasad loved a challenge. Their courtship began mid-morning, in the tea houses around College Street, over masala chai and samosas, then moved on to lunchtime showings of first Bollywood and then Hollywood movies, where they would come out blinking into the afternoon sun and go on to Tulika's ice-cream parlour to eat ice-cream sandwiches and nutty delights. Then finally it reached the home straight – dinner at Amber or Silver Grill, followed by a romantic stroll around a moonlit Victoria Memorial. Hariprasad decided where, and Hariprasad decided when. Rekha did as she was told.

Rekha had never thought about her own pleasure and Sachi had never thought about it either. She had been a silent recipient of dry, closed-mouth kisses and a motion which was not even animal but mechanical. Although it didn't really worry her, as she was quite indifferent to any activity of that nature. When Hariprasad first kissed her, she leaned back, her eyes shut and her lips shut even tighter, as she had seen her screen heroines do. He tried to wrench her mouth open with his own, but to no avail; she wasn't that way inclined, and would rather have been watching television. Besides, she knew it was only white *actresses* in *those* films who kissed like that. And she was not only a respectable woman, but a respectable widow! But although she didn't want to, and was well within her rights not to, in time she gave in. She couldn't defy him. She wasn't allowed to.

Why did Rekha never rebel? Because her father didn't think her capable of it; rebellion is a parasite feeding off the blood of disapproval.

When Rekha was fourteen, she had attempted to be defiant. Her life was not tailored to her needs or wants; it was a badly fitting off-the-peg suit. The poor who live in the villages of India don't have the luxury of bespoke; she could either wear it or go naked. Her father Vishnu owned a grocer's shop in the commercial centre of the village, which comprised a sweet shop; a fabric and sari seller; two jewellers; two other grocers; a butcher; a fish-monger; a purveyor of cigarettes, bootleg alcohol and candy; and a bicycle repair man. Vishnu sold fresh local produce and occasionally, if he could get them, tinned goods imported from the city. He was the most popular shopkeeper of the three and the least prosperous. Whereas the other two had the sense to display prominent signs declaring, PLEASE DO NOT EMBARRASS ME BY ASKING FOR CREDIT, and only occasionally, at their strict discretion, gave credit to the lower-desk clerks who received their meagre salary at the end of the month,

141

Vishnu offered credit to everyone, even those who didn't ask. This was not due to some misguided business strategy to increase market share, but because he suffered from the terribly English affliction of over-politeness. Although it was something he only suffered from within working hours: at home he was a mean and rude man who treated his children like slaves and ran his household with ruthless efficiency. Rekha bore the brunt of his wrath; not only was she his first daughter after four sons, but she had inadvertently killed her mother upon her entry into this world, and was therefore the greatest disappointment of all. And dark-skinned to boot. How would he ever afford the dowry?

Year after year after year, Rekha followed Vishnu's orders. She studied for as long as he said, but when he told her to prepare dinner, she read not another word more. She ate until he told her to clear up the dishes; then not another grain of rice passed her lips. And when he told her to wake up in the morning, she didn't dare sneak another sleepy wink. She did what she was told, and besides, what else was there to do? Too much freedom can be a bane; it should be rationed as a luxury good. And when Vishnu's friends visited his house, they all complimented him on what a good job he had done of single-handedly raising such a daughter – clean, tidy, quiet, and a great cook – the women with the highest value are the women who realize their place.

Rekha wasn't very familiar with parties, and she most certainly wasn't on intimate terms with them. She had been invited to a few (although she hadn't been allowed to go), but they were small fry compared to Beauty Kumar's farewell party: the whole class had been invited to see Beauty and her parents leave for the city to cement their fortune. Beauty Kumar was anything but beautiful. The gods are always quick to punish presumptuous parents. And just like her parents, she was a fancy-pants show-off. It was said that you could hear her mother coming from the next village because of her jangling bangles. She was also rather in love with her voice, much like a blackbird at dawn, and as keen to display her fiscal superiority as a turaco is his plume. So when the invitation was issued, everyone accepted, eager to see her off. Except Rekha. She wanted to go but Vishnu refused her permission. Despite the fact that Mr Kumar was one of his most frequent customers (although he always paid late, if at all), his mind would not be changed. Rekha knew better than to ask again, but her fingers and toes tingled with rage. For the first time, a question bounced around in her head like a ball in a pinball machine, until it hit the jackpot and the words 'Why *not*?' resonated between her ears so loudly that she could hardly hear her father's orders. She had to put a stop to the ringing.

At half past two the following Saturday, after carrying out her household chores, Rekha decided to rebel. She would go to the ball. Telling her brothers that she was going to fetch some milk, she set off for Beauty Kumar's house, even though she didn't know exactly where it was.

No one noticed her absence until dinner needed to be made. Vishnu asked his sons where she was. They looked at each other, petrified, and told him that she had gone to fetch some milk. Vishnu went to the larder and looked on the cool shelf: the vat of milk was full. He asked them how long she'd been gone for. Again they silently consulted each other with their furtive glances: was it worth lying? 'Two hours,' they said, looking down at their feet. The closest shop was a ten-minute walk away. But for Vishnu, one plus one did not make two. He was solving a problem with an entirely different set of rules. It did not cross his mind for a moment that Rekha might have disobeyed him. In fact it was quite clear to him what had happened: being careless, she hadn't noticed there was enough milk, and then at some point on her journey to the shop she had been kidnapped. Clearly. In a matter of minutes, everyone in the vicinity was alerted, and they eagerly left their houses armed with torches (even though it wasn't dark) and sticks (to ruffle the undergrowth with) as if they were extras in a horror movie, the dirty excitement cackling in the air.

Ajit was the village idiot. Unfortunately, he wasn't simple, docile, good-natured, which is how people like their idiots to be served. He was stupid in a way which made people feel uncomfortable, especially women. His brain may not have developed but there was one part of him which most certainly had, they agreed in surreptitious tones, standing huddled in the market place, checking over their shoulders to see whether he was lurking in the shadows. Indeed, Ajit was often around; he hovered around groups of women like a wounded African wild dog, waiting for one of them to be separated from the herd so that he could pounce, although he had never been successful – as soon as a woman screamed he would let go, as if in surprise.

Rekha was lost. She wondered why she had thought that she could intuit her way to Beauty Kumar's house on Nandan Lane – it was the only street in the village which had a name, all the others were identified by a combination of numbers and letters. Beauty lived on the edge of the village; there the houses had windows that were covered by swirled iron instead of straight bars, and the porches were decorated with tubs of flowers. She stood in the middle of the road and looked around her. There was nothing to place where she was – just ranks of coconut trees and grass and bushes and the constant low buzz of insects going about their business. It occurred to her that she might be walking in circles – everything had started to look the same. She felt beads of perspiration form at her hairline and above her top lip. Her puffed-up feet throbbed crossly. Her sari blouse dug in under her arms. She was hot, tired, irritated. And she didn't even know how to get home. Already her rebellion was seeming like a bad idea, but worse was to come.

Ajit was also a champion coconut-tree climber. He didn't have enough money to buy food, but this hardly mattered: in the midst of cool paddy fields were patches of purple brinjal; shadowy magur fish dozed in the lazy khaki waters; the roadsides were rich with skinny branches weighed down by bulbous papayas, banana trees with their leaves flapping like elephant ears, and stately palms waving their long arms high up in the tranquil air.

It was a hot day, even by local standards, and Ajit was desperate for refreshment. What would be perfect, he thought, was a drink of coconut water, straight from the shell. And there was one road just outside the village which was lined with the best trees of all, bearing the fruit with the creamiest flesh and the most fragrant juice.

By the time Ajit reached the road, he was giddy from dehydration, and the landscape became a smeared canvas of green and brown and yellow, as if someone had run a mucky hand over an oil painting. Instinctively, he walked towards a coconut tree. The trunk, protected from the sun by the palm leaves, was cool to the touch. Ajit took the rag which he had stuffed into the back of his lunghi and wrapped it around his feet, then pulled himself on to the tree, easing himself up it with the skill of a monkey. At the top, he took out his machete and chopped a few coconuts to the ground, then tucked an especially small one under his arm, and climbed down. After hacking off the top, he poured the water into his mouth, until his thirst had been quenched. Placing the empty shell by the side of the road, he looked up and saw what seemed like an empty pile of clothes lying in the middle of the road. Making his rag into a knapsack, he gathered his coconuts, slung them over his shoulder and went to investigate – maybe the sun was playing tricks on his yellowing eyes.

Rekha's light-pink sari was filthy; damp from sweat and brown from dirt. She looked like a dying peony. Her face was ashen, but her chest rose and fell, so Ajit knew she was alive. He had the curiosity of a child, and prodded her lightly, as he would a pill millipede. She didn't curl up, but instead slowly opened her gluey eyes. He crouched over and pulled her up.

'Baba?' she asked dozily.

Ajit put her down again, and then sliced off the top of another coconut. Holding it in one hand, he managed to cradle Rekha in his other and started to pour the water into her mouth. Gradually, she came round and her eyes began to focus. And what was the first thing she saw? An army of villagers, armed with sticks, marching towards her, led by Vishnu. And what did Vishnu see? His daughter, lying in the arms of Ajit the Pervert, her clothes dirty and rumpled, her body withered. Nothing was said. The villagers rushed towards him like angry lava, snatching Rekha from him, then beating him with their sticks. Rekha became hysterical, screaming and crying, but every time she tried to say something, she was silenced and told repeatedly, 'It's not your fault, it's not your fault.' Finally, just as the beating was about to come to an end, Vishnu saw the coconut knife on the ground. Brandishing it, he walked towards Ajit, spreadeagled on the floor, held down by his arms and legs.

'You'll never do this again, you dirty sister-fucker!' he growled, and Ajit was left bleeding in the middle of the road. Rekha never rebelled again.

CHAPTER SEVEN

Ciara

Seph didn't do anything he didn't want to do. Born in early May, when the hollows in the woods were covered by a quilt of primroses, violets and bluebells, and squill arose on the coastal path along Red Bay, he was truly a son of Horus, and like other bulls, stubborn and determined. Even if he failed, it was his decision to do so. He couldn't remember a time, until Darshini, when he had been caught off guard; nothing came as a surprise to him. When he was fourteen and received a 'C' in his geography test, he admitted it was because he wasn't good at the subject, but that was because he didn't *want* to be. It was his decision.

A pupil of St MacNissi's College, which sat high above the Antrim coast road overlooking the Irish Sea, Seph both exasperated and fascinated his teachers. At times he would sit in during his fifteen-minute morning break and devour his textbooks. At other times he would skip class and be found on the seaward wall of the college, taking in the breathtaking view of the Mull of Kintyre. He had the agility of a butterfly; just as they thought they had him captured, he would flutter his beautiful wings and fly to the next flower. He was always in sight, always out of reach.

He was also the only boy ever to be given a detention in a school which didn't hand out detentions. The reason why he had been given detention was because he hadn't shown any remorse when he had been given the strap by Father O'Hanlon in his Religious Education class. The reason why he had been given the strap was because he had been caught passing a note. And the reason why he had been passing a note was because he felt like it. It read:

There was a young reverend from Red Bay,
Tried to grind his betrothed in the subway.
She said, 'No, you young goose,
Just try self-abuse,
And the other we'll try on marriage day.'

His teachers thought that he was disturbed; maybe there was some childhood trauma which he had buried? Father O'Neill set up an appointment for half an hour every Friday lunchtime, in one of the empty rooms of the disused boarding department where they wouldn't be disturbed, to discuss Seph's life with him. The room itself had cold white walls and was bare apart from two hard, not too comfortable chairs and a wooden coffee table which Seph took to resting his feet on; Father O'Neill thought that any other furniture might distract Seph from the task in hand, and believed that austerity encouraged focus. Seph found the sessions both amusing and interesting; he had wondered at which point he had become himself, but there were no stand-out moments, no great revelations, just the drip drip drip of time. He was a human stalactite. Father O'Neill gave up.

Seph didn't need friends, which is why everyone wanted to be one of his. His magnetism was that of volcanic rock. Why why why? Because. Some things are elemental, irreducible. Like in some strange logical problem, his qualities – kindness, generosity, strength, intelligence – were necessary but not sufficient explanation. He was proof that man is greater than the sum of his parts. He never barked; it was the possibility that he might bite, and bite hard, which meant that he could skip the lunch queue without fear of retribution, and was never grassed on for smoking. But it wasn't just fear, it was admiration, too – Seph inspired hero worship. They had competitions over who knew the most about him, who had sat next to him at lunch, who he had asked to play squash that afternoon.

Seph dealt with his fame with good grace and modesty. He saw it as a given, rather like a king views divine right. He didn't bellyache over the whys and wherefores. Kings should rule, not philosophize. It was this aloof power which made the girls shorten their skirts by hastily rolling over the waistbands when he walked past them. And dream about kissing him under the eucalyptus tree, which was the oldest in the British Isles and had seen its fair share of trembling mouths and tentative hands. Not that they ever had their chance.

On Seph's eighteenth birthday, Ciara organized a party for him. He hadn't asked for one. He didn't consider it a milestone in his life or even something to celebrate. But he didn't want to upset his mother by telling her so. Her eyes looked bright for once; he wouldn't put the fire of her enthusiasm out.

It was meant to be a surprise, but as he lay in bed on a Saturday morning and heard her busying herself in the kitchen, cooking far more than for just the two of them, he guessed. Not that he let on – he didn't want to ruin *her* surprise. He looked at his watch, it was midday, and wondered whether to stay in bed. He reached into his bedside table, where he kept four pornographic magazines, his mile swimming certificate (all the other medals he had won had been left at the side of the pool after the race; he knew he had won – why would he need a token to remind him?), an assortment of pens in varying stages of decay, and a packet of cigarettes and a box of matches. Seph prided himself on not being a person of habit, and would therefore not admit that he was a habitual smoker. He said he was not an addict, he chose to smoke. He could give it up any time he liked. Neither did his mother acknowledge that he smoked. She often walked into his bedroom and commented on the musty air, pushing the windows open and saying earnestly, 'Fresh air – good for the body and the mind!' but she couldn't bring herself to link cause and effect.

Seph lit a cigarette, took a drag and looked at himself in the mirror opposite his bed. He watched his bicep curl as he lifted the cigarette to his mouth, then prodded it lightly, and pursed his lips. Then he extended his arm and pushed against his tricep, which resisted his touch. He smiled. As a swimmer, his biceps weren't as worked out as his triceps. He ran his left hand over his tiled belly and pulled the thin puppy skin away from the muscles. *Good*, he thought. *Good*.

He tiptoed downstairs and picked up the post from the mat. Apart from the occasional bill, there was rarely any post for Ciara – no invitations to parties, no postcards from friends lying on sun-drenched beaches or skiing down Toblerone peaks, no flimsy airmails from distant relatives. Not even any companies asking her to sign up for a loan; it was as if she didn't exist at all. When he was younger he would wonder why; now he felt sad. He flicked through the post: it was all for him.

Seph went back upstairs silently, stretching past the creaky stairs, enjoying feeling the pull in his hamstrings. Settling back in bed, he pulled out a paper knife from his bedside table, ready to slice; he liked envelopes to be opened neatly.

He set aside the hand-delivered envelope stuffed with cash (he earned money from working as a bouncer at a couple of the local bars. Until now he had been underage, but no one cared) and the obvious junk, and whittled it down to a pile of five he-wasn't-sure-whats. Five: a swimming newsletter detailing upcoming events. Four: a fanzine from a band he had once liked. Three: a reminder to book a dentist's appointment. Two: another reminder to book a dentist's appointment. One: a birthday card signed 'Conor Murphy'.

Seph took a deep breath, but he felt as if he were on the top of a mountain, the thin air offering no relief to his tightening lungs. The greeting read 'Happy Birthday, son.' Son? He was a son to only Ciara. She had told him that his father had been an officer in the army and died on duty. He had once asked to see photographs, and she had cried and cried and cried. He hadn't asked again. There were no further clues apart from the postmark that said 'Kerry'. He stared hard at the writing. It was extravagant, sprawling, eating up the paper, just like his own. The cross of the 't's, piercing all the other letters through the side, the squirl at the top of the 'C', the fullness of the cups on the 'B', it was all his. He shut the card and put it in his bottom drawer. He didn't have a father. It was his choice not to have one. He lit another cigarette and inhaled uncontrollably, even though he wasn't addicted.

Ciara O'Shea's and Conor Murphy's courtship had lasted four months. Ciara's mother Mary had disapproved right from the start. 'I'll tell you one thing, my girl,' she said sternly, 'no good will come of that man.' Ciara's father Tim didn't say much. He never did. He thought words complicated matters. Most things could be sorted out by a glare or a quick back-of-the-hand. But as the family sat round the dinner table one evening, eating in silence and listening to the radio, he said to no one in particular, head still down, pushing an unidentifiable vegetable around his plate, 'He'll be your undoing, that lad will.' Everyone knew who he was talking to, and who he was talking about. No one said anything in response. And then he looked up and glared at Mary, snarling, 'What is this shite you're dishing out?' All the kids looked at their food and wolfed it down, so that Mary would escape Tim's palm. It was a close call.

Ciara was neither rebellious nor stubborn. She didn't even think she knew better than her parents. So why did she keep on with Conor? Because at last she had found someone on whom to lavish her attention, and someone who accepted it. Before Conor, no one and nothing had wanted Ciara's love. She was born to serve, but couldn't find a master. Her need to love was too anxious; her watery eyes were filled with it, her stooped shoulders were burdened with it. When her brother Tim Junior had his nose bloodied in the playground and she sought to comfort him, he pushed her away. Her arms didn't seem to have enough strength to offer solace. Instead he limped to his other sister, Evangeline, whose arms glowed with warmth and cosiness.

The smell of desperation is sickly sweet, like burnt syrup, at first enticing, then repulsive. Despite the odour of glycerine soap which she scrubbed with (cleanliness is next to Godliness, her mother told her), Ciara reeked of it; her pores exuded it like a liver does bile. But Conor Murphy had had a blocked nose for eighteen good years. Even though he worked in the docks, he had never smelled the salty sea nor the stagnant oil. With wolverine green eyes and a seductive snarl, he had bedded most women in a five-mile radius. They gave themselves to him easily, desperate to be Bathsheba to his King David. But his power was not derived from wealth or status or intellect. It was raw and immutable, and he sweated it through every pore. And Ciara was assaulted by it.

In Ciara's last term at school, Sister Anne O'Sullivan of the Loreto Convent had told her whole class about the mystery of life. Her predecessor had warned the girls of the *dangers of kissing*, but she would tell them the whole affair. It was His Will that they hear it.

She stood solemnly at the front of the classroom and leaned on her desk. Ciara sat in the front row, mesmerized, waiting to be told The Truth. Sister Anne began:

'Sex is holy. Sex is sacred. We know that sex is holy because God uses it, joining his divine and creative power to the love of a man and a woman to bring forth new life into the world. No two people ever work so closely, hand in hand with God himself, as when they become co-creators with God and bring forth new life into the world.'

She looked around her class. There was no sniggering, but rather a weariness which she did not expect from sixteen-year-old girls on the cusp of womanhood. How little they had lived, and already they were bored, she thought sadly. Then she continued in a more sour voice, as if someone had poured a whole tube of sherbet dip into her mouth:

'Although many people are probably not thinking about this at the time that they engage in sexual relations, God is very present in this life-giving act, whether a pregnancy results or not.' Sister Anne took a pointed breath and then continued in a tremulous voice, her heart beating faster, her breath becoming shallower, 'Because sex is so sacred and beautiful, God has filled it with meaning. Every act of sexual intercourse is intended by God to express love, commitment and an openness to life. If two people are ever uncertain about whether engaging in sexual activity is the right thing to do, they need to ask themselves if love, commitment and an openness to life are present in the relationship. Sexual activity is a gift that we give to another person to whom we have committed our lives.'

Sister Anne released her breath and looked beatifically at her flock of sheep, silent and respectful. Just as she was about to ask the girls to open their biology textbook at page fifty-six, the female reproductive organs, she heard a voice pipe up, 'Sister, like, how would *you* know?' The tone was calmly callous.

No one made a sound. *You, you, you* reverberated around the classroom, a sneering love song. The mocking silence wrapped itself around her white neck and tightened its grip. *God*lovesme*God*lovesme she repeated to herself noiselessly, as she reached down into her skirt pocket and massaged the reassuring beads. The moment collapsed.

Conor met Ciara in the summer after she finished school, when she was sad sixteen and prickly with unfulfilled desire. She was at a ceilidh where he had danced every dance and she hadn't danced one. He saw her in the shadows from the beginning, and wondered who she was. At the end of the night, he stared at her with such intensity that she froze, unable to run away.

When the other girls heard that he had asked Ciara out, they bristled with envy and resentment, and the question 'Why her? Why not me?' was sobbed into many a pillow that night, and pouted over at shower-time as they soaped their own budding breasts and wondered what it would be like to have his fingertips, and not their own, trailing over their nipples.

No one else had ever shown any interest in Ciara, so when Conor Murphy *told* her that he was taking her out, she couldn't say no, because she hadn't had any practice. At first, he was polite, charming, burrowing his way under her skin imperceptibly, like a Bilharzia worm. She wouldn't understand the damage until much later. But then, just as she was finally about to escape a lifetime of drowning and come up for air, he pushed her head under the water again. Realizing his command over her, he would taunt her with comments about her imperfections until she curled up into a ball, but like a baby hedgehog her spikes were soft and white and offered her scant protection. Then he would coax her out by offering her tidbits of flattery and encouragement. But the weaker she grew, the more she needed him. And then there were the things he did to her, which she could not tell anyone about, not even God. She knew it was wrong, but she couldn't, no, *wouldn't* ask him to stop. It started with a kiss, which is how it always starts.

'Can I give you a kiss, then?' Conor asked, his face so close to Ciara's that she could feel his moist breath, which was laced with whisky. She didn't say anything; she was too afraid of giving the wrong answer.

'Well?' he soothed. And then his lips were on hers and his hands were in her hair and his body was pressed up against hers. She had never felt anything like it. His kisses were gentle, then urgent, then insistent; probing, then light. She felt dizzy and her knees buckled, but he kept her pinned up against the wall with his arms. Finally he pulled away and said casually, 'I better get you home, then.'

Ciara didn't want to go home. She wanted more. And she was ashamed of herself. The more she went out with Conor, the more she read her Bible. The more pleasure she received, the more guilt she felt.

After two months of trying to touch her *there*, and being refused entry, Conor thought he would try blackmail. When he had his hand nudged away again, he pulled back from her completely, then stood a distance from her, lighting a cigarette, looking away. The warmth from his body left her and she shivered, crossing her arms to keep herself warm.

'You know I'm not allowed,' she apologized nervously.

He gave a dismissive shrug.

'Look at me,' she pleaded, but he wouldn't.

'I bet that sister of yours would let me,' he said, turning his head to give her a sniping semi-glance and then turning back.

Ciara felt sick. NO. Waves of acid lapped at the ravaged walls of her belly. She walked towards him; this time she wasn't going to lose. He studiously ignored her, even when she cupped his face in her hands. She stood on her tiptoes and gently kissed his temples and his forehead, and then took his worn hands in hers and grazed her lips over his knuckles, peering up at his face desperately.

Suddenly he pushed her to the ground, and all she could see in front of her was cracked earth and the first yellowing leaves of autumn. She didn't scream, because she didn't want to. For the first time in her life, she felt completely alive. There was no one else to take away this moment; it was entirely hers. Both her hands were held over her head and pinned down by one of his hands. The other reached under her skirt and pulled her knickers down. The weight momentarily lifted from her body and she heard the whisper of clothes and a zip being pulled. Then the heaviness was on her again and her mouth tasted the grass. And then she felt the most exquisite pain. She remembered Sister Anne's words and her spirit soared. God was *in* her; she had finally felt the presence of her Maker. This was His Will.

She got up and tidied herself, brushing the dirt from her bare legs and picking out the tiny bits of grit embedded in her palm. The sash of her skirt had ripped and all she could think was how mad her mother would be when she saw it. Between her thighs felt damp and sticky. She turned her back to Conor, who was tucking his shirt into his trousers, and carefully hitched up her skirt, tentatively feeling the tops of her inner thighs. When she looked at her fingers, they were smeared with blood the colour of a wilting rose.

162

                              *   *   *

Two months later, when the curse showed no sign of
appearing, Ciara told Evangeline. Her sister seemed
unsurprised by the implication of the news, and
asked with a hint of incredulity, 'Did you not use
anything to protect you?'

'You know we're not allowed!' Ciara answered.

'You're not allowed to be shagging before you're
married, either,' Evangeline replied mockingly. 'You
better tell Mother.'

'What am I going to tell her?' Ciara wept.

'Tell her what you did,' Evangeline sneered.
'Won't she be proud of you then!'

'Didn't I tell you no good would come of that boy?'
Mary said to Ciara, who sat with her head down,
steady trickles of murky water running from both
her eyes and her nostrils. 'And I'll tell you another
thing: you are not going to bring shame upon this
family. As soon as you're showing, you're going to
visit your aunt until you recover from your illness.'

'But what about the baby?' Ciara whimpered.

'The baby'll be taken care of by a nice, decent
family. There are plenty of good women around who
can't have one of their own.'

'What about Father?'

'I guess I'll have to tell him,' Mary said with a
cavernous sigh.

That night Ciara lay in bed clinging to herself, her arms wrapped tight around her belly, as she heard slapping and screaming and shouting in her parents' room next door, and then much, much later the bed creaking steadily. She looked over to Evangeline who seemed to be asleep, her face still and peaceful, without a care in the world. Placing her palm on her stomach, she was filled with joy. She didn't care what her parents thought; she would run far, far away where they wouldn't be able to find her. She would not give her baby up. She was carrying the son of God.

Ciara's wedding had occurred frequently in her watery head, but nowhere on dry land. She took up more dream space in one day than others would in a lifetime. She thought of her dress – an ivory cotton A-line dress with Mountmellick embroidery on the bodice and skirt. She fantasized about the moment when the Claddagh would be slipped on her slim ring finger, the same ring that Richard Joyce had made as a slave and had given to his fiancée on his arrival home. Her bouquet would be made up of crimson roses and ivy. She would walk down the aisle decorated with foxgloves, to Bach's 'Jesu, Joy of Man's Desiring'. Like many of her type, she had been infected with marriage fever, which just like hayfever is carried through imperceptible pollen, all around but invisible to the eye. Perplexingly, although the local men breathed the same air, they rarely if ever suffered from this tenacious infection.

Ciara had once walked past St James's Church in Ballinora as a wedding was taking place and, mesmerized, had sneaked up to the door and listened to the service. The groom, a beautiful man with black curls and jade eyes, had vowed:

'O Christ, by your five wounds, by the nine orders of angels, if this woman is ordained for me, let me hold her hand now, and breathe her breath. O my love. I pray to the top of your head, to the sole of your foot, to each side of your breast, that you may not leave me or forsake me. As a foal after the mare, as a child after the mother, may you follow, and stay with me till death comes to part us asunder. Amen.'

Ciara had never forgotten these words. In her loneliness she would repeat them to herself, to bring her comfort. And when she learned of the baby in her belly, she repeated the words like a novena: nine times a day for nine days. On the tenth day, a decision was made. After seething red silence at each mealtime, and angry accusations which got lost in the carpets and the curtains, never to be answered, Tim, drawing himself up to his full height like an angry grizzly bear, stood in front of Ciara and bellowed, 'Where does the son of a bitch live then?'

For once, Ciara was not scared. She touched her belly as if it contained an amulet which would ward off all evil. She said Conor's address as if she were reciting a poem. She didn't notice Evangeline narrow her eyes and steal away.

Tim grabbed his best coat, made out of golden shearling, which he usually only ever wore to church, and marched out of the door. Mary followed, her head held high, her lips pursed. The other children fidgeted and looked at their feet. The dog barked but was silenced by a quick kick in the ribs. They all stopped singing, canaries in a toxic coalmine. They didn't know exactly what was going on, but they knew enough not to ask.

Tim rapped on the door as impatiently as a bailiff. Mary hid her shame in the upturned collar of her sheepskin coat, although it was too warm to wear it. There was no answer. He looked in through the window but was confronted by only a dirty net curtain and his own surly reflection.

'Tim, it's not even six yet. Maybe he's still at work,' Mary reasoned, her voice as fragile as a china doll.

'We'll wait,' Tim replied. 'Get back in the car.'

They sat in the car, not a word or glance between them, for four and a half hours. Mary dared not; Tim would not. They watched each colour and noise of the evening pass, from the shepherds' red sky to the lovers' twilight murmur. In the close confines of the car the heat stuck to them like chocolate-covered caramel, sweet and sickly. Spreading over their arms and legs and chests and backs, mingling with the sweaty leather car-seats, to give the acrid smell of a dead animal baking in the sun. Mary looked out of the window, longing to wind it down, but she was afraid to move. Even her breathing seemed too loud.

At last, when hope had disappeared into the darkness, Tim said something under his breath. Mary wasn't sure what, but her stomach felt hollow all the same. Instinctively, she put her hand up to protect herself, but nothing came. And then she covered her face with both her hands so that he wouldn't see her tears, which were born of both relief and fear.

They went back to a quiet house. Not even the dog barked when they walked through the front door. The kids' bellies were empty but their hunger had left them. Ciara sat looking out of the window, her arms protectively curled around her tummy, her knees hunched up to her chest.

Tim paced the floor; no one risked moving, even Ciara's four-year-old sister, who desperately needed a wee and had her legs crossed so tightly that they were numb.

'The bastard didn't even come home,' he said to no one in particular. He walked to the sideboard and took out a bottle of Connemara single malt, which was usually reserved for St Patrick's and Christmas Day, births and deaths. He poured himself a large tumblerful, took a gulp, then another.

'He's probably out getting arseholed!' he snarled, walking towards Ciara. He stood behind her, and stood and stood. She could smell the alcoholic haze as he breathed out heavily through his mouth. It was the smell of arguments, screaming, shouting. Then he drained his glass and went to bed.

Ciara went to bed last of all. After Tim left the room, Mary went to the kitchen and warmed up some milk, and the kids drank it in silence, cupping the beakers with both hands and trying to eat their malted milk biscuits without munching too loudly. Ciara stayed where she was. Even when Mary put a glass of warm milk next to her, she continued to look out of the window, until Mary picked it up, muttering 'Waste not, want not,' and drank it herself. None of them said goodnight to her as they made their way to bed; they were too exhausted.

It was only when she finally crept to bed herself, careful not to wake anyone else, that she realized. She hadn't switched the light on, so as not to disturb Evangeline, and had slipped out of her clothes and into bed in the dark. At first she couldn't tell quite what the difference was. She lay there, rigid, as if there was a burglar in her room. Something wasn't right. Something was missing. It was Evangeline's breathing, light and graceful. She turned her head and looked at the other bed. It seemed flat, as if there was no one in it. Ciara froze. She got up, tiptoed to the wall and switched the light on. Evangeline was not in her bed. And the room seemed slightly different, too, as if it had been rearranged. Ciara's first instinct was to wake her mother and tell her, but something stopped her. Not that she wanted her sister to come to any harm, but . . .

The question was asked at the breakfast table by Tim Junior, between mouthfuls of cornflakes.

'Where's Angel, then?'

Mary looked at Ciara, and said, 'Go and tell that sister of yours to get out of bed and down here.'

Ciara got up from her seat and went up the stairs, even looking into the room, knowing all the time that she wasn't there. She came down the stairs, and said with a slight shrug, 'She's not there. Maybe she's gone out early.'

'Evangeline, gone out early – that'll be a first!' retorted Mary, and went back to her toast.

From the other end of the table, Tim, with blood-shot eyes and uncombed hair, growled, 'I'll be seeing to that boy of yours today,' as if he were a policeman about to catch a criminal.

Ciara wrapped her arms around her belly and kept her mouth shut.

After work, Tim went down to the docks and enquired about Conor Murphy's whereabouts. The men eyed up Tim and decided that he looked big enough and rough enough to deserve an answer.

'He's run off, hasn't he?' smirked one of them. 'With a girl.'

Tim felt his ears redden. 'What girl?' he demanded.

The same man took a drag on a roll-up, and whilst exhaling said lasciviously to his friend, 'What's her name, Jack?'

'Evangeline, isn't it?' Jack replied timidly; he didn't know who to be more afraid of, his friend or Tim.

The first man turned back to Tim and repeated, 'Yeah, that's it. Evangeline. Angel, some people call her. Bit of a –' he stopped for effect, 'well, you know, a tart.' He took another drag. 'Although she looks like butter wouldn't melt in her mouth. You know the sort.' Another drag. 'Why, d'you know her?'

'No,' replied Tim. 'I don't.'

That evening, Tim broke the news to the rest of the family around the dinner table, as they filled their mouths with beef stew and champ (there was always too little of the former and too much of the latter), the scallions bought fresh from the market that day.

'Evangeline's gone,' he stated, in a manner that

welcomed no questions. Tim Junior chewed on a piece of beef until it was a dry fibrous mass and he couldn't swallow it, mulling over what his father had said. Surreptitiously, he took the meat from his mouth and dropped it to the floor for the dog, which was sitting by his chair. Mary, sensing that he was about to ask a question, stared at him with all her might, but he seemed oblivious.

'Gone where?' Tim Junior asked pensively.

As if he hadn't heard the question, Tim announced, 'We won't speak of her again in this house.' Then he took his last bite, pushed his plate away, got up from the table and walked past them, only stopping to say to Ciara, 'I told you no good would come of that boy.'

Later that night, Mary walked into her daughter's room and sat on her bed. She remembered Ciara as a baby, and wondered how something so weak and small could now be carrying a life itself. She stroked her daughter's hair tenderly and her eyes filled to the brim with tears of regret.

'Ciara,' she whispered, 'you're not going to be marrying that boy of yours.' Taking a deep breath she looked at the empty bed, then back at Ciara, and caressed her cheek, but there were no tears on it. God had given Ciara a baby, it was His gift to her, and it was all she needed. For once, she felt strong.

* * *

A week later, Ciara was on her way. She had only one suitcase, containing her clothes and a few toiletry items, and a small handbag, which contained the notes Tim had taken from a roll stored in a shoe box in the back of the wardrobe, a piece of paper with her aunt's phone number, and four photographs – one of Conor, one of Evangeline, one of the dog as a puppy, and a formal portrait of her family. Everyone except Tim – who remained in his comfy chair, listening to the radio – went to see her off at the bus station. She was to take a bus from Cork to Dublin, then from Dublin to Belfast. No one in the family had ever travelled that far. She kissed them all farewell, the children clinging to her legs and wrapping themselves around her; it was the first time they had shown her such affection.

'Bring us something when you come back!' they all chimed. She disentangled herself and nodded, 'Course I will!', knowing that she would never see any of them again. Despite being with child, she felt that she could run faster than any of the king's horses.

At Belfast, instead of calling her aunt to pick her up, she went to the ticket desk and bought a ticket for Cushendall. She had heard a local story about the ghosts of two young lovers who would walk together, hand in hand, along the grassy laneway on summer evenings, and conjured a romantic story about never-ending love and till death do us part. What she didn't know was that the young girl had become pregnant, and in desperation and fear of what the locals would think, she had taken her own life by hanging herself in a nearby barn. The young man had discovered her body, and unable to live without the love of his life had hung himself beside her. As only God has the right to take life, they were not buried in the graveyard itself, but at its entrance. But her ignorance turned out to be her redeemer.

Ciara's curse was her blessing. Everyone took pity on her frail frame and sorrowful eyes, and just as the diners in Greek tavernas throw scraps to the scrawny cats, people gave her work, and paid her over the odds, even when they weren't sure she was capable. But she proved herself more than capable; strengthened by the purpose that the life inside had given her, she worked tirelessly, always thinking of the baby she was now responsible for. There was no time to be selfish and think of herself.

People didn't know of her background and couldn't bring themselves to ask her. They saw her swelling tummy, but didn't judge it; with her virginal demeanour and air of sadness, she elicited sympathy, not scorn. And her regular church attendance was duly noted, too, along with the fact that when she said 'Lord, graciously hear us' after the bidding prayers, she seemed to mean it more than anybody else. But they weren't happy *not* to know either, so they created a story for her, to make themselves more comfortable, to make her less of a stranger. So across shop counters, over bar tops, on doorsteps, at the bus-stop, travelled the whisper that Ciara, the poor wee thing, had lost all of her family in a tragic accident. No details were given; they were unnecessary, and besides, the past was best laid to rest, and hadn't the unlucky thing suffered enough already, God love her.

So it was with much rejoicing that Seph was born. Into her sad and dark life had come a ray of light – proof, if ever proof was needed, that God was kind and merciful. Whilst she cradled him in her arms, they came bearing gifts. First of all was the doctor, who examined the baby, then gently hung a gold chain with a locket engraved with Saint Joseph around his neck. Next along teetered Sinead Murphy, the wife of the local businessman, who always wore full make-up, even to attend con-fession. She brought with her a jar of Frankincense cream, which she said would help with cradle cap and any other skin ailments the baby might suffer from. Then came the publican, who slid a few notes into Ciara's clammy hand, and said with a wink (or was it a twitch?) and a nod, 'Something for the boy.'

Last was the sheep farmer, Joseph, who brought with him a lambs-wool sweater which his wife had knitted for the baby. Ciara was so delighted with the gift that she decided to name her baby son after him. Seph, son of God, had come into an adoring world.

Ciara was too busy in the kitchen to notice that she hadn't seen Seph all day. She had painstakingly pre-pared all of his favourite dishes. Although she always did. They would sit, with Seph at the head of the table, and she would watch anxiously as he put every forkful into his mouth. As he ate she would talk, about broken domestic appliances, neighbourly disputes, and human-interest stories from the local newspaper which Seph hardly listened to. She told him stories of other people – of how the Gilroys were going on holiday, and the Edens had a new car – but if Seph interrupted to ask her about *her*, she was vague, unsure. She had always been a passenger. But when at the end of the meal he said, 'That was lovely, Ma. Thank you,' her heart would swell so much that it filled her stomach, and she herself had no need for food.

It had taken all her strength to organize this birth-day party. She had written the invitations with her own anxious hand, taking the names out of Seph's address book, and asked them to reply to the pub where she worked – if she received post at home it might have made Seph suspicious. When everyone replied in the positive, it brought tears to her eyes, and she carefully stored each of the responses in her dresser's bottom drawer. Seph had been blessed with popularity, something she had been praying for since she had held him in her trembling arms when he was a baby.

When she went up to his room in the early evening, she walked into a fog of smoke. Through it she could make out a Seph-shaped mass still in bed.

'Seph?' she asked, but her voice seemed to lose its way in the mist. She walked to the edge of the bed and sat down on it. Seph was propped against the pillows, his eyes closed. She looked at his broad shoulders and strong arms. The freckles which played on his arrogant nose. She touched the curve at the base of his throat and ran her hand along his collarbone. Her body had produced *this*. Her weak insignificant body. Her sunken chest filled with pride like gale-force wind blowing into the sails of a wrecked ship. He put his hand on Ciara's and opened his eyes.

'Mother.' His voice was even deeper than usual, cigarette-ravaged.

'Happy Birthday, Son,' she said, gazing beatific-ally into his storm-blue eyes. 'Get ready and come down. I've cooked a special birthday dinner for you.' She could hardly contain her excitement.

'OK, give me a few minutes to wash up,' he said, and Ciara smiled again and left his room.

He wanted to go back to sleep. He closed his eyes again and then opened them crazy-man-wide and jumped out of bed. He took a shower, turning up the heat so much that it stung, allowing the shampoo to run into his eyes so that all of the sleep and tiredness and melancholy was washed out of them. Whilst dressing, he practised making surprised faces in the mirror, but he couldn't make his mouth turn up – it kept drooping – and his eyes refused to twinkle. He blinked several times, but every time he opened his eyes, the darkness remained.

Come on, he chastised himself as he walked down the stairs, *come on*. But when he walked into a room of people all waiting for him, cheering, shouting, 'Happy Birthday, Seph! Seph, Happy Eighteenth!' and he heard his name said with such love and affection, he smiled without choosing to. And even if it was only for a moment, it was a genuine smile.

He stood in the middle of the room, regal, as his loyal subjects came forward proffering gifts. His mother came last, card in hand, her face beaming. He opened it, his face neutral. On the front, a black and white photograph of a young man, James Dean style, standing next to a sports car. On the inside: *Congratulations on this special day, Celebrate in every wonderful way!* Seph wondered how long it had taken for someone to come up with that. The exclamation mark depressed him even more, a kind of Smile, smile, everybody's looking.

Everyone looked at him expectantly. He felt as if he should break into a tap dance.

'Thanks, everyone, for coming, then!' he managed. 'Let's get drinking!' And the table lined with bottles of beer turned into a stretch of overlapping people.

Mia Connolly didn't really know anyone at the party. In Cushendall, she was an outsider, a Belfast lady from Malone who had married the local hardman Gerry Fitzgerald and moved into town. Gerry owned Gerry's, one of the bars in Ballymena, where Seph worked. Out of the three bars in town, Gerry's was the fanciest, attracting the prettiest girls and the prettiest boys. The bouncers even had a uniform – a black suit and a white T-shirt. There was rarely any trouble, and the worst it came to was drunken men urinating in the street. Except for the once.

Brian Flaherty didn't usually visit Gerry's. He was a trouble-maker and preferred Duke's, where the alcohol and girls were cheaper. But to celebrate his thirtieth birthday, he decided to go. He hadn't anticipated queuing, and bristled. His friends tried to calm him down.

'Oh now come on, Bri,' they pleaded. 'It's not such a big deal.' Brian said nothing and cracked his knuckles.

Being the boss's wife, Mia did not have to queue. She was an ethereal-looking woman, neither beautiful nor ugly, but with the possibility of both. With her pale skin and claret hair, she looked vulnerable. But what was vulnerability to Brian Flaherty? When Seph allowed Mia through, he shouted out, 'Fuck! Why is she going in without queuing? You think you're someone special, do you?' And within a moment he was at the front, reaching for Mia's dress.

And then he was on the floor.

'Jesus,' he said, looking surprised, lying down, arms and legs outstretched. 'Jesus.' He tried to pick himself off the ground, but he couldn't. 'Fuck, I think something's broken,' he groaned.

Seph's face was impassive. 'Call Gerry out, will you?' he said calmly.

Brian was so shocked that when Gerry asked him how he had been injured, he agreed with everyone else that he had fallen on Seph's fist. Seph himself remained silent. Gerry looked round at a circle of faces. 'How was that, then?' he queried. No one said anything. 'Are you *sure* you fell on his fist?' he asked Brian, spraying his face with spit and sarcasm.

'Sure I'm sure,' Brian whimpered.

Seph hadn't asked anyone to protect him or lie. But just as with a Rorschach inkblot, where people could see rabbits or demons, a flower or a penis, in Seph they saw royal-blue courage instead of bull-red aggression, and concrete integrity instead of steely indifference. And Mia was no different. She thought of him as a palimpsest, and wanted to scrape off the new paint with her fingernails and see the original marks. She wanted to solve the puzzle, turn the key.

At the party, Mia stood and watched as Seph circulated, awaiting her turn. She fiddled with her hair, bit her lips and straightened her skirt. She was a thirty-five-year-old woman with the colour of a fifteen-year-old in her cheeks. Seph asked her where Gerry was. She replied that he was away on business for the weekend.

Later that night Seph slipped out of the back door. His mother had been asleep for at least an hour, and she would be asleep when he returned. He walked to Mia's house at a steady pace. He couldn't crush her by not turning up; he had said he would and it was his duty to. She answered the door in a flimsy nightdress. He picked her up, but not knowing where he was going, he ended up in the drawing room with its batwing drapes and reproduction furniture. Placing her on a deep over-stuffed sofa, he went to dim the lights, and when he turned back she was naked, lying on her side, top leg at a right angle to the body in order to produce some sort of curve.

Her skin was watery, translucent, like skimmed milk. Her nipples, no different in colour from her chest, buttons sewn on to a rag doll's dress.

He wondered what to say to her. He didn't want to tell her she was beautiful because he didn't think she was. And he didn't care enough to lie. He lay to face her and raised himself up on his elbow, resting his head in his hand. With the thumb of his other hand he ran down the ladder of her ribs, until his hand rested in the hollow of her waist. He felt momentarily contented, but then she pulled him towards her, and it was just a mass of heaving flesh. But with each thrust, he kept something back, not because he intended to, but because she was someone else's and he was a man who couldn't share. Instead of his heart and body becoming one, they separated like oil and water. But as Mia's feet arched involuntarily, her skin tingled and her eyelids fluttered, she couldn't help but hand over her heart, beating furiously, in its torn wrapping. Asmodeus balanced precariously on Seph's shoulder and chuckled; the seed had been sown. When he got up to leave, and she asked tremulously, 'When will I see you again?', he realized what his power was. And his weakness, too.

CHAPTER EIGHT

What Becomes of the Broken-Hearted?

Rekha had her palm read fortnightly by the chiromancer who sat in a shack just outside shyambazaar, next to the tobacconist who sold Chiclets chewing gum, chewing tobacco, regular cigarettes, and *herbal* cigarettes to those who knew to ask. She would sit cross-legged on a cushion flattened by a bounty of bottoms, and ask Babaji what her future held. Babaji was at least one hundred and fifty years old, although he looked older, and claimed that he was a descendant of the palm-reader who had been taught by the goddess Durga, who had herself been taught by Shiva, the Almighty. So he knew his stuff.

Rekha put down her fish-bags and arranged herself on the cushion, hastily wiping her grimy hand on the anchol of her sari before presenting it to Babaji. She always put out her hand palm down, and then he would lightly pat his fingertips on her knuckles, as if he were gently tapping a lotus flower to open it up, and she would turn her hand up. But instead of a pure white expanse, he was bestowed with a sepia parchment of skin, scrawled with deep brown lines from years of rolling roti using a splintered rolling pin, and scrubbing clothes in soapy water until they were threadbare. He held her hand and looked at it carefully, tracing the map of her life with his forefinger. After a good ten minutes (he liked to give his best customers their money's worth), he took his hand away, pulled out his dentures from the glass of water which was sitting next to him, spat viciously on the street, and then clicked his tongue against the roof of his mouth a few times. Then he began.

'A very big change is coming in your life. You will experience things you have never experienced before, maybe with someone new. You will be in the best of health, eating, drinking and being merry! Fortune is smiling upon you!' Babaji grinned, his perfectly arranged enamel shining from the crevice of his mouth like an opal mine. Quiet validation swept across Rekha's face; she had thought as much, and now Babaji had confirmed it. And she had already met that someone new.

'Thank you!' she said triumphantly as she wobbled to her feet. 'Thank you!'

Babaji detected the change of tone in her voice but didn't ask why; he was happy just to accept the tip she placed in his palm.

Now that her own romantic destiny had been fulfilled, Rekha knew that it was her duty as a mother to see that Mousumi's marriage was arranged. Sachi would have expected it of her.

Alliance invited from Kolkata-based Bengali, conservative, educated, preferably Doctor M.B.B.S, Engineer, or MBA; tall, at least 5'7", around 25 to 28, for single daughter, late father District Manager of large multi-national pharmaceutical company, height 5', feminine shape, very domesticated family girl. English London connections. Caste no bar. Box GW 9029, Statesman, Kolkata-700001. A89731.

Rekha admired her words in the matrimonial section of *The Statesman*. Although she was unaware of having done so, her paraphrasing of 'fat' to 'feminine shape' was worthy of a top advertising executive. She read each word carefully, underlining it with a fingertip as she went along. 'Caste no bar' she said aloud, pleased with how cosmopolitan and modern it sounded. She had had help from the neighbour living in the flat above with the Bengali to English translation, but apart from that it was all her own work. She drew a large red circle around the advertisement, and left the newspaper open at that page, lying on the table, so that she could take a read of it every time she passed and be reminded of her literary flair.

Hariprasad, however, was less than impressed with Rekha's bid to marry off Mousumi. He had been sitting at the table with a cup of cha and a stack of iced biscuits when he had noticed the red circle. It made the purpley-blue vein at his right temple swell so furiously that it looked as if a worm were trying to hatch out through his skin. He read the words over and over again, trying to vacuum them up with his eyes, willing them to disappear. But they wouldn't budge an inch, and glared back at him defiantly.

Rekha, as pleased as a schoolgirl gaining full marks in a spelling contest, beamed as she handed the newspaper to him, and asked him to take a read. She didn't notice the way his hands gripped the paper so tightly it crumpled, nor the fact that the words were smudged from where he had rubbed them with a humiliated and sweaty palm. Hariprasad pretended to read. He looked up and smiled a tight, false smile, the skin by his eyes smooth and unwrinkled. Rekha grinned back; she had never learned to read people.

That night, Rekha lay awake in bed, looking up at the ceiling, her eyes half-closed. Her fantasies of being a bejewelled maiden had long gone, her dream now was to be mother of the bride. It was the most important thing she would ever be. Where would the wedding take place? What food would she serve? What would she wear? Which jewels? Questions bloomed in her head like velvety pansies in the Kashmir Valley. Focus would water those flowers and Purpose would bathe them in sunlight. So taken was she with visions of herself in a widow's cream raw silk sari, embroidered with seed pearls, that she didn't notice that Hariprasad, who would fall asleep with his hand tucked between the rolls of flesh of her belly, was lying on the other side of the bed with his back to her so she couldn't see the bonfire burning in his eyes, and she couldn't see the Catherine Wheel of jealousy spinning around in his tummy, the sparks reaching as far as the top of his head and the tips of his toes.

At the end of week one, Rekha had received five responses, which she was both pleased and relieved about. And five was a lucky number for Mousumi. Out of a readership of nearly two hundred thousand, the figure might not seem so impressive, but what Rekha didn't know couldn't harm her. What pleased her most was that they had all written back in English and not in Bengali script or, even worse, phonetic Bengali using the Roman alphabet (*Ammee bhalo achee* – I am well). She sat at the dinner table with its cracked Formica top, rested her swollen feet on the rung of the chair, and put the responses into order: one engineer, one doctor, two government clerks and one teacher. The engineer, a Mr Prabir Sarkar M.Eng, was a thirty-eight-year-old divorcee; Rekha scowled – had he not read the advertisement closely? The doctor, Pulak Banerjee, fulfilled all the criteria – Rekha puffed out her chest and smiled, placing the letter to her right with some ceremony. The other three were, in turn, too old, widowed, Dalit (she could tell from the surname – the phrase 'caste no bar' had its limits!). Who were these unsuitable timewasters? Her mouth composed itself into a sulk and she rubbed her nose in irritation. But having only one on the shortlist, Rekha reluctantly reread the bio-data of the two clerks and the teacher, her head high, the letters held at arm's length, as if she were touching something contaminated. She wondered what kind of life they would be able to provide for Mousumi on their government salaries. Love or money, love or money, she thought to herself. Money won – narrowly, of course! The doctor it was.

Then, as her spoken English wasn't up to scratch, she gave Hariprasad the responsibility of making meeting arrangements with the gentleman. He was more than happy to oblige.

Hariprasad gave himself an hour; although he was convinced of his power of persuasion, he didn't want to take any risks. He told Rekha where she would be meeting the doctor – in public, for safety reasons – and the time, an hour later than the time he had given the gentleman himself. So, Dr Banerjee was directed to the Nalban Boating Complex, inside Salt Lake City. He was a suggestible young man, and when Hariprasad proposed they take a ride on the lake in one of the paddle boats, he was quick to agree. He seemed timid – his gestures were twitchy, he didn't say much, his laughter was nervous. Hariprasad was certain that he had never had a girlfriend before.

Hariprasad began by explaining that he was Mousumi's uncle on her father's side, and that as her father had recently died, God bless him, he was helping her mother with the matchmaking. Dr Banerjee wobbled his head from side to side in understanding. Hariprasad then went on to describe Mousumi.

'Do you know how beautiful she is?' he asked, as if the doctor should have already been in receipt of that information.

'Very?' Dr Banerjee ventured timidly.

'Very?' said Hariprasad raising his voice. '*Very!*'

He paused. 'No, not very, but *extremely*,' quickly correcting himself, his voice another fraction louder. 'Indeed, not extremely, but *impossibly*!' Quietening down to his original level, he adjusted the collar on his shirt and lifted himself from his seat for a moment so that he could pull his trousers up to sit even higher on his waist. He elaborated, 'Five feet eight and like this . . .' He made the outline of a Coca-Cola bottle with his hands. 'Not like this,' he demonstrated, exaggerating the Coca-Cola bottle's curves, 'but like this.' Again he made the shape, carefully pausing his hands to show what a small waist Mousumi supposedly had.

Dr Banerjee looked slightly nervous, his hands gripping the oars so firmly that his knuckles turned white, and nodded quickly.

Hariprasad went on, 'Men chasing her here. Men chasing her there. Although none suitable yet, so we placed the advert. Although she is,' he stated with some conviction as he jabbed a finger in the doctor's direction, 'a woman of the world.' The doctor winced, but Hariprasad continued, now in a more avuncular tone, 'Nowadays, women have their needs. You understand what I'm saying? They have *needs* . . .'

Dr Banerjee paled visibly and paddled so hard that the boat veered off to the left and crashed into a shikara full of picnicking grannies.

When they reached the bank, Hariprasad asked when a suitable time would be for the doctor to meet Mousumi.

Looking down at his feet, Dr Banerjee replied, 'Babu, please forgive me. Your niece sounds wonderful and any man would be lucky to have her as their wife, but I am a simple man with simple tastes, and I don't think that I would ever be able to satisfy a woman so exceptionally beautiful and talented. Please, Sir, I ask that you understand my position.'

Hariprasad looked shocked, then disappointed, then sympathetic. 'I understand,' he said thoughtfully, shaking the doctor's hand. 'I understand.' The two parted company.

Rekha took along with her the best photograph she could find of Mousumi. In it she looked black and plump, but the chubby god Krishna himself was dark, having been born at midnight and taken the colour of the night, and if it was a good enough colour for a god, it was a good enough colour for any mortal.

She waited for fifteen minutes, checking her watch every two for the doctor, who was nowhere to be seen. Hariprasad was very organized, so he could never have mixed the time up, she thought. She went for a walk around the lake, looking to see whether anyone fitted the doctor's description.

Finally, she went to the man at the helpdesk, and asked whether anyone had been inquiring after her.

'No, Ma'am,' he answered, barely looking up from his newspaper.

'Are you sure?' she pleaded. 'The gentleman was meant to be meeting me here at least half an hour ago.'

'Ma'am,' he answered, staring her square in the eye, 'I said, no man for *you*.' He held her gaze for a moment, and then went back to his newspaper.

Rekha sniffed a little, then straightened her sari and said with as much sarcasm as she could muster, 'Thank you very much for your help, Sir!', and marched off.

Tuhina was a great believer in assimilation. The first thing she had done after booking Mousumi's plane ticket was to buy her a Bengali-to-English phrase-book. And ever since Mousumi's arrival, she had spoken to her only in English – 'How will she learn, otherwise?' she chastised Prakash, who thought communication was more useful than learning how to say 'Do you speak Bengali?' in English. Tuhina thought Prakash was being too soft. Prakash thought Tuhina was being too hard.

Every morning, Mousumi brought her phrasebook down to the breakfast table with her and pretended to consult it whilst looking at the newspapers. Tuhina and Prakash would leave for work, and then, soon after, Darshini would leave as well, despite it being her school holidays.

Every day Darshini planned something to do – perhaps a visit to the Renoir Cinema for an afternoon of delightfully obscure films, or buying a foreign fashion magazine from RD Franks on Market Place and reading it under a tree in Regent's Park with a couple of pieces of frangipane flan from Patisserie Valerie. Occasionally she would take a walk, starting at Trafalgar Square, going down the Strand and Fleet Street and finishing at St Paul's, taking in its splendour and amusing herself by whispering in the Whispering Gallery, before dropping in to the office and pleasantly demanding to be taken out for a coffee by either Tuhina or Seph, whoever was available. Sometimes she would spend the whole day in the Bond Street shops, dressing up in extravagant outfits and modelling them for both the other customers and the shop assistants, who were bewitched by her cheekiness and lack of affectation.

Meanwhile, Mousumi stayed at home, suffocating herself with the sound of her own breath. Since their aborted tour of London, Darshini had only invited her out once again, to a showing of Tian Zhuangzhuang's *Springtime in a Small Town* at the Renoir. Darshini bought them each a bar of Green &

Black's organic milk chocolate, which Mousumi managed to guzzle by the time the trailers had ended. Darshini gracefully broke off small pieces and made hers last until the end of the film.

Mousumi sat back in her seat, put both her forearms on the chair rests and awaited the film eagerly. She was only allowed to go to the cinema in Calcutta as a very special treat, when her father told her to go because he wanted some time alone in the house. (Although, Mousumi used to muse, he wasn't alone, her mother was in the house, too!) Or if her father had had a particularly good day at work, which happened about once every two years, he would take the whole family out for a movie and ice-cream. Darshini, Mousumi had noted, went to the cinema whenever she felt like it. She peered at the screen intently, waiting for some singing and dancing. She waited for one hour and fifty-six minutes and it didn't come.

Darshini loved the film, and was unusually vocal about it. 'How gorgeous was that!' she exclaimed as they left the screening room. 'All those beautiful muted colours, it was just *dreamy*.' She smiled at Mousumi and added, 'Really gentle and subtle.'

Mousumi didn't want gentle and subtle. She wanted loud and garish. 'But nothing happened in the film,' she wanted to say. Where were the shoot-outs in back-street alleyways, and wounded heroes wiping blood from their foreheads, and women gyrating in Alpine meadows? As she was thinking this, Darshini caught her off guard, and asked, 'So, did you enjoy it?'

Mousumi's immediate response was to shrug, non-committal. Then she realized what she had done, and tried to rectify her response by saying something else.

'Umm . . .' she mumbled. 'But . . .' she continued hopefully, but it was too late. Her initial reaction had already registered with Darshini.

'Oh,' said Darshini, disappointed. 'Never mind.' She didn't say another word to Mousumi for the journey home.

After that, Darshini never invited her along; she thought that Mousumi would just be an irritation, much like a piece of toilet paper stuck to the bottom of her shoe. She liked having herself to herself. She would never have refused had Mousumi requested to join her, but Mousumi never invited herself along; she was someone who always waited for others to ask. From then on, she would stand at the window until she saw Darshini's mane disappear from view and then go and search around the house, an archaeologist looking for clues about the nature of the inhabitants – a photo album filled with pictures of Tuhina and Darshini and no one else, fastidiously labelled with date and place; a cupboard full of champagne flutes, brandy snifters, shot glasses, crystal tumblers, a port decanter.

But the room which especially interested her was Darshini's bedroom. Mousumi had never had her own room, and Darshini's, with shelf after shelf of magazines and books, racks of clothes and shoes, bottles of perfume and jars of fragrant creams aroused both inquisitiveness and envy. Mousumi thought of her own meagre wardrobe and her nearly empty wash-bag and her two pairs of shoes – one pair of flat, buckle-up sandals and a pair of flat, buckle-up shoes – and it made her feel unfulfilled.

At first, she was carefully curious – everything was returned to its place without a hint that it had been moved. But then she became purposefully sloppy – leaving lids off jars, taking books and magazines from the shelves and not putting them back, leaving drawers open. She visited the room every day, and as time passed she became angrier, determined to destroy it, Belial in the House of God. She tore pages out of the meticulously kept magazines, destroyed lipsticks by screwing them into their lids, rifled through papers, tearing up letters which she couldn't understand. And when she tried on Darshini's clothes and they wouldn't fit, tears ran down her face. Her bitter, inarticulate rage flew round the room like a hurricane.

At first Darshini was confused – maybe she had

forgotten to put the lid back on the jar or return the magazine to the shelf; but when she found her torn clothes and broken lipsticks, she was both bemused and perturbed.

Mousumi also started taking items. Only small, mind. At first, a purple eyeliner with a gold lid. Darshini noticed, but didn't mind, as she had a Noah's Ark of make-up – two of everything. Then Mousumi took a small pair of red glass earrings, cheap but pretty, which she wore for ten minutes each night before she went to bed. Darshini noticed, but didn't mind, because she didn't wear them much any more. Then a little badge disappeared, which Seph had bought for Darshini from the Tate, reading 'Work of Art'. Darshini noticed, and did mind, but only a little bit, just because it was a gift from Seph. It *had* to be Mousumi, she thought, but she couldn't come up with a motive; neither had she seen her with purple eyes or red ears. And it seemed such a ridiculous thing to accuse her of. So Darshini said nothing and waited; Mousumi might as well have been screaming into a vacuum.

A month and a half in, Mousumi found Darshini's lingerie drawer, which was in a hidden compartment of the wardrobe. It was filled with scraps of lace, delicate pieces of silk embroidered with flowers, barely-there pieces of mesh and ribbon. As she felt the material with her fingertips, she prickled with resentment. Rifling through the drawer further, she found what looked like a scroll, tied up with a deep crimson silk scarf. She untied the scarf unusually carefully, and looked at what it held. Her hands trembled and her heart beat faster. It was a thin magazine with two women on the front cover, both naked, caressing each other, with superimposed stars covering their nipples and groins. Mousumi opened it, her eyes and mouth opened wide. Inside, the stars were gone. She slowly turned page after page, fascinated and disgusted. She had never even seen her *own* body in such detail. Then she came to a page near the back which had a photo, taken from the side, of a woman kneeling on a bed, her arms stretched in front of her, her head hanging between her shoulders, her wrists placed one in front of the other to form a cross and then tied to the iron headboard with a scarf. Behind her was a man, his penis fully erect, just about to enter her. She couldn't imagine something so big ever fitting inside her. Next to the photo was a Post-it note, with an arrow pointing at the scarf. It said something she couldn't understand. She ran to find her phrasebook and raced back. 'To match your lipstick,' she frantically translated. And in the bottom right-hand corner, 'S x'. Mousumi felt shame, then panic. She hastily shoved the magazine back in the drawer and fled the room.

When Mousumi went to bed that night, her bedroom seemed slightly different. Something, imperceptible to the eye, had changed. She took off her clothes self-consciously and looked in the mirror at her robust bra and colossal knickers and the rolls of flesh in between. To her, the things she had seen in the magazine, and her body, seemed mutually exclusive. She took off her underwear, turning away from the mirror so as not to disgust herself, and put her nightdress on. Climbing into bed, she was just about to turn her bedside lamp out when she saw something sticking out from under her pillow. She lifted it up and suddenly she felt as if the room was filled with invisible eyes, all staring at her. There was the magazine, and on it a note. Mousumi reached for her phrasebook and, heart pounding, looked up the words: 'Keep it for yourself – you might learn something.' Her face reddened, humiliation wriggling in the veins of her cheeks like hatching maggots. All night, she struggled to sleep; her body sweated dread and disgrace, and her dreams strangled her. She never went into Darshini's room again.

Tuhina came home exhausted. She had started to become tired more easily recently. She wondered whether it was her age. Though she was only forty-five, the ambition which had kept her in the office until four in the morning, and back in again by seven, was beginning to pale. The espresso thrill of the early days had lightened to a cappuccino pleasure, light and frothy, but it wasn't enough. There was no motivating desperation any more. What would she do if she retired, she mused. Read books? Learn another language? Redecorate the house? How does one find meaning and satisfaction in a satin or matt finish or the perfect shade of green? She walked around her home slowly, trying to calculate just how much time she had spent in it. First of all she went into the den, where Darshini had left the television on, humming quietly. She scanned the room, searching for the remote control to turn it off. She lifted the assortment of magazines – *Vogue*, *W*, *Q*, *Self Service*, *Amelia*, all Darshini's – from the low black lacquered table, but it wasn't there. Distracted from her task for a moment by the earrings the model on the cover of *W* was wearing, she picked the glossy up and flicked through it. Pages were missing and photos had been cut out; Darshini must have stuck them in one of her scrapbooks, Tuhina thought to herself, the corner of her mouth lifting slightly. Then she put it down and started looking again. Next she kneeled in front of a large wooden cupboard, which years ago Darshini had taken it upon herself to paint gold. Now the paint was flaking off in places, but Tuhina thought it looked even better that way, and she rubbed the door tenderly with her hand. She pulled the handles and a swell of objects came tumbling out: colouring pencils, old tattered exercise books, sequins, a bodiless doll with a ribbon in her hair, a broken plant pot in the early stages of restoration. At first, the skin between her eyes pinched together, but then she shook her head lightly and put the things back into the cupboard as neatly as she could manage.

Finally she found the remote control under the seat of the large Victorian mahogany-framed sofa, which she had had re-covered in a deep crimson silk and was scattered with hand-embroidered cushions. She picked one up, and saw that the needlework was fraying – it was the cushion that Darshini always tucked between her legs whilst watching TV. Tuhina rubbed a loose thread between her thumb and forefinger and then shrugged half-heartedly, plumped it up and put it back down. She turned the TV off and wiped the screen gently with her hand to clear it of static.

Next she padded slowly upstairs. She ran her hand over the bannister, noticing that it didn't gleam as brightly as it once did. She stopped at one particularly dull spot and rubbed it vigorously with her hand to try and restore the shine. She stood back, tilted her chin up and peered down her nose, and nodded. Satisfied with her work, she continued up.

In her bedroom, Tuhina slipped off her shoes and lay on the bed, looking up at the ceiling. There was a crack. She looked at it for a long time, stretching her arms over her head and rubbing her feet against each other. She bent her head to one side and decided it was an artistic crack, then wrapped her arms around herself, gave herself a quick hug and jumped out of bed. As she walked around the divan, straightening the duvet, she noticed the corner of something poking out from under the mattress on Prakash's side. Pulling at it, she discovered a magazine, *FHM*. She flicked through it, un-impressed by the stacks of heaving, oiled breasts and women bending over wearing nothing but g-strings – they all looked so cheap. But she was even more unimpressed by the fact that Prakash considered this porn. It was so typical of him, she thought – he didn't even have the balls to buy the real thing. Aggravated that he was so gutless, she left the magazine lying on his bedside table.

As she wandered around the rest of the house, she took in everything carefully, picking up details she hadn't had time to notice before: the scratch on the hall dresser, probably left by Prakash's keys, although she had told him numerous times to put them in the blue Venetian glass bowl; the damp patch in the ceiling above the sixth stair; the dusty cobweb hanging in the corner of the study. Not that she minded.

She came to a stop in the kitchen and rested her elbows on the counter. She rubbed her eyes and tried to work out how many times she had cooked a proper meal for her family since Darshini was old enough to eat solids. Not a quick omelette, but starter, main and dessert. Her eyes moved up as if they were trying to search her brain, but she couldn't find an image stacked away in her 'Meals' folder. However, she pointed out to herself, she did take her family out to lots of wonderful restaurants, which made them a lot happier than any half-baked soufflé she could rustle up.

Looking at her watch, she wondered where the others were. It was eight thirty, and there wasn't a sound. She walked back downstairs and stopped by the phone in the hall. Picking up the receiver, she held it to her ear, wondering whether she should call, but then decided against it. Back in the kitchen, she noticed a piece of notepaper stuck to the fridge with a magnet: 'All – not in for dinner tonight, gone to cinema with friends, D.' Removing it, she folded it neatly and then put it in the bin. What about the other two? She was quite hungry and wanted to sit down for dinner.

At nine, Prakash and Mousumi waltzed into the

kitchen, where Tuhina was now nursing a glass of red wine and a junior-sized packet of pretzels which she had fished out of the bottom of her handbag. They looked invigorated, as if they'd been for a brisk walk.

'Where have you been?' she demanded, her belly rumbling slightly. Tuhina's belly had barely rumbled once in the last twenty years of marriage. Dinner had always been on the table (or at least in the oven) when she had come back from work.

'We're getting fit together!' Prakash replied, jolly, determined.

'We went to walk,' Mousumi added, smiling.

Tuhina flinched at the slight syntax error, and opened her mouth to correct her, but then closed it again and swallowed drily.

Tuhina had been asking Prakash to take some exercise for ten years, although she had given up in the last five, but he had never taken her up on her suggestion. Now, he was rosy-cheeked and wearing trainers and a tracksuit. Mousumi stood beside him and watched Tuhina's expression. Self-consciously she wiped the sweat from her forehead, and then wondered where to wipe her hands. She tried to pat her tracksuit pants subtly. 'Long walk!' she added, stretching her arms out, hoping to impress Tuhina. Then she suddenly realized that there were damp patches under her arms and, embarrassed, rapidly clamped them to her side.

'Well, good for you!' Tuhina said with as much vigour as she could muster, narrowing her eyes at Mousumi's sudden movement. And then, as if it were merely an afterthought, 'So, what's happening for dinner?'

'I thought we'd get takeaway tonight,' Prakash answered, whilst fixing himself and Mousumi a drink. 'Chinese?'

'Chinese is fine with me,' Tuhina said quietly, although what she actually wanted to eat was Prakash's homemade pan-fried scallops (which she would have picked up from Billingsgate fish market on her way to work) with Pernod and coriander sauce, followed by butterflied lamb (which he would have bought from their local butcher that lunchtime) marinated in lemon, thyme and garlic, served with olive-oil-properly-mashed mash. And if Prakash had had an especially good day at work, flourless chocolate cake with crème Anglaise. The thought made her mouth water, then, unpredictably, her eyes. 'Chinese is fine . . .' she repeated, sotto voce.

'Chinese, Mou?' Prakash asked. Mousumi simply grinned and nodded.

After dinner, Tuhina went to read some case notes in the study. Half an hour later, feeling thirsty from the salty Chinese food, she went downstairs to fetch herself a drink. On the way to the kitchen, she stopped in the doorway of the sitting room and saw Prakash and Mousumi sitting on the sofa. It was so deep that they both sat cross-legged on it, like children at assembly. She and Prakash never sat on the same sofa any more, Tuhina thought. In fact, they rarely sat in the same room, apart from at dinner.

Prakash and Mousumi were so engrossed in whatever it was they were talking about that they failed to look up and notice her. Tuhina listened as carefully as possible; Prakash was teaching Mousumi English. The blind leading the blind, Tuhina mused cruelly, but not without basis – Prakash's sentence structure was idiosyncratic, to say the least. It constantly annoyed her. And now he was passing on his mistakes, scribbling, in his doctor's illegible handwriting, incorrect phrases ('he ate a bean on a toast', 'those stupid peoples') and quirky expressions which he believed were in general usage, but were actually of his own making. There was no sign of the Bengali-to-English phrasebook which she had bought.

Something about the set-up irked her; and the longer she stood there unnoticed, the more it bothered her. For a start, she felt left out. Not that she would have wanted to join in, but it would have been nice to be asked. Secondly, she couldn't recall ever seeing Prakash taking that much interest in teaching Darshini; she herself had always taken care of that. And thirdly, wasn't that *her* sofa? She had chosen it, had it made, bought it, decided where to place it. And now they were sitting on it. Together. Without her. Suddenly she felt inclined to interrupt.

'Er, Prakash?' Tuhina never said 'Er.'

Prakash looked up. 'Hmm?'

'Er, I think the light in the study's gone. You need to fix it.'

'Now?'

'Yes, now. I need to find a book in there.'

'OK, hang one minute,' Prakash said, transferring the notepad, dictionary and pen from his lap to Mousumi's. 'I'll just go and get new bulb from the pantry.'

Tuhina walked upstairs to the study and turned the light out, wondering what to do. She stood with her back to the switch, covering it, so that Prakash wouldn't try it himself. He came armed with a step-ladder, a tea-towel (so he didn't burn his hands) and a new bulb, and walked straight past her to the centre of the room.

'Hold,' he directed. 'This wobbles.' He unscrewed the bulb carefully, handing it to Tuhina as she steadied the ladder with her other hand, then took the other one and put it in. 'Now see,' he told her, motioning to the switch. She guiltily walked back to the wall and paused for a brief moment before turning the switch on. The light worked. 'Good!' Prakash exclaimed, climbing back down. Gathering his things, he walked past Tuhina, who was still holding the broken light bulb which wasn't really broken. She stood there for a long time, cradling its fading warmth.

CHAPTER NINE

Too Much Protest

Darshini had been on the phone to a man who had recently climbed Everest. As usual, she had randomly picked his name out of the phone book and called. He had assumed she was a member of the press, and spoke to her at length about the challenges of climbing and the 'physical and mental stamina' needed, and anything else which he thought would make good copy, but what had caught her attention was his description of actually being on the mountain. Darshini had lived her life in a city of lofty government buildings, grand churches and towering office blocks, where people spent their lives looking up, and now she wanted to go somewhere where she could look down. So she began to plan her expedition; she thought Seph would accompany her. A little smile appeared on her face as she daydreamed of being on top of the world.

His answer was 'No,' without any hesitation. She hadn't expected this, and eyed him with curiosity.

'Why not? You haven't taken any holiday this year, you said so yourself.'

'Because I don't want to.'

'Why not?'

'Because I don't.'

'But *why*?'

'*Because.*'

They had met at Curfew Tower; Seph joined the group last. They pretended not to notice him, but the girls' freckled faces flushed with longing. One of them, Elaine Patrick, or Ellie as she was known, was especially besotted.

'All right, Ellie?' Seph asked casually, and the whole of her body ached.

They stayed outside the tower for a while, milling about like a swarm of gnats, until Seph said, 'We better get going, then,' and everyone followed him. The weather forecast was warm and sunny, the perfect day for trekking up Lurigethan mountain in the Glens of Antrim, which had once been home to the fêted warriors Finn McCool and his son Ossian, and was also the preferred residence for the wee folk in the area. It had been Ellie's idea, and although she had contrived to make the trip seem as casual as possible, she had made very sure that Seph made it by mentioning it to all his friends. They picked up their rucksacks and started on their way.

Seph had also brought along Meghan, a six-month-old black Labrador which had been a gift from him to his mother to keep her company. With her kohl-lined coal eyes and a pleading gaze, everyone wanted to stroke her and be her favourite, so as she bounded up Lurigethan they all followed her.

The mountain wore a majestic green robe, lit up by buttery rays of sun, and in the distance they could hear the silver waves spraying the shingle with salty water as they breathed in the fresh glen air. After an hour or so, they stopped for their picnic. Ellie sat down next to Seph and then lay back on the grass. Seph continued to stroke Meghan, oblivious to Ellie. So she sat back up, whipped her top off and lay back down again. The other girls looked at each other, but said nothing, and when the boys laughed nervously, she shot back, 'What? I'm hot! All right?' with a little too much protest.

Seph turned to see what the fuss was about and saw the pale skin of her shoulders, and her adolescent breasts, which hardly needed covering, jutting irately into little triangles of white cotton, and felt embarrassed for her. 'You'll get sunburnt with that pale skin of yours,' he said, avuncular in tone, and then turned back to stroke the puppy. Ellie's failure set her mouth in a fish's pout and narrowed her emerald eyes, but she didn't give up.

They packed up their belongings and set off for the fort remains at the top. Meghan was still full of energy and raced ahead of them until she was out of sight. When they next saw her, they came to a standstill. She was sitting about three metres away from a Fairy Thorn, her head tipped back, her ears alert, and whining, a haunting, desperate sound which echoed around the glens and gave them goose-pimples, despite the warmth of the sun.

'What's going on?' one of the girls asked nervously.

'It's the skeogh,' answered Kevin Quinn, who was a farmer's son and the quietest of the group.

'Ah, don't be so dumb,' Ellie piped up. 'Who believes in that kind of shite!'

'But look how the dog's howling,' insisted Kevin.

'You're not telling me you believe in fairies, are ya?' Ellie retorted, her voice full of bravado; this was her chance to impress Seph, and she wasn't going to miss it.

No one said anything. She continued, made braver by the lack of comeback, 'It's just a tree, for Christ's sake!' Then mockingly, 'You don't really think there are fairies living under there, do ya?'

'Just leave it, will you?' Seph said calmly, his voice displaying just the slightest dip of annoyance. 'Let's carry on up to the top.'

'Come on, Seph,' she teased. 'It's only a tree, surely *you* can't be scared . . .' Meghan continued to whimper. Ellie walked past her and stood next to the Fairy Thorn.

'Come away from there, Ellie,' Seph said, his voice showing the slightest strain. But Ellie would not, and determined to show Seph how fearless she was, she broke off a twig. 'See?' she taunted. 'Nothing's happened.' She nonchalantly threw the twig on the ground.

Meghan stopped wailing and ran off. Ellie, determined to keep up her show of bravado, chased after her until they were soon both out of sight. The rest of the group turned to follow her, but as they climbed they started to shiver as clouds gathered and a cold breeze blew in from the sea.

'I think we should head back,' Seph said, looking up at the darkening sky. 'Ellie?' he shouted, cupping his hands around his mouth. 'Come back! Ellie?' His words echoed eerily, but the plaintive request was eaten by the vast space. He hooked his fingers inside his mouth and whistled, hoping that Meghan would hear. 'Meg?' he cried out. 'Meg?' She was an obedient if playful puppy, and he had never had to call her name more than twice before she came bounding back. There was no response.

Suddenly there was a huge bang, as if a car had backfired, and the black skies opened and lashed them with fierce rain, soaking them to the skin. Fat streaks of lightning shot through the sky and the clouds clapped with thunderous applause. Through the drum beat of the rain, they could hear the gush of the rivers and waterfalls as they swelled with water. They all huddled together in the open air, unable to move. Up on the mountain, everything else looked so small and far away. It was as if they were on the front line of the world, the first to face His wrath. There was nothing to hide under, nowhere to shelter.

For the first time, Seph was scared. But he knew that he had to keep looking for Ellie and Meghan. Pulling away from the others, he continued up the mountain, praying to a God he didn't believe in, the rain lashing his face. As the storm continued unabated, he thought of his mother, who had no one but him, and tears flowed down his face, masked by the continuing downpour. He thought about the father he hadn't met and the wife he hadn't married and the children he hadn't been a father to, and the tears came stronger. Then, through the tumultuous noise, he heard a strange mourning noise. He stopped to listen, trying to work out exactly where

213

it was coming from, then ran in that direction.

She must have slipped. In such bad weather it would have been easy to lose her footing. Seph looked down from the edge of the rock and saw her twisted body in the stream below, her legs outstretched so it appeared that she was in the middle of performing a grand jeté. At last she looked calm, all her bluster and fieriness drained away. Her lips had already started to turn blue and her face was as ghostly as a Kabuki dancer's. Meghan stood by the body, her front paws resting on Ellie's ribcage, howling and wagging her tail for attention.

'Meg!' Seph called. She looked up at him and barked anxiously. 'I'm coming!'

There wasn't anything Seph could do, although he tried, and when the rest of them finally caught up they found him sitting by the side of the stream, cradling Ellie's body, with Meg curled around him trying to keep him warm. The girls started to cry and the boys' bottom lips quivered from the cold and shock. They would need the coastguard to come and pick the body up. Seph was the only person willing to stay with Ellie – the rest of them were spooked, and trembled at the thought. So for another hour, whilst the others went back into the town to raise the alert, Seph sat with her, and Ellie, who had in life dreamed a thousand times of being held in his arms, had her wish granted in death.

214

* * *

Seph couldn't tell Darshini why he wouldn't go with her. Wasn't it the same as her saying she was scared of clowns (ever since watching Stephen King's *It*) or bubble-bath (*she* didn't know why; it was because she had once put her hand through the bubbles and the hot water underneath had scalded her)? No; to him those fears were funny, endearing even. They didn't turn Darshini into another person; they added to her uniqueness. But he believed that his trepidation would make him seem a weaker person. He didn't want her to think he was pathetic. He equated being masculine with having no weakness; he had an irrational fear of fear. Darshini would have understood, but he didn't give her the chance. She had thought his 'No' was a childish protestation, and that he wouldn't change his mind simply because he was being stubborn. So she had stormed off to his bedroom, and now he had to make up with her.

He sat next to her on the bed, and tried to appease her. 'It's not that I don't want to go on holiday with you,' he said, stroking her leg. 'I just don't want to go on a mountain-climbing expedition.'

'Fine,' she said dismissively.

Seph realized that words wouldn't suffice. He pulled his shirt off and then kneeled near Darshini's feet, gently prising her legs apart. She didn't stop him, and seemed slightly responsive, the muscles in her thighs faintly flexing. Seph gently kissed the crease at the top of her inner thigh and Darshini lifted her hips up, sliding down the sheets, her body arching like a cat that needed to be stroked. He pushed her hips down with his hands to hold her still. He enjoyed the physical power he had over her. He could do what he wanted. Hooking her legs over his shoulders, he looked up at her prostrate body: the dip between her hipbones, the plane of her breasts, the soft underside of her chin, exposed from throwing her head back. Gently, teasingly, he pulled her knickers down. Slowly, he ran his tongue between the grooves of damp flesh and then sucked the delicate skin into his mouth. He felt Darshini's hand on the back of his head, lightly pulling his hair. Pinpricks of sweat formed a tingling line down his spine. He licked more insistently as she tried to place herself against his tongue. The command he had over her made him hard. She was all *his*.

Probing her with the tip of his tongue, all he could hear was her stunted breath and a soft sigh. Still he made her wait for him to touch her where she was desperate to be touched. Finally, when she was so wet that her skin glistened like petrol-stained water, he moved away and kissed her on her parted mouth. She went to grab at him but he pinned her arms over her head and looked into her furious eyes. She tried to move her arms but couldn't. Frustration marched through her body like an army of fire ants. He leaned in to kiss her, but she turned her head to the side. This act of futile defiance made him love her even more. 'Ssshh,' he whispered, 'ssshh,' as if to calm an irate animal. This infuriated her further and she lay totally still for a moment before trying to lift her whole body, but Seph anticipated her move and threw his leg over her thighs. His knowing smile elicited a groan of exasperation.

They lay there for a few moments, her angry, unfulfilled body rigid, and he a poacher staring into the face of a trapped tigress. He ran his free hand down her body, which bristled with rage, and then resting his forearm on her hipbone touched the small nub of flesh, which expanded on contact, contrary to her will. This was what aroused him the most: having more control over her body than she herself did. He started rubbing her slowly, firmly, rhythmically. Her eyes closed with pleasure but he wouldn't unpin her until he was sure she wouldn't run. When her breathing became so shallow that she was gasping for air, he lifted his leg from her. She didn't retaliate. He continued to stroke her, harder, harder, until he felt her whole body convulse. His hand was crushed between her thighs and her smooth brow furrowed into an expression of deep thought, although she was thinking of nothing.

217

Finally, she said petulantly, 'We're still not friends.'

'That's OK,' Seph replied, pulling her against his body and nuzzling the back of her neck.

'I *mean* it.'

'That's OK,' he repeated, overwhelmed with adoration for her, wrapping his arms around her even more tightly. He wanted to tell her about the others. And then he could forget about them for ever.

CHAPTER TEN

The Goodwill Mission

Prakash had had enough. The fan in his room was broken and the ammonia smell of geriatric patients hung in the close air. He pressed the bell on his desk and sighed, rubbing his already tired eyes. There was no response; it must have broken again. He heaved himself out of the chair and walked through to the reception area. Peering over the top of a pile of medical notes, he scanned the waiting room: so many people, so much loneliness, he thought. They sat next to each other, elbows and knees accidentally touching in moments of careless-ness, each encased in a clear dome of their own like a sheet of bubble-wrap. Prakash felt like squashing the bubbles between thumb and forefinger and screaming, 'Wake up!' Only a few of his patients had proper medical conditions which needed treating. The rest had invented or imagined illnesses to give structure to their day: go to the doctor, fetch prescription, go home, pop pill, watch daytime television – a human cake with misery as its icing – pop pill, pick up screaming grubby kids from school, warm up plastic dinner in the microwave oven, pack screaming grubby kids off to bed, watch evening television in a fog of smoke, pop pill, go to sleep. What makes people live life to the full is knowing it is finite; what makes life pointless is lack of purpose, and these people had no purpose. They clogged up the room like cholesterol, waiting for their prescriptions of painkillers, sedatives, sleeping pills. The grass-green tablets, the sky-blue capsules: this was the only colour in their life. They were prisoners, but they were their own keepers, too.

The most depressing of all were the elderly, with their loose crêpey skin and doddery steps, ignored by even their own, desperate to be heard, their slack-jawed babblings barely intelligible. But where were their families to listen to their tales of war and woe? They had sons and daughters, grandchildren, great-nieces and -nephews, but on their family tree the boxes filled with their names were joined by the faintest of dotted lines, if at all. In a world of each man for himself, there is no room for duty or obligation or love. Life is a diamond which reflects a different colour depending on the light that is shone on it; in the grey winter days of old age, it appears to be no more than a piece of broken glass.

Mrs Blackmore was one of Prakash's favourite patients. A proud old woman with wispy white hair, she refused to die, much to the annoyance of her family, who begrudgingly visited her twice a year – at Christmas and on her birthday – at a nursing home just off Clapham High Street, despite living only an hour's drive away. They were too busy with ballet lessons, piano recitals of Bach's minuets, and extra maths tuition to pay any attention to the woman without whom they wouldn't exist. Despite years of neglect, she stood strong, a flowering ocotillo in the Californian desert. Prakash admired her resilience. So when she came into his consulting room that morning, her face drawn and her normally rouged cheeks sallow, it was a sad sight, and he felt sorry for her, and then annoyance at himself for feeling it, because she wasn't a woman who would want to be pitied.

He tried to help her into the chair, but she wouldn't have any of it, pushing him away with a twisted hand, and taking a few minutes to bend her knees and ease herself into the seat. Prakash waited patiently; he knew the value of independence. He asked her the routine questions and her answers were the same as usual. He warmed the stethoscope in his hands and then gently lifted her top and

221

listened to her chest; her breathing was normal. He asked her to lie flat on the couch and pressed her abdomen: there was no tenderness or pain. He knocked her knees with a hammer: her reflexes were fine. He checked to see if she had suffered a stroke, but when he scratched the palm of her foot, her big toe shot defiantly upwards. But despite all this, she said she felt unwell and lethargic. All he could write in her notes was 'general malaise'; he asked her to rest and come back in a couple of days. When she hobbled out of his office, his mouth drooped.

Mousumi was bored. Since the pornographic incident, she had become too nervous to explore the house. Now when the others left the house, she would creep from room to room, scared even to sit down in case she left an indent in the sofa or displaced a cushion. When she used a piece of crockery, she would meticulously wash it, then dry it until it gleamed, taking great care to put it back exactly where it had been placed, without nudging anything else. She didn't even dare change the channel or volume on the television – every morning she would watch the same programmes at the same volume sitting in the same place on the same sofa, creating her very own groundhog day.

It was only when Prakash was around that she felt free to do what she pleased. So that morning, after sitting very still for an hour, Mousumi decided that she would pay Prakash a visit – she thought that he might be pleased to see her. And she decided to take him lunch.

She had never made a sandwich before, but she had figured out that that was what people in England ate for lunch. And she wanted to do her best to show that she was learning. So she looked in the fridge, and took a guess. Taking four slices of bread, two for Prakash, two for herself, she spread them with mayonnaise, making sure that the pieces were covered right to the crust. Then she neatly chopped up uncooked frankfurters into little rounds, and lined them neatly on the bread. She placed a piece of ham on top of each piece, neatly trimming round the edge for a perfect fit. Ready-grated mozzarella cheese followed, finished with a dollop of tomato ketchup in the centre. Satisfied with her creation, she cut the sandwiches into triangular halves, and wrapped them in foil. Putting everything away neatly, and wiping the crumbs from the bread board, she put the sandwiches in a bag and prepared to leave.

Just as she was about to close the door, she realized that she didn't really know where she was going. Prakash had pointed out his surgery a few

223

times whilst they were driving to the supermarket, but Mousumi had neither a photographic memory nor a great sense of direction. She stood in the doorway and wondered what to do. She didn't want the sandwiches to go to waste, but she considered that she could always eat both of them herself. Then she decided that she wanted to leave the house, and with no idea of how she was going to find Prakash's surgery, she slammed the door very definitively behind her.

For once, luck was on her side. She recognized shops and restaurants and flowerbeds, the garage that sold old Mercedes and BMWs with fluorescent yellow star stickers in their windscreens declaring their price, and even the old tramp who slept on the bench outside the bookie's, clutching a beer can, with his feet wrapped in plastic bags and his dirty woollen hat pulled over his eyes. And since she had started walking with Prakash, she was less out of breath than usual.

Prakash was both delighted and surprised to see her. Darshini and Tuhina never visited him at work. He had been sitting on his own in his consulting room, reading his MMs book and thinking about Mrs Blackmore, when she had appeared in his doorway.

Rosemary was standing behind her, looking quizzical. 'She says she's here for you,' she said, raising an eyebrow. 'She says she *lives* with you!' she continued sardonically.

'Yes, yes, yes, yes!' said Prakash, perking up. 'Come in, Mou! Thank you, Rose Mary!'

Rosemary looked slightly perturbed for a moment, but then shrugged her shoulders and closed the door.

'So,' Prakash asked, rejuvenated, 'to what I owe this pleasure?'

Mousumi didn't understand, so she simply handed him a sandwich.

'Lunch!' he exclaimed. 'Wonderful!'

Whilst they both sat munching on their interesting sandwiches, Mousumi's visit gave Prakash inspiration – they would be Mrs Blackmore's family! They would visit her, take her little tiffin boxes of spicy potatoes and tarka dhal, read her human-interest articles from the community newsletter and stroll around the park listening to stories of her life back in the days of the Raj.

When he told Mousumi his idea she responded enthusiastically, nodding her head and smiling. So he asked her whether she'd mind sitting in the waiting room whilst he took his afternoon surgery – there were plenty of magazines to read, he said, which would help with her English – and afterwards they went to his favourite grocer's in Brixton, both of them feeling motivated and light, with a bounce in their step. The evening sunlight bathed everything in a warm ochre glow. A group of men stood on the street corner, the light turning them into sculpted ebony statues, gold glinting at their throats and wrists, the soporific smell of herb lazing around them. A couple of girls strolled by, their mountainous bottoms wrapped in slices of denim, speaking into garish over-designed phones, their bejewelled nail-tips creating crescents at the side of their face.

Prakash rummaged in the half-empty crates outside the shop, looking for his treasure. He picked up a sweet potato, rubbed its dusty red skin with his thumb and then popped it into a brown paper bag, which Mousumi held dutifully. Next he moved on to the ladies' fingers, their green gloves slightly crumpled from the heat of the day, pressing them gently to check they weren't too firm. An aubergine was inspected the same way a diamond is scrutinized by a gemmologist, held up to the light, peered at from every angle.

When they arrived home, Prakash laid his purchases on the kitchen table and poured himself a congratulatory glass of whisky and Mousumi a congratulatory glass of lemonade. Mousumi took a seat at the table. The sight of the harvest in front of her warmed her insides.

'Would you like to help, or are you too tired after

this afternoon's walk?' Prakash asked her pleasantly. Mousumi nodded eagerly. Prakash was the only person who had ever given her any duty or responsibility. She had helped him wash the cars and had developed a talent for drying them so no water marks were left. When he clipped roses from the garden, she arranged them in vases, taking extra care to strip them of their thorns. When they came back from the supermarket, he would unpack the bags and she'd load the fridge, meticulously sorting the food into meat, fish, vegetables, dairy products, juices, condiments. She especially liked to rearrange the fridge magnets after each shop.

Prakash didn't look at her fat body and fat hair and see laziness or incompetence or docility; he just saw someone who liked food. Not so Tuhina, who was repulsed by the acres of flesh and thought of her late brother with his flabby body and flabby mind. 'Mens sana in corpore sano' was engraved on the back of a plaque which she had received for being the best all-rounder in her final year of school. Mousumi could tell from Tuhina's tone of voice, a cool weightless timbre, like aluminium, that she was a hindrance even before she tried to help. And she didn't have the guts to ask Darshini; before Mousumi even dared look at her, her whole body blushed and her mouth dried.

'Where are you going?' Darshini asked casually, as

Prakash and Mousumi strode past her and Tuhina armed with carrier bags full of clanking metal tins.

'We're going out!' Prakash answered, his new ally making him bold.

Darshini raised her eyebrows at Tuhina. Tuhina gave a little shrug. Even with his back turned, Prakash sensed the two-headed tigress was flicking its tail, but he felt safe.

Mrs Blackmore was delighted by the visit. Prakash and Mousumi brought all the seasons with them: the bright elation of spring, the sun-kissed torpor of summer, the crisp freshness of autumn and the sparkling magic of winter. She was like a deaf person who could suddenly hear Pamina's lament *Ach, ich fühls*. They left her with a smile on her face and in her belly. The next day she flushed away all her pills. The staff at the nursing home were aghast – but she was alive again.

The news spread and soon every person worth his grey hair and dentures was clamouring for a visit, especially from Mousumi, who was so different from the gum-chewing, lemon-sucking teenagers who wiped the floors for three pounds an hour, so unlike the jobless girl-women who pushed past them on the street, their trousers slung dangerously low on their waists, cussing and sneering as they pushed along babies, neither black nor white. Here was a girl who showed respect to her elders, listened to their stories, told amusing ones of her own, and wore decent clothes which covered her body! With her, they were taken back to another time; a slower, gentler time, with gin and tonics on the lawn, and dancing the Charleston.

Mousumi had never had such a captive audience. These men and women, with their failing hearing and toothless grins, didn't seem to notice her dark, greasy complexion and her unfashionable clothes. With them, she didn't feel self-conscious; she felt free. Free to become the person she was in her dreams. So came the stories – all of them extra-ordinary, and all of them invented. Prakash happily translated.

Never had one of so few years lived so much. From dining on tandoor-roasted quail with nawabs, to tasting the crystal waters of Gaumukh with her own tongue; from trekking through the eerie night forest of Sunderbans, glinting with flame-coloured eyes, to diving in the clear, warm turquoise waters off the coast of Bangaram; from lounging with louche movie stars on the low canary sofas at Athena, five-hundred-rupee daiquiri in hand, to visiting the gem palaces of Jaipur, adorned with princess-cut sapphires – the tales came as fast as the Tamur river. Not that Mousumi ever planned on lying, but flights of fancy just came out of her mouth like leaking sewerage from a burst pipe. She was always briefly anxious in case someone challenged her – once, walking down Park Street in Dharamtalla, she had walked past St Ignatius's Church, and there was a big yellow sign with black writing which translated as 'White lies get tanned from exposure' – and she had a funny feeling in her stomach, like when she ate deep-fried battered chillies. But the emotion soon subsided and the stories were free to flow.

They even made the local newspaper, on one of the inside pages, between an advertisement for an African spiritual healer who could solve all romantic, career and health problems and an article about the rise in muggings in the area.

Pictured above are local doctor Prakash Majumdar and his niece Mousumi Sharma, who has come to visit us for a holiday all the way from India. Prakash and Mousumi have recently been bringing some cheer to the old folk in the area, by paying them lunchtime social visits and cooking them delicious Indian fare. In the photo, Prakash is holding a bowl of one of his speciality dishes: sag aloo chingree.

Tuhina, who had made the *Financial Times* a few times, congratulated them with a warm over-delighted smile and a sniff of indulgence, much like

230

a mother congratulating her child on his first painting – to be stuck on the fridge door with a novelty magnet and then miraculously lost after a month.

Prakash had the article framed and hung it up in the kitchen. Darshini watched him hammer the nail in, and said coolly, 'Well done, Dad,' then went back to reading her book, adding after a moment's thought, with subtle condescension, 'Nice frame.'

But Prakash didn't care. He had Mousumi now. She listened to his cricket commentary with interest. Like him, she supported India, not England. In the past, there had been polite discussions about loyalty between Darshini and him, pivoting on passports and blood, which had ended in the most unsatisfactory outcome of agreeing to disagree, like a see-saw balancing uncertainly. And when he complained about the partiality of the English umpires, Mousumi certainly didn't say, 'Oh, Dad, *give* it a break!' and roll her eyes with casual contempt. She didn't judge him for talking about his patients at the dinner table, whilst Tuhina scowled at him and said through pursed lips, 'What about patient confidentiality?', leaving him feeling sheepish and unable to gnaw on his curried lamb bones. It was not that Tuhina didn't enjoy the anecdotes; simply that she thought she ought not to. Mousumi, on the other hand, found his stories amusing and interesting and would ask him for another: 'One more, Kaku; just one more!' When Prakash hadn't had a particularly entertaining day, he would tell Mousumi old stories, which on repetition did not lose their charm for either the teller or the listener. One of his favourites was the story of a woman who had come in with a permanent headache. Prakash had told her that maybe she hadn't been having enough sex. Joke! The two-headed tigress didn't even bother to roll her eyes, but Mousumi giggled; she was delighted that Prakash thought her mature enough to mention the s-word in front of her. Sachi never would have, although she had sometimes heard him making dirty jokes about melons and bananas in the sitting room, late at night, his friends all with glasses of whisky in their hands, belly-laughing.

Strengthened by the cooperation of a co-conspirator, Prakash suggested a trip to the seaside. He had been to Blackpool once with Tuhina when they had first married. One of the nurses he worked with had said that it was a fun place, and Prakash had thought, Why not? When they arrived there, he had found the place quite enchanting. The arcades filled with jingling-jangling slot machines and their waterfalls of coins, their flashing lights and lurid carpets embedded with cigarette butts; the pier with its vinegar smell of fish and chips and burned-hair candyfloss; the promenade with its peeling handrail and boxes of begonias; the amusement park filled with rickety rollercoasters and chubby dodgems. What fun! Tuhina hadn't thought so. She hadn't said anything, but then she hadn't needed to. Her distaste was evident in the way she delicately picked the superfluous knobs of batter from her fish and dropped them on to the creaky wood. The way her eyes glazed over when he pulled three sets of cherries, and she said politely, 'Oh, well done' (the randomness of gambling didn't appeal to her). The way she wouldn't drive the dodgem car, even when Prakash had said, 'Go on, go on, it's funny!' But now he had someone on his side.

'Would you like to go to the seaside this weekend,' Prakash said lightly, looking up from his plate.

Darshini stopped pushing a pea around her plate and looked up as well, perturbed. 'The *British* seaside?'

'Yes, Darshini,' he said, enunciating every syllable, 'the *British* seaside.' He turned to smile at Mousumi, who smiled back, not knowing quite what was going on.

'Mum, can't we go to Nice or somewhere instead? France is much nicer.'

But before Tuhina could answer, Prakash said,

with an authority he'd never shown before, 'It's not up to your mother. *I* am asking.'

There followed a slightly bewildered and somewhat irritated silence.

'Well, in that case,' Darshini said pointedly, 'no.' The 'no' was careless, as if Prakash's invitation had required little consideration.

But Prakash hadn't lost yet; he still had his secret weapon. 'And what about you, Mou?' he asked sweetly, as if Darshini's rejection mattered not. 'Would you like to go?'

She looked at her uncle and smiled. 'I will love to!'

With a pleased grin, he looked at Tuhina and said, 'And what about you?'

'Sorry,' she said, gazing up from her plate, her tone more gentle than usual, almost pensive, 'but I have to work this weekend.' She put her fork down, and by way of explanation said, 'Big deal going through at the moment.'

'That's OK,' he said quickly and graciously, his shoulders pulled back, his chin jutting. Then he turned to Mousumi and said, his top row of teeth showing, 'Looks like it's just the two of us, then!'

Darshini stopped eating, exhaled deeply through her nose, like a bull confronted by a red rag, and cleared her plate from the table. Tuhina chewed on

234

her lips slightly, and left the rest of her food, although she waited until Mousumi and Prakash had finished eating too before she left the table.

Mousumi started having a great time as soon as they got into the car. She loved sitting in the front passenger seat and choosing which radio station to listen to. And she was especially pleased that, when they stopped on their way at a drive-through McDonald's at one of the service stations, Prakash gave her the responsibility of placing their order and let her lean over him and speak into the micro-phone. Even licking the quasi-chocolate doughnut icing off her fingers made her happy.

When they reached the coast, Prakash parked in one of the side streets – not well-lit, he observed, and in a run-down area, noticing the wrecked bicycle propped against a crumbling brick wall, but the NCP was full and he didn't want to waste their time looking for a better parking space when there were rides to be ridden and hotdogs to be eaten. Mousumi wholeheartedly agreed.

Mousumi prickled with anticipation. She was wearing one of her best shalwar kameez, which her father had intended for her to wear to special family occasions – crimson and adorned with circular little mirrors around the neckline and sleeves. She was so excited that she didn't even feel the drawstring around her waist digging into the pliable flesh of her tummy.

She had never been to the fair before and was overwhelmed by the noise and the bright lights. It took her at least ten minutes to decide what ride to go on first. In the end, she decided on the Ferris wheel. They went on it three times in a row, clapping every time they reached the top. Next they shrieked with laughter on the waltzers, screaming for more as the boy spun their carriage round even faster, and feeling dizzy but elated when they got off. After that, Prakash bought them sticks of rock – Mousumi chose bright pink, he chose green – which they sucked for five minutes and then discarded, wiping their sticky fingers on their trousers. Then Mousumi saw a glass box full of stuffed toys. She had never had one. Prakash noticed her looking at them with both interest and wistfulness.

'Do you want one?' he asked.

'You buy one?' she replied, immediately hopeful.

'Er, not exactly,' Prakash said, realizing what he was getting himself into. 'I have to win one,' he said, slightly nervous now.

'Yes, please,' said Mousumi.

'Right then!' Prakash exclaimed, thrusting his hands into his pockets to see how much change he had.

It took him fifteen goes at £1.50 a shot – after the

first five attempts he had to go to the candyfloss vendor and swap a twenty for change. But Mousumi didn't weary and was just as excited each time Prakash, concentrating deeply, nudged the joystick this way and then that in an attempt to pick up a toy. Finally he managed to manoeuvre the mechanical claw to grab a penguin with flashes of orange on its cheeks. Mousumi jumped up and down as he handed it to her, and then rubbed its furry white tummy against her cheek – she had never felt something so soft before.

After eating a hamburger with extra onions, and an extra slice of cheese for Mousumi, and watching a teenage boy, who had minutes earlier been loudly decrying his friends for not daring to go on Equinox, disembark and promptly vomit over himself, they decided it was time to go home. With Prakash holding a bag of toffee popcorn: dessert, he said, for after the hamburgers, and Mousumi gripping the penguin, they walked back to the car.

As soon as they turned on to the street where the car was parked, Prakash noticed a group of teenage boys standing by his car. Instantly his pace slowed. Mousumi carried on, oblivious, and Prakash had to reach out to pull her back. She looked at him, inquisitive. He didn't know what to say. He couldn't hang back and wait for them to leave now that he was with Mousumi.

'Oh, nothing,' he fibbed, and they continued to walk.

The gang had now noticed the couple, and had stopped their banter to stare at them. Mousumi didn't realize. Prakash did, but didn't know what to do about it. He thought that the best tactic was probably to ignore them and hope that they left him alone. Mousumi waited at the passenger door for Prakash, who was nervously fumbling round in his pocket for his keys. The boys noticed his trembling hands and eyed each other up, sly grins on their faces.

'Can I have some of that popcorn?' one of them asked nonchalantly.

Prakash stopped fumbling, but didn't dare turn around.

'Didn't you hear what I said?' the lad repeated.

Prakash's heart pounded furiously. The boy took advantage of his indecision and grabbed the bag of popcorn out of Prakash's hand.

'Nice of you to offer,' he snarled, picking out a kernel and popping it in his mouth.

Mousumi had watched the whole scene unfolding, not really understanding what was going on. What she did understand was that the boy had taken the popcorn and it wasn't his. Marching fearlessly round to him, she snatched the bag and said, 'Thank you!'

The rest of the group sniggered. In humiliation, the boy shouted, 'You fat bitch!' but Mousumi refused to look at him. Prakash, emboldened by Mousumi's bravery, found his keys quickly and opened the door. He even managed to drive away without stalling.

Mousumi didn't say anything on the journey back about what had happened. She was just pleased to have her dessert. And when they arrived back home, she took her penguin and placed it on her bed, at the top, in the centre of her pillows, and sat and gazed at it for a while, smiling, bits of toffee stuck in between her teeth.

Another suitable candidate had been found in the P.O. Box. This time it was an engineer (ranked after doctor, in terms of eligibility, but before lawyer). Very nice, thought Rekha, looking at the reply, very nice indeed. Indeed, this man seemed an even better catch than the last – Fate must have engineered his no-show! Again, Rekha requested that Hariprasad set up a meeting; he was more than happy to oblige.

They agreed to meet under the banyan tree in the Botanical Gardens, and Hariprasad recognized the man straight away – he seemed a confident sort of chap, neatly groomed, wearing a sports jacket despite the temperature, his hair slicked down with Brylcreem. It would take more to scare him off.

Hariprasad introduced himself as an investigator. Putting a brotherly arm around the engineer, he whispered, 'I'm a private detective.'

The man tried to pull away, but Hariprasad's grip was firm. 'And I think you'll want to know what I am going to tell you about this woman.'

As Hariprasad told it, Mousumi was of the Latrodectus family.

'Latrodectus?' asked the engineer. 'I thought she was a Sharma.'

Hariprasad laughed a superior laugh. 'My dear boy,' he answered – he often took on the speech pattern of an English gentleman when elaborating – 'the Latrodectus family is of course known more commonly as the black widow spider family. You *have* heard of the black widow spider, haven't you? You do *know* what the female does to the male?'

By now, the engineer's brow had broken out in a cold sweat. 'Yes,' he replied, trembling.

But Hariprasad wanted to be sure, so went on as cordially as possible, 'So far, the girl, who goes by the name of Mousumi Sharma, has married six men, all of whom have died in mysterious circumstances, all of them having left their entire wealth to her.' He paused dramatically to let the information sink in, then continued, 'I wonder what Oscar Wilde would have to say about that? More than careless, eh!'

240

The engineer dropped his act and became the little Indian mummy's boy he really was. 'Thank you, Dada,' he said, clasping both of Hariprasad's hands. 'Thank you for saving my life!' And then he ran away as fast as he could.

The bus and taxi journey from Rekha's flat to the Botanical Gardens was not a pleasant one. Squashed into a beeping tin box, Rekha began to sweat, big damp patches forming under her arms, a curtain of perspiration forming along her upper lip. The taxi wasn't much better either: rolling the window down to let in some fresh air, she was hit by a gust of oily dust and had a sneezing fit, which made her kohl-lined eyes water and smudged her mascara.

By the time she made it to the shade of the banyan tree, Rekha was a wreck. 'This is not how a mother-of-the-bride should look,' she thought miserably. She was also fifteen minutes late. She felt as if she had let Mousumi down. Reaching into her bag, she pulled out a wet-wipe and tried to tidy herself up as much as she could, and then applied a coat of lipstick to add some colour. But the engineer didn't appear. Glum and antsy, she made her way home, huffing and puffing, her sari, which had been freshly pressed that morning, now grimy around the edges and full of creases. Once again, despite all her efforts, she looked like a fisherman's wife.

* * *

241

Tuhina stood in the porch and looked at the moon through the blue stained glass of the panelled window. It seemed fitting that she was going out with Prakash for the evening. For business purposes, of course – some charity dinner for some hospital, raising money for the paediatric ward. Prakash was a sucker for kids – he liked their simplicity; he conflated it with integrity. She was tired and would rather have stayed in, but she hadn't been a dutiful wife in a while, and needed to put some effort in. 'I even have to put in face-time at home,' she thought to herself wryly. She looked at her watch and frowned. She had been ready and waiting for ten minutes. And despite the fact that Prakash had been all set before her, they were now going to be late. Again.

He had said to her, 'Hurry up, hurry up, we don't want to be late!' the minute she had walked into the house, even before she had had chance to take her jacket off. And then, when she had hurried up, and was ready to leave, he had said, 'Sit down, sit down, we don't want to be early!' and had gone to make himself his fifth half-cup of tea. Her temples hurt, and she massaged them gently with her fingertips.

Finally, Prakash made an appearance. 'So, you're all ready to go?' he asked her.

Tuhina didn't bother to reply. At that moment

Darshini came running down the stairs, and was about to kiss Tuhina goodbye when Prakash, with a surprised look on his face, said sternly, 'Where are you going?'

'I'm going out,' she said, scrunching up her nose. That much, she thought, was obvious.

'With who?'

'Seph.'

Him again.

'And what about Mou?'

'What about her?'

'Well, where is she?'

Darshini shrugged and rolled her eyes, irritated by the questioning. She looked at her watch – she was already running late.

Questioning, thought Prakash, wasn't working; commanding might. 'You're not going out without her.'

'*What?*'

'You can't leave her alone in the house.'

'Why not? She's stayed in the house on her own plenty of times!' Her logic.

'This is different.' His logic.

'Why is it?'

'Because it is. And that's the end of it. You can either take Mou with you or you're staying at home.'

Darshini looked at her mother, whose eyes were glinting dangerously. Tuhina bent down and kissed

243

Darshini's cheek, whispering, 'Please don't say anything more.'

Prakash caught Darshini's gaze and held it, as if he was daring her to disobey him, but she said nothing else. Walking out of the door, he tried to put his hand in the small of Tuhina's back, but she shrugged him off.

Darshini stood and leaned against the banister, sticking her tongue into the side of her cheek, then running it back and forth along the edge of her teeth. She didn't care about disobeying her father – he deserved it – but she didn't want to upset her mother. She could of course go out and be back before her parents, but this relied on Mousumi covering for her. And considering her tenuous grasp of the English language, she might not even understand the concept. But she really didn't want Mousumi to meet Seph. She was embarrassed. Embarrassed to be seen with someone who wasn't like her. Someone who was fat. Ugly. Stupid. Boring. But she would never admit to this, even to herself, so she told herself that they had nothing in common, and what would they have to talk about? Seph's arid, unforgiving sense of humour would alarm Mousumi and make her even more nervous than she already was – she had Mousumi's best interests at heart. And besides, they wouldn't like each other, she was certain of that, so what was the point?

At that moment, Seph called. 'Where are you?' he quizzed. He knew she always ran late and had started to tell her to turn up fifteen minutes early to compensate for the fact, but this time she was half an hour late; he wasn't angry, he was worried.

'I'm still at home,' she said awkwardly.

'What d'you mean, you're still at home? I'm sitting in the bar waiting for you!' and then, suddenly worried, 'Everything's OK, isn't it?'

'Yeah, everything's fine.' She hesitated.

'So are you on your way, then?'

'Um, not exactly,' she answered, chewing hard on her lower lip.

'Well, what's the problem?' Seph's tone of voice was new to her – it indicated impatience.

'I have to babysit,' she said, trying to keep her voice calm, her fingers drumming desperately against the phone receiver.

'Babysit? Babysit who?'

'Mousumi.'

'She's old enough to look after herself, isn't she?'

'I know; but Dad said that I have to look after her.'

'Well, bring her along.' His impatience was turning into exasperation.

'I can't.' A tiny spot of blood appeared on her lip. It tasted sweet.

'Why not?' Pause. 'Well?'

Darshini rubbed her arm, trying to smooth her feathers. 'She doesn't drink alcohol.'

'Well, she can drink coke or have an orange juice!'

Then impulsively she replied, 'Actually, I think we'd better just leave it for tonight.' Blood spurted from the gash where she had cut off her nose.

She heard him take a deep breath, inhaling the sulphuric smell of her childish obduracy. 'OK, fine then,' he said, seemingly unmoved.

No, no, no, no. She wanted him to plead, to cajole, to say how much he wanted to see her. She felt, whisper it, whisper it, *needy*. The distinction between want and need is only ever intuited post denial.

'Well, give me a call when you're free,' he continued. His voice implied detachment.

'Fine,' she said, with a tentativeness which he mistook for indifference.

'OK, bye then.'

Seph ended the call and stared hard at his drink. *Fine?* What did *fine* mean? He took it for Collins dictionary's thirteenth (unlucky for some) sense: ironic, disappointing or terrible – *a fine mess!* She had intended the fifth meaning: satisfactory – *as far as we can tell, everything is fine.* He felt he had cheated himself. He had wanted to plead, to cajole, but he had done that once before and he wasn't going to do it again. He was a man of his word, especially those words he said to himself.

Darshini stood in the hall, and her annoyance congealed into something heavier, something more viscous, like anger. Now, she thought, her nostrils flaring, her eyes darkening, *now* that stupid girl had caused an argument between Seph and herself. It was all Mousumi's fault. Darshini was furious.

CHAPTER ELEVEN

Love

Where was she? Where? Mr Chatterjee couldn't see her any more. Where was the beautiful, delicate jasmine flower whose fragrance had so intoxicated him? Where was the soft, silken voice which had once made his breath short and his cheeks hot? The arousing sweet-nothings had turned into disheartening nags about Anything and Everything and the rest of their extended families. The once graceful dancer's body had lost its elegance. The haunting profile had sagged. And what was left was not even worth a scavenger's salt. How easily the eyes fall in and out of love. But what upset Mr Chatterjee most was that he had nothing left to say to her, even though they talked at each other all the time. She made constant requests for more money, a bigger flat, a faster car. And as her requirements became larger, his resources became smaller.

He had thought that he had managed to weather the storm, but it wasn't the storm which was the problem, it was the persistent, demoralizing rain which followed that finished him off. He knew that his living arrangements had never been whole-heartedly approved of, but they had at least been quietly tolerated. Having a wife in another city may have been deemed a curiosity, but it had not been seen as a disgrace. Keeping a mistress in a government-owned apartment was, however, beyond the pale. Mr Chatterjee belonged to a party which promoted family values and linear love. It was unacceptable for a party member, and a very senior one at that, to so brazenly go against the party grain. And as a Hindu nationalist, to *go with* a Muslim woman was abhorrent (if not, others thought to themselves, really quite thrilling and something they wouldn't mind trying themselves).

The attack, when it came, was based on an illegitimate use of the 'if–then' operator. If, the Prime Minister said to his secretary, *if* Mr Chatterjee's own wife could not trust him, then neither could the party. Mr Chatterjee's affair had clearly proved him to be an irrefutably deceitful person. Proposition A: Mr Chatterjee was not honest. Proposition B: all politicians must be honest. Conclusion: Mr Chatterjee should not be a politician.

It was harder pushing him out than they thought

it would be – did the man have no shame (another sign of his moral corruption)? They started by zealously undermining him at any opportunity, even if it meant destroying the party's credibility and making a laughing stock of themselves in front of the opposition parties, who were so entertained by the Punch-and-Judy-like show that they were content to remain spectators, believing that the government had enough rope already. No one could make head nor tail nor front nor back of it. The Health Minister, a hunch-shouldered, secretive man, accused Mr Chatterjee of spending too much on humanity-destroying guns and missiles, whilst people were dying from lack of clean water. The Employment Minister accused him of not building an artilleries factory which should have provided training and jobs for a thousand men, who instead were sitting at home, penniless, unable to feed their families. The Agriculture Minister accused him *of* building an artilleries factory, thus using up valuable, fertile land which should have been used to grow food for the starving masses!

At first, Mr Chatterjee was unrepentant. His private life was no one else's business. So there! His personal matters were not to be conflated or confused with Mother India's affairs. But despite his level-headed protestations, it was the beginning of the end. Nothing he said was of any import any more – where once his pompous, swollen chest and thunderous walk had inferred authority, they now implied a man with delusions of grandeur, who was too arrogant to admit his shortcomings. Even his minions, who had once cowered in his wake, now sniggered behind his back. When he asked his researchers for information, their output was slipshod and incomplete; he couldn't do the work by himself – there was too much of it. He was a lion with a bleeding leg; the hyenas were waiting until he was too weak to defend himself, and only then would they attack.

The final straw came at the end of a particularly wearying week. Mr Chatterjee's once plump face now drawn and gaunt, his nails bitten to the quick, he was asked by a particularly irreverent journalist whether courting a Muslim courtesan compromised, if not outright contradicted, his Hindu nationalist beliefs. Turning an unusual shade of puce, he shouted gruffly, 'I'll have you fired for your impertinence, you little bastard!' The Press, which had so far kept its distance, rounded on him for attacking one of their own. He had nowhere left to turn. So in the end he was hung for his hypocrisy; it was a lesson to practise what you preach. The day he had put that woman above his job was the day his career had finished. But, he consoled himself, love conquered all, did it not?

*　*　*

On Saturday morning, Ciara left another message on Seph's phone; she called him daily, even though she rarely had anything to say. He listened to her with gloomy weariness: she was looking forward to seeing him next Saturday and asked him to catch an afternoon flight so that he would be in Cushendall in good time – she liked to eat early, around seven. Seph hated eating early. He thought it rather pedestrian, although he had never told her this. Some little things are disproportionately hurtful. Honesty can sting like a paper-cut.

Seph didn't want to go home. When he was there, a heavy lethargy descended upon him like a surly nimbostratus, and all he did was watch television and eat. And Ciara never thought of anything to do; Seph knew he was no longer a child who needed to be entertained, but he wished she would do it for herself. But she didn't have any interests to weigh her down; she let herself be carried along like a plastic bag in the wind, being caught on twigs and park benches before being swept away by another gust; worthless, useless.

The less Seph saw Ciara, the more expensive his gifts had become when he visited. He always went to Harrods – to Ciara it emphasized what a success her son was, and she never failed to look pleased when she saw the forest-green bag with the antique-gold lettering. He always bought her the same kind of present – perfume or soap, unoriginal, reliable. He could never tell whether her smile was genuine or dutiful; neither did he care any more.

Seph had been in real trouble once before. Not the kind of trouble which served you a slapped wrist and a stern telling-off, but the kind of trouble which brings silence and concern and theorizing. Or at least *should* have, if anyone had known.

The beating itself wasn't particularly drawn out or vicious; it was a quick and efficient assault which left the victim with one cauliflower ear, one split lip, two bloody nostrils and a mild'n'creamy concussion.

Along with other bits and bobs of work, Ciara worked as a barmaid in the local pub, Johnny Joe's. It wasn't *her* local, though, as she never drank in it, only served. Not that she was part of the furniture; she had never fitted in, ever since the day she had walked in nearly nineteen years ago, hat clutched in hand, asking whether there was any work going. She was like a painting that had been hung just slightly unevenly – there was something about her that made the punters feel uncomfortable, although they couldn't work out what. But they all liked her, were kind to her, would help her out in any way they could. So they mumbled about her amongst themselves, but when they went to the bar they smiled at her, and said, 'Thanks, pet,' when she passed them their pints. And they were careful not to curse around her; when Ards put another one past the Braidsmen in the Cup Final to win two–one, and Johnny exclaimed indignantly, 'What the fuck was that?', he was soon reprimanded by Big Ronan with a 'Don't fuckin' swear in front of the lady!' Neither was she harassed by drunks told to finish their drinks on a Friday night, or chatted up by men waiting to be served. Even Fat Annie with frizzy red hair and stout breasts was chatted up. She was especially popular at closing time, when she left the pub for ten minutes and then came back, her make-up slightly smudged and her bosoms heaving. The other girls looked her up and down and then ignored her, whilst clearing away the glasses and emptying the ashtrays, but Ciara always had a kind word for her.

The admirer was an outsider. None of the village men had ever seen or would ever see Ciara in that hazy light. She seemed too delicate, as if an appreciative glance would wither her with its heat. But as Jim McGelleghet took a seat at the bar, his fishing rods propped up in the corner, he saw a slim wisp of a woman, with fine milky skin and eyes as pale as mist. He was an old-school charmer; his strength lay in his silences. His stare, which was timed just right and of the correct intensity, made women rub their lips together and look away half embarrassed, half aroused. And even when they weren't looking, they could still sense it.

'A pint, please, young lady,' he said.

Ciara turned around to see whether he was talking to Fat Annie, but he was looking at her. Young? Lady? Immediately her cheeks flushed. 'A pint of what?' she asked tentatively.

'Guinness, of course!' he said, his eyes cheeky, his smile wry.

'Course,' she said, flustered, reaching for a pint glass.

He didn't take his eyes off her once as she pulled his pint with shaky hands. She wanted to tell him not to watch her, that it made her nervous, but she couldn't pluck up the courage, and bit her lip anxiously. Every time she furtively looked at him, his eyes were on her. She couldn't understand why he was staring. Her heart beat faster.

As she put his drink down in front of him, her hands trembled a little and the creamy froth spilled down the side of the glass.

'Sorry –' she said, going to reach for a cloth, but before she had the chance, he picked up the wet glass, took a sip, licked the froth from the top of his lip and said, 'Not to worry,' with a generous smile.

He laid a five-pound note out in his palm, so that she had to touch his hand to pick it up. She fetched his change and was about to hand it over to him when he said, 'Keep it.'

'Oh –' she said, surprised, and was about to put the money in the tip glass when he summoned her with his index finger and coaxed, 'Come here . . . just for a minute.'

She moved towards him cautiously, unsure of what he wanted.

'A little bit closer,' he smiled, until she was about a foot away from him. Then he reached over the bar, touched the side of her face with his fingers, and brushed her lower lip with his thumb. She was too shocked to ask him what the hell he thought he was doing. He knew she would be.

'Look,' he said, holding up his thumb for inspection. 'Your lip's bleeding. Only very slightly, though.'

She looked at the tip of his thumb, which was tinged watery red, and then touched her lip self-consciously. 'Thank you,' she said, although she wasn't sure what she was thanking him for.

She continued to serve the other customers, but was aware that the whole time he was looking at her. She started to spill drinks, give customers the wrong change and forget their orders.

'Everything all right, love?' asked one of the

regulars. 'You're a bit absent-minded tonight.'

'Sorry,' she said, flustered. 'Just rushed off my feet.'

The pub was half empty.

When she passed him for the umpteenth time, he asked her, 'So, when does your shift end?'

'My shift?'

'That's what I asked, isn't it?' he said gently.

Ciara shrugged and bit her wounded lip again. 'About eight thirty,' she whispered.

'Well, would you do me the honour of having a drink with me when you're finished?'

'Umm . . .' she mumbled, biting her lip again.

'Come on . . .' he cajoled. 'What harm's one drink going to do you?'

'All right then,' said Ciara, because she wanted to, giving him a shy smile.

'Young lady?' he called as she walked away. 'You haven't even told me your name.'

'Ciara.'

'And I'm Jim,' he said with a grin which was both threatening and disarming.

Seph came into the pub at eight thirty with some of his friends. No matter how busy it was, Ciara would always notice when Seph came in, and would wave at him and smile. But this time she didn't.

'Who's that your mother's talking to?' asked Eoin.

257

Seph looked over his shoulder to see who he was talking about. He didn't recognize the man. 'Don't know,' he said dismissively, although he turned around again to see if he could get a better look.

'Maybe he's your mother's new boyfriend?' asked Luke suggestively, raising an eyebrow.

'Shut the fuck up now, why don't you?' replied Seph coolly, although his annoyance showed in the flicker of his eyes.

'Just joking, mate!' Luke said immediately. 'Don't take everything so serious. Christ!' He didn't want to get on the wrong side of Seph.

'Both of you shut up, and let's get a drink,' intervened Eoin, nervous.

'Fine,' said Seph.

'Fine,' said Luke.

But everything was not fine. Half an hour later, when his mother had still failed to notice his presence, Seph started to become agitated. Who was this other man whom his mother was paying so much attention to? She had never mentioned any men to him. She didn't have any friends, really, let alone male friends. And she was behaving differently; she seemed less diffident than usual, more assuming. She was not only listening, but speaking, too. And what was that – was she *giggling*? Seph felt disgusted, as if he had seen something he shouldn't have. Jealousy festered in his brittle heart.

'You're drinking a bit quickly tonight, aren't you?' asked Luke. 'Thirsty?'

'What does *that* mean?' queried Seph, frowning.

'Nothing. I just meant that we've only been here for about half an hour, and you're already on your third pint.' Seph didn't reply, and ran his finger around the rim of his glass. He didn't much feel like talking. He wished he'd never come. His fingers couldn't keep still, moving the coasters around the table, twisting the cellophane wrapper from a cigarette packet into knots, knitting themselves together when they could find nothing else to fiddle with.

Ciara agreed that she would have lunch with Jim the next day. It would have to be lunch because she had to make dinner for Seph in the evening. He had suggested they take an appetite-rousing walk around Glenariff, then head to a cosy pub for lunch. No one had ever taken Ciara out for lunch before. Her belly felt souffléd.

Fifteen minutes before last orders, Jim left with a bounce in his gait. Fifteen seconds later, Seph left too, his step heavy.

'Where are you going?' asked Eoin, as Seph pulled his jumper on over his head.

'Home.'

'But you haven't finished your drink.'

'Yeah, I don't feel too well. See you lads tomorrow.'

Seph caught up with Jim quickly and patted him on his shoulder. He wasn't sure what to say; his mouth felt dry.

'Yes?' Jim asked, friendly. Maybe, he thought, Seph was lost.

'Was that Ciara you were talking to in the pub?' Seph asked, his voice laced with poison.

Jim's weathered face scrunched up in puzzlement. 'Yes?'

'Yeah, she's my mother,' Seph said, as if this explained his presence.

Jim remained puzzled, and responded unsurely, but as jovially as possible, 'Oh, really, she's your mother, is she? She didn't tell me she had children.'

'Oh, really?' sneered Seph. He was the most important thing in her life; of course she would have mentioned him.

Jim sensed that Seph needed to be appeased, but he couldn't tell why. 'No, but I'll tell you what, son – that mother of yours is a wonderful lady,' was his best attempt.

Seph knew that; Ciara was his mother, after all – he didn't need to be told what she was like by a stranger. And that was it.

Jim McGelleghet didn't know what had hit him. It was entirely unexpected and he was too shocked to defend himself. He went reeling backwards, but Seph pulled him back to standing position.

'Son?' stuttered Jim, incomprehension imprinted on his face, as Seph pulled his fist back again.

Eoin and Luke were the first to hear the kerfuffle as they walked out of the pub. They ran towards the men and pulled Seph away from Jim.

Seph shrugged them off. 'I'm fine,' he said roughly. 'Let go of me, would ya?' He started to walk back to his house.

Jim, his blood leaving a Hansel and Gretel trail behind him, disappeared into the night.

Standing in the street, Eoin asked Luke, 'What was all that about?'

'Haven't a clue. You don't think it was anything to do with what I said, do you?'

'About what?'

'You know, about that bloke being his mother's boyfriend?'

Eoin shrugged. He didn't know. He didn't want to know. To question their idol's behaviour would have muddied the esteem in which they held him. They never spoke to each other about it again, or told anyone else.

Ciara never saw Jim again. She didn't know why. But she believed it was her fault.

CHAPTER TWELVE

Darshini and Seph

It wasn't a big cut, or even a deep cut, but it was certainly a bloody cut. That's what happens when you mix bare feet and a broken beer bottle. The beer bottle was from the barbecue which Prakash had arranged. Tuhina was normally in charge of entertaining, but this time Prakash had taken the initiative to arrange the party himself. He didn't even ask for the two-headed tigress's permission, which he usually did under the guise of asking for her *opinion*.

'We're having a barbecue tomorrow evening,' he had said with curious confidence. 'Priya and Neal are coming. And Rose Mary and her husband Patrick. And Patricia with her new baby. Her husband's just run off with another woman, you know, so this will cheer her up! And lots of other people, too. *Lots* of other people!'

'Really, darling? That's lovely!' Tuhina responded, wondering since when had Prakash organized anything. *She* was The Organizer. Then, with a little furrow between her brows, 'Who's Rose Mary?'

'She's my secretary!' he said sternly. 'You've met her at least five times before!'

'Oh, of course,' she said unconvincingly, tucking a strand of hair behind her ear and looking down. He meant *Rosemary*. She wondered whether to modify his pronunciation, but he was already on the cusp of disagreeable and a correction was unlikely to help.

Prakash looked at Darshini. 'And what about you?'

'Sorry, Dad, can't make it. Going out with Seph.' Her answer was not rueful; it was happy, carefree. She was going to see Seph! Seph, Seph, Seph! (She had made a conciliatory phone call, promising to bring along both the silk scarf he had bought her and a bottle of fragranced oil which he had taken an especial liking to.)

'Can't you invite Seph here?' he asked. 'Or is that too much to ask?'

The skin at the corner of Darshini's eyes crinkled instinctively. She felt a slight lump in her throat. Her father had never questioned her like that before. She did whatever she wanted. That was the way of her world. 'I don't want to,' she said, stubbornness disguised as indifference. It was the best she could come up with.

'Mou,' he said, ignoring Darshini's answer, 'let's go and marinate the meat!' He got up from the sofa and then, his back turned, mumbled as a parting shot, 'And who the hell is Seph, anyway?' It wasn't heard, but wasn't really meant to be heard, either.

So the meat was marinated and lots of people turned up, and they all said what a wonderful evening it was, with the grass dry and warm underneath their bare feet; how wonderful the food was, so painstakingly prepared – Prakash, dear, you *must* let me have that recipe for the lime and coriander salmon, you simply *must*; and most important of all, what a wonderful host Prakash was, assisted ably by the charmingly shy Mou, who told such wonderful stories about India – we really *must* visit some time soon, *mustn't* we, darling? It sounds so exotic! And, oh, where's that beautiful daughter of yours? Ah, a boyfriend – well, she's coming up to that difficult age, isn't she?

She's always been difficult, thought Prakash, although he hadn't always thought that.

By eleven, it was becoming chillier, and the women started rubbing their goosebumped shoulders and making noises about getting home. Mousumi thought she would help Prakash by clearing up in the garden. Unbuckling her sandals and slipping her chubby feet out of them, she went about it slowly and steadily, her legs heavy; she felt slightly tipsy from the one glass of punch she had drunk. She didn't like alcohol, or at least she thought she didn't like alcohol, having never tried it, but the feeling from the slightly funny-tasting fruit juice was not unpleasant, and she wandered about the garden picking up empty plates smeared with tomato ketchup and mustard as if she were a pre-Raphaelite maiden plucking blooms from a rosebush. She didn't notice the broken green bottle lying discarded in the grass.

It hurt as it cut her, but then the pain seemed to subside, and she continued around the garden, not really aware that she had injured herself, leaving a snail's trace of blood behind her, which it was now too dark to see. It was only when she went back inside and stood on the cream limestone tiles of the kitchen floor that Miss Colchester, who had never married and didn't have a first name, noticed and said loudly, and with just a touch of drama, 'Good Lord, child! What *have* you done?'

Prakash looked over at the blood and at Mousumi, assessed the situation and said calmly, 'Sit. You have cut your foot?' He didn't think it was a particularly big deal. Early in his career he had worked Up North, near a coalmine, and after a particularly nasty accident there had been witness to a foot detached from its owner. So he was undismayed by a mere cut, although the blood had already attracted several guests who were keen to see what was going on. Nothing like a little gore to raise interest. After fetching the first-aid kit, Prakash kneeled at Mousumi's feet and cleaned the wound, then stuck on some steri-strips in a crisscross pattern before bandaging it up. Mission complete.

'Oh, well done, Prakash!' said Miss Colchester, as if he had just performed open-heart surgery. 'Aren't you a little star!'

'Yes, yes, Prakash, very well done to you. Crisis averted,' said Neal, nodding sagely, his sixth gin and tonic in his hand.

'Well, I'm pleased it wasn't anything life-threatening, no,' said Priya to Mousumi, rubbing her shoulder. 'Broken glass can be very, very dangerous . . .' she continued, spilling a little of her vodka (large) orange (small) into Mousumi's lap.

Tuhina stood in the corner of the kitchen, near the pantry door, and looked at the scene. She didn't feel like making conversation.

Darshini and Seph's Saturday evening had been far less dramatic. They had managed to persuade a restaurant to let them take out the food (it was Darshini's eyelashes which had clinched the deal):

empanadas, mechadas, platanitos, paella, moqueca (enough for four) – they both had an irrational fear of not having enough to eat and consistently over-ordered – and then lay on the sofa all night, eating, watching movies and having all sorts of sex: tender, rough, playful, intense. They hadn't even bothered to move to the bed. The laziness of one indulged the laziness of the other.

But on Sunday, Darshini, full of beans – Seph was exhausted, he thought it was because he was getting older – had left his flat before him to go shopping. Seph had worked out early on in their relationship that she liked going shopping on her own, after she had made disparaging comments about the type of men who could be found looking morosely at their posing other halves, saying wanly, 'Yes, that looks lovely on you!' and 'No, I *swear* you don't look fat.' So after breakfast she had ventured out into the Sunday sunshine, agreeing to meet him back at his flat at two thirty, which meant three with her timing.

Seph needed to go shopping, too. Instinctively he headed to the Guerlain counter at Harrods – Ciara didn't recognize the name so assumed it was luxury, and it sounded French, which conjured up images of soignée Parisian women with glossy chignons and a line of pearls at their haughty throats. He bought her a bottle of Mitsouko, which came in a reassuringly ornate bottle, something she would understand. Not that she ever dabbed the perfume behind her pale ears; instead the bottles would sit neatly in her dressing-table drawer, and be admired from time to time – she didn't think herself worthy of them.

As the saleswoman wrapped the box, Seph looked at her carefully. She glanced up intermittently and smiled at him. She was coy, flirtatious. 'Who's the lucky lady, then?' she asked suggestively. He didn't answer her, pretending he hadn't heard. The etchings around her eyes, the coral lipstick which had bled into the fine lines around her mouth, the skin which had started to hang under her chin like an iguana's leathery jowls; Seph felt his mouth dry as he thought of all the others like her. He wished his memories were pencil drawings, instantly erasable, but they were drawn in indelible ink. As she leaned over the counter to find the sticky-tape, he peered at her legs. They were white, blotchy, with an almost luminous glow to them. He felt repulsed by them, by the thought that they could ever have been wrapped round him. Not hers, specifically, but legs like that. Regret and Disgust tangoed in his belly. He felt like gagging. The incessant noise, the crowd – a gaggle of brightly coloured hundreds-and-thousands swarming over the floor, the overpowering smell of a thousand different flowers, the lights bouncing off the glass counters and crystal bottles and shiny powder cases; Seph felt dizzy and sick. He grabbed the bag from the assistant and without even saying 'Thank you' turned to leave.

Just as he was about to go, he saw Darshini at another counter standing talking to an unknown man, whitish, twenty-fiveish, good-lookingish. Seph had never met any of her friends, but he looked too old to be one. They were both laughing. He kept touching her arm. Darshini kept throwing her head back and wrapping strands of hair around her finger. The man put his hand on her shoulder and kept it there. *Stop touching her*, Seph thought so vehemently that the words nearly exploded out of his mouth, *stop touching her*. Suddenly he realized how little he knew about her. She was just talking, smiling, but he wanted her to pay attention only to him, to talk only to him, to smile only at him, and he felt a deep stomach-clenching jealousy. His face reddened and his jaw clamped as he gnawed on his nails, tearing into the delicate skin around them. Seph felt like grabbing Darshini and hiding her inside himself, where she existed only for him. The more he looked, the more agitated he became. The sound of the other shoppers was drowned out by the throbbing in Seph's head. His fists clenched in anger. The -ish man kissed

Darshini lingeringly on the cheek and made his way through the other shoppers. *How dare he kiss her?* Seph thought, *how dare he*, as he followed the man outside.

The pavement was heaving with people, and Seph had to push them out of his way as he struggled to keep up. Motorists beeped their horns as he crossed blindly in front of them. Shouts of main roads became whispers of residential streets. The jungle of people thinned; Seph picked up his pace. He had forgotten that he was a man who never got annoyed, whom it was impossible to upset. He had vaccinated himself against reacting a long time ago, as if his face had been gazed upon by a gorgon. But now his waterproof skin had sprung a leak. He continued to follow the -ish man. He hadn't even formulated what he was going to do or say; his train of thought had fallen off the rails.

Then, without warning, the man turned around and said quite calmly, 'Excuse me, but can I help you?'

Seph came to a stop and glared at his questioner. The slight crinkle at the sides of the man's eyes hinted at puzzlement. Seph felt Rage transform itself into its distant cousin, Embarrassment. He had nothing to say. His brain was pathetically blank, the mental equivalent of a flaccid penis. He looked hard at the man's face and then turned and walked away.

On the Tube home people gave Seph a wide berth, although the train was filled to the brim with shoppers. There is a point at which awkwardness is trumped by fear, and with Seph's clammy brow, shaking hands and face drained of colour, people thought he was on drugs and kept their distance, not wanting to provoke him. A small inquisitive child went up to him, but was quickly reprimanded by his mother, who hissed, 'Leave the gentleman alone!' and pulled him back by the scruff of his neck.

When Seph made it home, he lit up a cigarette. He had an empty feeling in his stomach and a fierce urge to speak to someone – anyone. His finger hovered over the keypad of his phone, but he wasn't sure what he needed to say and who he needed to say it to. He was paralysed; the only action he could carry out was lifting the cigarette to his mouth, inhaling, pulling it out, exhaling – trying to bring some order to his trembling hands. Wanting to impose a pause on his actions, he quickly smoked another cigarette, the Saturnic rings slowly rising above his head, evaporating, only to be replaced by more.

Darshini arrived a couple of hours later and was immediately overcome by the smoke which stung her eyes and angered the back of her throat. Throwing open the windows, she asked quizzically, with an amused expression, 'Have you been cooking?'

271

Seph couldn't cook. Or as he would have it, *didn't*.

'No,' he spat. The word was ugly, at once dismissive, the verbal counterpart of a shrug, and at the same time hostile, a narrow-eyed dirty look.

Darshini picked up on it straight away. 'Why are you being mean?' she asked matter-of-factly.

'I'm not,' Seph said meanly.

Darshini felt a sudden lump in her throat, and pressed the inside corners of her eyes to stem her tears. Then she picked up her bags and went to leave. But as she opened the door, Seph jumped towards it and slammed it shut. The sound made her drop her bags and she tried to turn around, but Seph had pinned her to the door with his body. Pulling her hands over her head, she tried to wriggle free, but her wrists smarted, just like when she was twelve and Joe Letts in the year above had given her a Chinese burn.

She felt Seph's hand reach under her skirt and push her legs apart, roughly moving her knickers to one side. The weight momentarily lifted from her body and she heard the whisper of clothes and a zip being pulled. Then the heaviness was on her again and her hipbones were pushed into the door. And then she felt a piercing pain, and her eyes filled with water, and this time her hands weren't free to stop her tears. And at that moment, she wished that the coin had landed on tails.

She left without a word. And when she slammed the door, the air in the room had left with her and Seph felt suffocated. He stood still, trying to compose himself, his head light and confused. When he finally moved, he looked at his watch: a whole hour had passed. He went to the kitchen, poured himself a large glass of whisky and made his way back to his room, taking the bottle with him. He buried himself in his bed, cocooning himself in his duvet like a parrotfish protecting itself at night. He fell asleep with the glass in his hand, and in the ashtray the last of his cigarettes dying on the heap, like a pile of poached ivory tusks.

It was the first time they had been together alone. Tuhina couldn't relax; she felt like a stranger in her own home. All she wanted to do was to eat her brunch and read the Sunday newspapers, but she felt that Mousumi needed entertaining. So despite the fact that Mousumi knew where everything was in the kitchen and was perfectly capable of making herself something to eat, Tuhina insisted on preparing it herself.

'So, what would you like, then?' she asked warmly, looking at her watch and then frowning slightly – it was nearly three, which was either a very late lunch or a very, very early dinner, and

Tuhina liked things to be on time. She smiled a quick smile – *Hello, my name's Tuhina and I'll be your server today!*

'Toast and cheese. Please.' Mousumi tried her best to remember all the rules Prakash had taught her – 'Please' after a request, 'Thank you' after its fulfilment. She sensed that Tuhina was keen on correctness.

'Toast and cheese?' Tuhina repeated, and then quickly corrected herself, 'A cheese toastie, you said?'

Mousumi smiled and nodded; she was less likely to get it wrong that way.

'Actually,' Tuhina continued, 'I think that's a little boring for a Sunday. Hmm . . .' She rummaged through the cupboards. 'Don't you?'

Mousumi smiled and nodded again.

'OK then. Well, what about pancakes? Or perhaps scrambled eggs with smoked salmon?'

Mousumi recognized the word 'eggs'.

'Eggs,' she said timidly.

'Eggs it is then!' said Tuhina, pleased, walking to the fridge; Prakash wasn't the only good host.

Mousumi felt like retching. The moist, pink flesh, raw, uncooked, cosied up to the bobbly eggs. She watched Tuhina take her first mouthful, munch on it thoughtfully whilst reading the front page of the *Observer*, and wash it down with orange juice. She felt the back of her jaw tighten. Tentatively, she put her fork into the mound.

Tuhina looked up from the paper and asked, 'Everything OK? Eggs are good, aren't they? From some organic farmer in Hampstead. Or maybe Hampshire. One of the two. Prakash would know, I suppose.'

Mousumi smiled and nodded. Tuhina was still watching her, so she gripped her fork tightly and lifted some smoked salmon to her lips, breathing out so she didn't inhale the smell. She put it in her mouth and moved the food to the back of her tongue, where her taste buds were least sensitive, and chomped on it like a horse, then counted down from three in her head, and gulped. She smiled at Tuhina, and slipping, said in Bengali, 'The food is very good.'

Tuhina acknowledged the praise by giving a quick, sharp smile. 'The food is very good' was not a difficult construction. She frowned at Mousumi's table manners, grimacing at her spastic-like grip of her fork, the way she ate with her mouth open, grinding her food with her back teeth. It was all so bloody horrible to look at. And Prakash hadn't helped. For twenty years he had used cutlery to eat Indian food with, but since Mousumi's arrival he had started to eat it with his hands again. He's turning into a native, Tuhina thought. He had even started to buy hilsa fish again, despite the fact that a) it stank the house out, and b) it had so many bones that choking to death was a distinct possibility. And not only that, but when Tuhina had studiously picked at a piece with her knife and fork, he had winked at Mousumi – here comes a joke – and asked Tuhina, mockingly, whether she was too posh to use her hands? To which she had replied, calmly, that, no, she wasn't, but she didn't like having yellow-stained fingernails at work – it wasn't very professional. That had wiped the smirk from his face.

Tuhina's head started to get hot. She downed her juice and went to the fridge for more. With Tuhina's back turned, Mousumi quickly scooped a few more forkfuls into her mouth and swallowed without chewing, and definitely without tasting.

She was saved unexpectedly by a phone call from a stranded Darshini. As Tuhina went to answer the phone in the hall, Mousumi made the bravest decision of her life. She picked up her plate, tiptoed quickly to the bin and scraped her food into it, picking up a few empty cartons and packets to cover it with, like a cat hiding its shit. She was even careful to leave a few scraps on the plate for authenticity.

'Can you pick me up?' Croaky voice.

'Why? Where are you?' Tuhina closed her eyes and saw a busy high street anywhere in London.

She squeezed her eyes tight, hoping to see a distinctive shop or a landmark, but nothing came into her vision.

'I'm not sure.' Breaking voice.

'Well, beautiful, I can't pick you up if I don't know where you are.'

Sniff, sniff, sniff. 'Near Farringdon.' Sniffle.

'Well, what about I pick you up from Farringdon Tube, then?'

'O-o-o-kay.'

'Are you OK?'

'Y-y-y-es.'

'OK, I'm on my way then.'

'Do you want to come with me to pick Darshini up?' Tuhina called from the hall, out of politeness.

'Thank you, no,' Mousumi called back.

Thank God, thought Tuhina.

Thank God, thought Mousumi.

CHAPTER THIRTEEN

The Sandwich

His head throbbed, the unbearable pressure building up at his temples as if someone was trying to push his eyes out. His mouth was parched and it hurt every time he moved. With great effort he turned his head to see if Darshini was lying next to him. No. Very slowly, he rolled into the centre of the bed and pulled the duvet over his head. It was half past ten and the sunlight streamed through the window. He remembered glass after glass after glass. Fuck, he thought to himself, *fuck*. He should have been at work. He called the team assistant and told her he was ill, asking her to pass the message on to Tuhina. He didn't dare tell her himself.

At midday he could not sleep any more of his hangover off. His lips were glued together by thick white saliva. His throat felt raw. He got out of bed and walked to the kitchen. The place seemed musty and arid. He walked to the window and opened it wide to freshen the room. Everything felt dirty. *He* felt dirty. He really needed something to eat, but there was nothing in the fridge apart from a hibernating bottle of champagne and some depressed onions. Darshini often went to the local patisserie on Monday morning, queuing with office workers to buy croissants and pains au chocolat for breakfast. She said it was a cheering start to the week. Seph pressed his lips together, closed his eyes and imagined himself lying on his back, as he usually did, with Darshini pressed into his side, as she kissed his temple and traced his lips with her fingers, sweet and oily from the butter-soaked pastries. He opened his eyes and the reality crawled under his skin like an angry centipede.

He got up, made himself a restorative cup of Kenyan tea and gulped it down, despite the heat, trying to clear his tarred throat. Then he started to feel sick, so he rushed to his bedroom and pulled on his never-normally-crumpled clothes, grabbed his wallet and ran to the local greasy spoon. Seph really didn't want to be sick. He thought it showed a lack of control. Sprinting down the road, he saw a huge Marlboro billboard, which made him wheeze. It was the beginning of the day, and already he was shattered.

When Seph returned home, he tried to call

Darshini. His heart froze as a bodiless cold voice said pitilessly, 'This mobile phone has been switched off.' He felt lonely and scared and empty. Wandering around his apartment, he looked for traces of her, but there was nothing; she never left anything behind, not even a toothbrush. He looked under his bed in case a pair of her knickers or maybe a bra had fallen under it. He pressed his face to the pillows, trying to smell her, but the linen had been changed the day before. He nuzzled the back of the sofa where her neck would have touched it, but he could smell only last night's smoke. Despondent, he ran a bath. He never took a bath, always a shower, but he wanted to wallow. Opening up his bathroom cabinet, he found a bottle of bath oil which he had never seen before. He opened it up and sniffed it cautiously. It was her smell – a giddy mix of tuberose, gardenia and jasmine. He inhaled deeply. The smell calmed him down, and he poured the oil carefully under the hot tap. Seph left the bathroom door open and a cobweb of steam floated through the apartment, lightly scenting everything in its path.

But the respite was only temporary, and as Seph sat on the sofa after his bath he decided that there was nothing for it but to go to Darshini's house. He knew that Tuhina would be at work, so he wouldn't bump into her. And he assumed that Darshini's dad would be at work, too. It was a good time for him to go. He went to his bedroom and pulled out the Post-it note that had her phone number and address on it. It still vaguely smelled of perfume.

It was Mousumi who opened the door. Seph was slightly taken aback. He was confused by the person who confronted him. She reminded him of the girl in his local corner shop, who always struggled to reach his twenty Marlboro Lights from the top shelf of the rack behind the counter, had bushy eyebrows, a faintly shiny complexion and wore the same kind of tunic and trousers outfit that battled to contain her bulk. His first thought was that she might be the cleaner, although she seemed slightly too young for that.

'Erm, hi,' he said. 'Is Darshini in?' He looked behind her into the hall, but no one appeared.

'Darshini out,' Mousumi said.

'Ah,' he replied, stalling for time. 'Well, you must be . . . Darshini's cousin then?' He realized that Darshini had never told him her cousin's name.

'Yes,' Mousumi said, warming to the handsome man on the doorstep. She liked his accent, too. 'Cousin-sister.'

'Well, would you mind if I came in and waited for her?' he said, edging forward.

'Er,' Mousumi hesitated, 'OK.'

She showed him through to the sitting room and,

281

once he'd settled down on the sofa, asked, 'You take tea?'

'Yeah, I'd love a cup,' he replied, a little solemnly.

While Seph sat wondering what Darshini might have told her cousin-sister, Mousumi went to the kitchen, apprehensive but excited, her hands fluttering as she tried to decide what order to do things in. This man was her first guest and she wanted to impress him with her hospitality. Maybe she could make him a sandwich – Prakash had seemed to like his well enough. Fingers jittering slightly, she buttered two slices of bread and then looked around for something to put on them. Opening the fridge, she peered inside, her eyes flitting from jar to jar. Then she noticed something new, something she hadn't seen before. It looked like a tin of shoe polish, made of shiny black metal with a matt pink paper label displaying an image of a fish on it. Smiling broadly, she placed it on the worktop before returning to the fridge and taking out her standard condiments – mustard, ketchup and mayonnaise. On the meat shelf there was a packet of Serrano ham, but it looked uncooked to her, so she picked up some cheese instead. And some leftover roast chicken from the night before – when Prakash had made chicken stuffed with cheese and ham it had tasted delicious, so she supposed it would be a fine combination for a sandwich, too.

Neatly lining up her products, she began the layering process, making sure that no millimetre of bread was left uncovered. Finally, she opened up the special tin and hovered her nose above it. It smelled slightly fishy, but in a pleasant way, like the sea. Satisfied, she neatly spread the dark-grey beads of caviar in a perfect circle in the centre and then clamped the other piece of bread on top.

Fifteen minutes later, proudly carrying a tray with two cups of tea, two bowls of pickled-onion Monster Munch (Mousumi had developed a taste for them) and a sandwich for Seph on a side plate rimmed with gold flowers, she re-entered the sitting room. Seph was bemused – he hadn't expected such effort. He took his cup of tea and a bowl of Monster Munch and put them down on the side table. Mousumi remained standing. She nodded towards the sandwich.

'Oh, for me, too?' Seph said, surprised. 'Well, thanks a million.'

Mousumi grinned, but still she didn't move. She liked looking at him up close. She thought he looked gentle.

Seph glanced at the tray again to see if there was anything else she wanted him to take, but it was empty. Unsure why she would not sit down, his forehead crumpled and he tentatively said, 'Thank you' again.

The sound of his voice broke her trance and, blushing, she mumbled, 'Pleasure for you' and shuffled to the chaise on the other side of the room – she wasn't used to sitting close to men who weren't her relatives.

Seph looked across at her, and thought how incongruous she looked. The smooth curve of the rollback on the chaise arm was in stark contrast to the rolls of flesh which gathered around Mousumi's middle when she sat down. The garish synthetic patterned tunic she wore looked coarse in comparison with the understated pistachio-green raw silk cushion she was resting against. Seph concentrated on the cushion. He could imagine Darshini's glossy hair fanned over it as she lay back, reading one of her magazines. He imagined that she would insouciantly sling one of her legs over the back of the chaise, and swing it casually. Thinking of her brought his attention back to the matter in hand, and he looked back at Mousumi.

'So, I guess Darshini told you what happened,' he said hesitantly, looking at his watery reflection in his tea. His fingertips burned as he touched the hot china cup but he didn't put it down. Mousumi wobbled her head from side to side. Seph took that as a 'yes'. Mousumi meant 'no'.

'Right . . .' he mumbled, chewing on his lip, his right leg involuntarily bobbing up and down.

'Right.' He paused for a moment, collecting his thoughts. 'I don't know how to explain it,' he said, looking up at Mousumi. Putting the cup down, he ran his fingers through his hair, shrugged and shook his head. 'I was just being a complete cunt.' He hadn't meant to say 'cunt' but it just came out of his mouth.

'Cunt,' Mousumi repeated, smiling. She hadn't heard the word before.

'Well,' he apologized, 'not a cunt; even worse than that . . .' His face reddened with shame, and he covered it with his hands. He seemed close to tears. 'Listen,' he said, suddenly straightening up and smoothing down his shirt. He fixed Mousumi with a firm gaze. She stopped munching on her Monster Munch, and pushed the soggy ball into her cheek.

'Just tell Darshini I came to try to say sorry, and tell her to call me. OK?' He got to his feet. Mousumi nodded vigorously. As Seph got up to leave, he realized that Mousumi was staring at the uneaten sandwich. She was looking at it because she was now quite keen on eating it herself, but he thought that it was because she was upset. So he picked it up, and started to munch on it quickly. It was on his third bite that he hit the middle. His face stopped still. Mousumi was still observing him carefully. He couldn't work out what the hell was in his mouth. She smiled at him, and he tried to smile back.

Instead of speaking, he simply waved at her and then ran to the door. As soon as he got outside, he spat out and leaned down, looking perplexed at the unidentifiable ball of dough on the floor. Then he walked away at speed.

Mousumi had been watching him through the window and saw him spit out the sandwich. Her heart sank. Now he would think she was a bad host. Grumpy, her mouth set in a sulk, she sat back down cross-legged on the chaise and finished off her bowl of Monster Munch, chewing moodily. But then suddenly she slammed the empty bowl down on the floor and marched into the kitchen. She would not be defeated.

Darshini walked into the kitchen and set her bag down on the counter. Opening up the fridge, she found, covered by clingfilm, a large platter of sandwiches, cut into little squares. Taking the platter out, she unwrapped it and examined the sandwiches more carefully. They all seemed to have different fillings. Sorting through them, and unable to identify some of the contents, she finally settled on one which appeared to be cheese and ham.

Mousumi was sitting watching television when Darshini came into the sitting room.

'You make the sandwiches?' Darshini asked, mouth half-full, brushing away some crumbs that had landed on her T-shirt. Not waiting for an answer, she continued, 'They're good.'

'You like?' Mousumi asked, hopeful.

'Yeah,' Darshini nodded as she walked to the bookcase.

Mousumi waited until Darshini's back was completely turned before asking hesitantly, 'Darshini?'

'Yeah?' Darshini replied, looking over her shoulder.

'Man came for you this afternoon.'

'What man?' Darshini asked, not particularly interested.

Mousumi had forgotten to ask his name. She wondered how to answer. 'Er,' she continued, 'he say, "Very sorry you call him".'

Darshini turned around sharply and spat out '*What?*', her eyes narrowed.

Mousumi tried to stay calm, although her palms had already started to sweat. She didn't want to get this wrong. She gulped, and said again, 'The man say he sorry. You call him.'

Darshini jutted her right hip out and put her hands on her waist. 'What did this man look like?'

Mousumi didn't know many descriptive words.

'Nice,' she offered, her face breaking into a smile as she conjured up the image of the man with the funny brown marks on his nose. Not a very eloquent description, but Darshini knew from

Mousumi's expression who the man was. Her face soured.

'What exactly did he say?' she interrogated, her voice hard. But putting Mousumi under pressure made her even more nervous. Sitting down on the chaise, even at a distance Darshini seemed to tower over her, and she cowered, edging further back into her seat.

'Well?' Darshini demanded, fixing Mousumi with her stare.

Mousumi's mind had gone blank. All she could say was, 'He just say "sorry". He say "sorry".'

'Really?' Darshini said, her tone softening. 'What *exactly* did he say he was sorry about?'

'Sorry for being a . . .' Mousumi hesitated, trying to remember the word. '. . . A cunt.'

Despite her fury, Darshini found this amusing. 'Sorry for being a cunt?' she repeated. Mousumi nodded vigorously.

'Did he tell you what happened?' she asked, try-ing to maintain a calm, even tone. Mousumi wobbled her head from side to side. Darshini took that as a 'yes'. Mousumi meant 'no'. What precisely had he told Mousumi, she wanted to know? What language had he used? How had he described what happened? Had he told Mousumi how her eyes had watered and her wrists had burned? Did he even know that himself? She bit on the inside of her lip

288

and her mouth dried. And out of everyone, Seph had chosen to tell *her*. She felt like crying.

Trying to stem her tears, she asked Mousumi stoically, 'So what do you think?'

'He nice,' Mousumi offered. It was all she could think of.

'He's nice,' repeated Darshini in disbelief. '*You think he's nice!*'

Mousumi wrapped her arms around herself and tucked in her chin – she had never seen Darshini mad before. She nodded meekly; she had lost her voice. Darshini couldn't bear to look at her, and turned to face the window, running her hands through her hair over and over again.

When she finally looked back again, she retorted, her voice firm but soft again, 'Well, quite frankly, it's absolutely none of your business, so don't poke your fat nose into other people's business! And if you don't mind, I don't want to talk about it again. *OK?*'

Mousumi was too nervous to do anything but nod meekly again.

In the morning, Seph reached across the bed. There was a space. He glanced at his watch. Seven. There hadn't been a phone call yesterday.

At work, he was distracted and lethargic. He had plenty to do but he put off doing it. He doodled on pieces of paper, absent-mindedly drawing hearts with arrows through them, then scribbling them out. He stayed in the office late, pretending to read *The Harvard Review*, and wrote in the margin of one of the pages 'Darshini Majumdar Loves Seph O'Shea' and then '01023, 1125, 237, 510, 61%'. The first girl he had kissed had taught him how to make the calculation. She had loved him 83 per cent. But Darshini loved him only 61 per cent. 'I must be doing it wrong,' he told himself.

Darshini hadn't told Tuhina what had happened, and despite her daughter's red eyes and sobs, Tuhina had not asked for an explanation. But she knew. Although, for once, she couldn't tell exactly what had happened: the image was distorted, like a photograph of a fast car taken with too slow a shutter. But she knew it was an unhappy image, and when she spoke to Seph her voice was laced with blame, though she tried hard to cover it. Seph, in turn, was too ashamed to look at her.

He returned to his flat late every night, trying to avoid being on his own. What was once palatial bareness was now barren emptiness. Even on Friday night, he stayed in the office till midnight, accompanied by the low whirr of dozing computers, and then went straight home, exhausted and down, walking past bars crammed with men wearing skew-whiff ties and women with laddered tights, all clambering over each other to reach the bar, like crabs on Christmas Island crawling to the beach.

He couldn't sleep and sat in front of the TV, the blue flickering light from it haunting his face. He wrapped a blanket around himself and settled down on the sofa. He was sure his mother would have something to say about sleeping on a sofa with no sheet. In the morning Ciara called, but he didn't pick up. He felt bad, but not bad enough. She left another message on his answer-phone. He felt at fault as soon as she said his name. She sounded deflated, but said that she was looking forward to seeing him that evening. The fact that she sounded so sincere made Seph feel worse.

On the plane, Seph couldn't even be bothered to respond to the air hostess whose bottom winked suggestively every time she passed his seat. He poured three miniatures of whisky into his glass and gulped it down. It seemed to have no effect.

When he landed in Belfast, he scanned his surroundings with a weariness he had never felt before. He popped his ears, pinching his sculpted nose together, keeping his full lips pressed tight, then blowing; but he still felt as if he was underwater.

Cushendall was like the faded print on an over-worn T-shirt consigned to the back of Seph's wardrobe. He looked out of the taxi window: the passing scene was a soft watercolour compared to the brash acrylic scream of London. The place was a dying spider, but it had wrapped the thinnest thread of silk around his heart and kept pulling him back. And the more he betrayed the place, the more he felt he was betraying himself; but he couldn't help it.

Ciara opened the door and hugged Seph immediately, almost clinging to him. In the background he could hear Meg barking. He gently pulled away from her and looked at her face. The only time she ever wore make-up was when Seph came home. It had the same effect as when an undertaker puts too much lipstick on an old woman. Underneath the facade of pink lipstick and over-rouged cheeks, he could sense her melancholy. He looked at her eyes carefully, and they mirrored her tone of voice on the phone: weary, morose.

He walked to his room, and stopped for a moment in the doorway. The room was as it always was, like the preserved lifeless room of a dead child. Too neat and too tidy. There was one print on the wall next to the chest of drawers: a photograph of a black 1975 E-type Jaguar, which he had cut out of a vintage-car magazine and covered in sticky-back plastic when he was about ten. The plastic had started to yellow and come away from the edges. On the bed there was a needlepoint cushion embroidered by his mother – 'Home sweet home'. The fact that the bed was single depressed him every time. *I am twenty-eight years old*, he thought to himself wryly. On top of the chest of drawers was an old tape-recorder. He turned it on and tried to tune the radio, bring some life to the room, but he could only elicit an irritating gurgle. He could hear his mother in the kitchen, filling the kettle. He was already counting the hours before he could go back to London, which made him feel guilty again.

He took off his jacket and hung it up in the wardrobe, which was empty apart from a few bent wire hangers, a deflated soccer ball and several odd socks. Ciara had obviously never opened it up otherwise the socks would have been paired off. Sitting on the side of the bed, Seph opened his overnight bag and put Ciara's gift to one side. He pulled out the few items of clothing he had brought: a pair of trousers, a couple of polo shirts, a jumper, socks and underwear. He could have left them in his bag, but he had once upset his mother by doing so. He opened up the top drawer and caught a whiff of something musty, like old-fashioned cough medicine. A sad smell.

In the kitchen, Ciara had laid the table as if she were expecting visitors, with her special crockery and fancy little cakes. *That's what I am now*, Seph realized. *A visitor*. He sat down across from her and picked up his coffee, which was instant: too watery and weak. Meg sat by his feet, her eyes shining, delighted that her master was back, and wagged her tail, her pink tongue rolling out of her mouth happily. He gave her a cheerless smile.

'Great coffee, Mother,' he said, taking another sip.

That evening, whilst Ciara was making dinner, Seph took a walk around the town.

'Aren't you going to take Meg?' Ciara called. On hearing her name, Meg immediately stood up and chased Seph to the door, but he pushed her eager-to-please face back and replied, 'I'm sure she's had enough exercise for today,' then shut the door. Meg's face dropped, but Seph didn't see that.

He started to walk, his feet heavy and his head hazy. Some of the bigger houses had no lights on (they were timed to come on for three hours between eight and eleven to deter burglars); they belonged to the doctors and lawyers who lived in Belfast during the week and often spent their week-ends holidaying in European cities, sitting in fancy restaurants, holding menus riddled with velouté, ballottine and escabèche, and laughing knowingly about the lack of a decent restaurant in Cushendall. To Seph, those houses seemed like the decorative gift boxes in shop windows at Christmas: wrapped with bright paper and tied with silky bows, but stuffed with tissue. He walked past a few of the smaller houses, which were closer together, with messier gardens, dogs barking, and pick-up trucks filled with building implements – bricks, spades, sand – parked in the drives, ready for Monday morning. Past the local garage, with trees in the courtyard, which had already closed for the day and always had a cover over one of the two pumps saying 'Temporarily Unavailable'. Past the tired seen-it-all chip-shop, with its grease-spotted walls and fluorescent lighting, where the fat girls congregated after a night out, arms crossed, shivering in their fuck-me dresses, their phosphorescent flesh glowing like a viperfish's skin. Seph shuddered at the memory.

He looked up at the sky; the light was beginning to fade and the green hills were turning blue, like the grass in Kentucky, as he headed out of town. He walked past fields of potatoes, their leafy canopies in neat rows, spaced three feet apart, like a parade of soldiers; past hills spotted with sheep, like balls of lint on a sweater. On and on and on. He was trying to escape – from what he couldn't tell. But then he stopped and turned around. There was no point. On his way back, he stopped on the coast road, in front of St Aloysius High School, which with superiority and wit they had laughingly renamed 'The Dunce Academy'. It didn't seem so funny now – the victory felt shallow. Seph didn't want to go straight home, so he thought he'd stop for a pint at his local. Just before he went in there was a moment of hesitation, although he didn't know why. No one looked at him, although he felt that everyone was watching him as if he were a thief. Guilt makes for paranoia. The pub was filled with faces he recognized but no longer knew. Old farmers with ruddy cheeks and thickened lumpy noses gulped down pints, licking the froth from their rosy lips, their fingernails still dirty from the fields and their pale Celtic forearms reddened by the sun. Seph looked at his own hands, smooth, soft, and hid them in his pockets. The younger men gathered in prides, with cement-splattered jeans and grubby boots, unflinchingly eyeing up the most buxom of the barmaids over the top of their glasses, their banter besieged by an army of superfluous expletives. On the table next to one group lay a copy of the *Sun*, opened at page three: Kirsty, nineteen, from Hull, now a sodden beer-mat. Seph leaned on the bar and looked down at the creamy crown of his drink. He felt uncomfortable, incongruous to the setting, as if he were an anthropologist observing the behaviour of an outlandish tribe. And he was ashamed of his own conceit.

When he finally went home, his heart was black with bitterness and cold with grief. He felt he was shedding people like old bark from a maple tree in autumn. No one knew him any more. Sitting next to Ciara, he felt drained; she was a black hole sucking the energy out of anything which came too close to her. He toyed with his food, which was fit for a king, and realized that although he was central to her, she was just on the periphery for him, a straggly thread on an otherwise neat hem. He needed to cut her off. He had a new set of clothes now.

CHAPTER FOURTEEN

A Case of the What Ifs?

Mrs Chatterjee had started to notice slight changes in Hariprasad. There was something restless about him – he had to sit on his hands to keep them still, and he frequently looked around the room as if his eyes were chasing an invisible fly. She couldn't work out why. She listened with extra care to what he was saying, but there were no clues there. Until one day, instead of reading the sports commentary to her (after international news headlines, before the arts reviews), he put down the newspaper and paced up and down in front of the bookcase, before picking up a volume of selected love poems. Then she knew, and a smile, both sad and joyful, pressed upon her lips.

'Would you like to hear a poem?' he asked.

'Of course,' she said, already knowing which piece he had picked. He began:

'I seem to have loved you in numberless forms,
numberless times,
In life after life, in age after age forever.'

Mrs Chatterjee looked down at her old hands, marked by brown spots, creased and dog-eared, the skin as thin as eggshells, and remembered the time when they had been plump and smooth and enclosed in Mr Chatterjee's hand, warm and adoring, whilst they sat in the back of a Black Ambassador, filled with the intoxicating smell of sandalwood, and crossed the floodlit Howrah Bridge. How infinite that moment had felt, the cool river breeze blowing in her face, her husband's balmy mouth against her neck. Life before him was irrelevant; life without him was inconceivable. The union of loving and being loved was the greatest treasure of all. A treasure which she had not hidden carefully enough, had allowed to be stolen. A treasure which she had never recovered. Her heart ached at the thought.

'Who is she, then?' asked Mrs Chatterjee gently, after he had finished speaking. Hariprasad looked up shyly from the book, like a love-struck teenager, and then beamed, 'Rekha!'

'Will I meet her?'

'Do you want to?'

'Of course, of course. Bring her next time you visit.'

* * *

For years, Mr Chatterjee's notoriety had put food on the table. But now, in his early seventies, he realized that not only did he not want to attend dinners where he was paid to reminisce about his life as Defence Minister, but no one really wanted to listen either; he was a tired old 45 rpm. Times had moved on.

As soon as Selina Rashid had become *the* woman, instead of the *other* woman, she had changed. It was a slow, creeping change; Mr Chatterjee hadn't noticed until it was too late. She had needed material security, not intangible love, and once she had it, the longing which had kept her sweet and eager to please faded away. Where once she would have received Mr Chatterjee's gifts with delight and gratitude, they were now standard and met with no more than a mechanical 'thank you'. Where once she would have kneaded his tense shoulders and kissed the back of his neck, before lifting her skirts and sitting in his lap, rocking back and forth, his face nestled against her bare breasts, she now grimaced theatrically if he so much as laid a finger on her, and if she ever did let him have his way, she would insist on keeping her bra and petticoat on, and lie still and stiff, like a dead insect, until he had finished his business, at which point she would roll over with a rather pained sigh and feign sleep.

Until one day he woke up and, seeing the cruel and indifferent body beside him, decided enough was enough. When he had been young and rich and important, he had never foreseen that one day he might be old and unrich and unimportant. He thought of his wife, who had loved him, whose neck had always yielded to his kisses, whose soft skin had always capitulated to his fingertips. His wife, whose most prized possession had been her College Street books, who had her limbs stretched and pulled by a Chinoise masseuse every Thursday afternoon, and took her coffee with two sugar cubes. He thought of all the little things which were big things. Then he made his decision.

After a late-afternoon snack of a samosa, an omelette, a mutton cutlet, a slice of triangled, buttered bread and a soporific lettuce salad, all polished off with a cup of sweet cha, aboard the Rajdhani Express, Mr Chatterjee settled down in his bunk with a book and pulled the scratchy blanket up to his chin. The chug of the engine soothed his mind as his eyelids gradually became heavier and heavier, and the vast plains turned red as they were cloaked in the last of the sun's rays.

When Mr Chatterjee woke up in Calcutta in the morning, he felt re-invigorated, as if he was once again a young man with a full head of black hair and twitching muscles, not an old man with thinning white hair and creaky bones. He struggled through the throng at Howrah station before hailing a taxi to take him to his house, which he hadn't seen for decades.

Hariprasad told Rekha the minimum: just that Mrs Chatterjee was a very dear friend of his, and that he would like Rekha to meet her. He asked the taxi to drop them off at the top of the street, so that they could walk down the tree-lined avenue.

Outside Mrs Chatterjee's apartment block stood a short, rounded man with thinning white hair, anxiously rubbing his hands together and nervously looking around him. Hariprasad looked at him closer and thought that there was something familiar about him, but he couldn't put his finger on it. Approaching him, he asked firmly but courteously, 'Dada, are you looking for something? Can I help you?'

The man smiled gratefully, but shook his head. 'No, no, I'm fine. But thank you for asking.'

'OK,' Hariprasad said, turning away, glancing behind him one last time to look at the stranger's face.

Rekha had never visited such an apartment before. She had never seen antique furniture, or Persian rugs, or book-lined walls. And she had never seen someone take such little milk in their coffee, which was poured from a cafetière – another novelty. She followed suit and nearly choked on the bitter, fragrant liquid – nothing like the sweet, creamy affair she served to guests herself. And cake from Mr Nahoum's Jewish Bakery in New Market instead of thin arrowroot biscuits. She scowled at the brooch of turquoise and pearl set in antique gold which Mrs Chatterjee had pinned to her pashmina – it wasn't like the jewellery which Sachi had bought her (on *very* rare occasions), shiny and garish, blaring like headlights from her ears and neck and wrists. Suddenly Sachi and his bellyful of petit-bourgeois sentiments overwhelmed her, and she was once again his wife, not the girlfriend of Hariprasad with his taste for foreign food and admiration of Guru Dutt. Attack was her best form of defence.

Hariprasad was surprised by Rekha's surliness; he had never been witness to it before. He was embarrassed, as if his prize bitch had crapped on his foot in front of the judge. Mrs Chatterjee, sensing Hariprasad's shame, tried subtly to engage with Rekha by asking whether she had read that day's front-cover news – no; whether she was a cricket fan, as there was a one-day international coming up which she was sure Hariprasad would be more than delighted to take her to – no; whether she had read any Jibananda Das; Mrs Chatterjee had only just discovered him and what a joy he was – no; and when she could think of nothing else, she asked her whether she would like more milk in her coffee – yes. Rekha's cursory answers offered only dead ends. There she was, being given the chance to air all the opinions which she had for so long kept locked inside her, to have her say at last, but she could come up with nothing more than the most humdrum of monosyllables.

'Well,' said Hariprasad, after an hour and a half of not much, 'we must be getting on. Rekha, you must be tired, you've had a long day.' He yawned, with an exaggerated stretch and an overblown exhalation. 'I could do with a nap myself!'

'I'm not tired,' Rekha contradicted.

'Yes, you are, darling,' he soothed her, as if he was speaking to a grumpy toddler, at the same time giving Mrs Chatterjee a knowing glance. 'Now let's go home.'

Hariprasad jumped theatrically to his feet, and Rekha heaved her bulk to a standing position by using her arms as levers. Mrs Chatterjee rose to her feet slowly but elegantly, despite her weight and rickety knees. Hariprasad went to touch her feet before he left, but Mrs Chatterjee waved him away. She was too tired and too wise to stand on ceremony.

Hariprasad got into the taxi with Rekha,

nonplussed by her display. He wondered what was wrong with the damn woman? He liked her malleable, docile. Not churlish and uppity. Maybe it was time to trade her in. She had only been a stop-gap anyway, he convinced himself.

He opened the window and looked in the rear-view mirror. The old man he had seen earlier was still standing there, rubbing his hands and looking up to the top floor.

Mrs Chatterjee had kept the same servant since her husband had left. When he opened the door and saw Mr Chatterjee, his mouth fell open in excitement, and he said, just to make sure, 'Sahib?'

Mr Chatterjee nodded his head, ashamed of himself.

'Come in, come in!' said the servant, ushering him inside. 'Didi!' he called ahead. 'You'll never guess who's here!'

As soon as Mr Chatterjee saw his wife, he dropped to his knees and placed his head in her lap. Her sari smelled of home. And then he sobbed and sobbed and sobbed.

'Don't cry,' she said. 'I forgive you.'

It was five in the morning, and silent. Darshini woke up for the fourth time since she had gone to bed, hot and bothered, and tiptoed to the bathroom. She felt as if she had a fever, a light film of sweat covering

305

her skin. With the cool blue light of dawn easing its way through the window, she stood in front of the mirror, naked, looked at herself, and thought, 'This can't be happening.' She placed her hand on her childlike chest and felt her heart pound. It sounded like a jungle beat, a beat to accompany the procession of a tribal king. She cupped her hands under her small breasts; they were so tender they could hardly bear to be touched. The draughts-piece areolas had darkened, now almost the colour of blackberries. She skimmed her fingertips over them and winced. Running her hands down to her belly, she interlocked her fingers and placed both palms level against her flat stomach. She rubbed it gently, as if commanding a genie to appear, breathing deeply. Already the fault-line, which started just below her belly-button and ran all the way down to her pudenda, separating the two plates of her stomach, had become more pronounced. She looked at her heart-shaped face in the mirror with its Cupid's bow of a mouth, but peering back was the face of someone else, much fairer, with a sculpted, freckly nose. Dreamily she reached out and traced the features of the other face in the mirror, and then it vanished. Her period was more than a week late. Seph, a son without a father, was now a father without a son.

Yes or No. They weren't opposite ends of the

colour spectrum, but from the same ink: two different spots on a chromatograph. Hope, Need, Desire and Fear mutated into each other, swapping outfits, pulling faces; Darshini felt as if she was at the fairground in the Hall of Mirrors, and everywhere she looked was another image, none of them the original. Her nonchalance was replaced by a deep bellyache. What if this, what if that? If this, then that; if that, then this. If if if if if. Ask too many questions and you're screwed, she thought. Look back, and it leads to an eternal regression: before you know it you're back screaming between your mother's sweaty thighs. Look forward and the progression only ends when you're on your deathbed, with the grim reaper holding his scythe to your neck. Choices can be plotted like airports on a flight map; so many departure points, so many destinations. The only way to avoid having to make a decision is not to travel.

Darshini's head was bound with possibilities and consequences. Every time she tried to untangle a knot, she created another one. Finally, she pulled a coin from her purse and rubbed it between finger and thumb, warming it up. She sat leaning against the wall, her knees pulled up to her chest, sheltering her stomach. Then, with a gentle flick of her wrist, the coin spun into the air and landed on the floor in front of her. She leaned over and looked at it. She went to her scrapbook and turned to the coin that had decided her date with Seph. She stuck this coin next to the other. The set was complete: heads and tails.

This time, Tuhina saw it all clearly. She saw the face, unknown yet familiar, in her dreams, and when she woke up her hands were clutched to her belly. And she felt a kind of sadness that she had only felt once before. Getting out of bed, she walked to the study and pulled out an album of photographs. It was one dedicated to her and Darshini. She came to a familiar picture: it had been taken on the beach when Darshini was three and a half years old, wearing a red gingham-checked swimsuit with a double frill around the hips, and in her mother's arms. Mother and daughter were gazing into each other's eyes. Tuhina traced the profile of her daughter's face with the nail-tip of her little finger. Her eyes filled with tears. She went to Darshini's room, but her daughter had already left the house.

The clinic was barely distinguishable from its neighbours, apart from the women with blank faces who went through its doors at regular intervals. Darshini was dropped off at the end of the road and walked the rest. She had been there once already for the consultation, but this time she felt relief, not fear. The choice had been made. Inside were mostly lone women, although some had come with friends, and just a few with their partners. Those men looked helpless, their carefree lives, their frivolous thoughts about football and lingerie models in magazines taken away by a moment of carelessness, a moment that could have led to nothing, but had now led to something, something which couldn't be ignored or denied.

There were three normal categories and one special one: a red star for very good work, a silver star for excellent work, and a gold star for exceptional work. Seph's exercise books had been filled with the last. The special category was for competitions, and the prize was usually chocolate. Even those who didn't normally receive stars were in with a chance of winning a special category prize.

Miss Scott was of a somewhat nervous disposition. She had started her teaching career in the Shankill area of Belfast, but had felt so intimidated that her health had started to suffer – she began to develop a stutter and high blood pressure. When she disciplined a boy for throwing the board-rubber at a fellow student and hitting him hard with it, the perpetrator's mother had paid her a visit, after hours, whilst she was marking the class's maths homework, and had said, leaning her clenched fists on Miss Scott's desk, 'Keep your filthy fenian hands off my wee boy, you hoor,' before glowering at her, then leaving.

Miss Scott, palpitating, left her job a week later; the school governors thought it unnecessary for her to serve the usual one month's notice. She decided to move to the countryside, hoping for both slightly more agreeable children and slightly more agreeable parents. Cushendall, she thought, was much more suited to her temperament.

The competition was to design a Father's Day card. Seph, loaded with crepe paper, sugar paper, cardboard, scissors, glue, sequins, glitter and colouring pencils, sat at the dinner table and thought very, very carefully about his design. He had even spent his own pocket money on the glitter and sequins. He wanted to win. Not for the chocolate, but for the winning.

'What are you doing?' Ciara asked him.

'Making a Father's Day card,' he said matter-of-factly as he decided on his colour scheme.

Ciara didn't say anything.

The other children's cards were typical fare: padded-out stick-men with dots for eyes and lines for mouths, kicking not-quite-circular footballs, fishing (foil for the water), holding golf clubs with shortened arms and mitten-hands, or behind the wheels of boxy and without exception red cars. On the inside they all read, also without exception, 'To the Best Dad in the world.'

Seph's card was the sky; half day, half night. The day was filled with sheep clouds (cotton wool), glitter rays of golden sun raining down from the top left-hand corner, and a rippled blue sky made up of strips of crepe paper. The night was filled with sequined stars and a huge foil moon against a black sugar-paper background. In the middle of the card was a face that Seph saw every day on the wall at home. The face had calm, forgiving eyes and a benevolent, half-smiling mouth. His hair was lush and wavy, and his full beard gave him authority. On top of his head sat a crown of thorns, picked out with golden glitter. Seph's card read 'To my Father, from the best son in the world, Seph O'Shea.'

At lunchtime, the cards were passed round the staffroom and appraised. It was agreed that they were all of good technical quality – fine use of foil, sweet wrappers, etc. – but Seph's stood out. His card was filigree compared to nuggets of gold. What a clever, clever boy to think of Him, the Universal Father. And there was something both wryly comic and charmingly wistful about his inscription. The winner was agreed on unanimously. Miss Scott gathered the cards back and smiled – what lovely children, what a lovely job!

The last lesson ended five minutes early for the presentation.

'Now I just want to say, first, that you've all done

very, very well,' *Yeah, right, get on with it*, 'and I'm very proud of you. All the cards are beautiful, and I can see you all made a lot of effort,' *Come on, come on, hurry up*, 'but the one card which really caught our eye was . . .' fevered anticipation, '. . . Seph's.'

Miss Scott held out a box of Butlers chocolates. Seph stayed in his seat. 'Seph,' Miss Scott coaxed, leaning forward, 'do you want to come up and take your prize?'

Seph slowly got up, took the box in both hands, nodded at Miss Scott to thank her, and returned to his seat.

'Let's everyone give Seph a round of applause, shall we?' smiled Miss Scott. The children clapped loudly. Especially Molly, who sat next to Seph and was hoping to share his loot with him.

Then suddenly a sulky voice retorted, 'But he doesn't even have a dad! Why should he win?'

'Sssssh!' exclaimed Miss Scott. 'Now you apologize to Seph, Iain.'

'No,' replied Iain defiantly, crossing his arms and tilting his chin downwards. 'Why should I? He *doesn't* have a dad.'

'That's quite enough from you,' said Miss Scott, flustered, her heart rate increasing. 'Go and stand in the corner, and face the wall.'

Iain pushed his chair away from his desk and

walked to the corner, dragging his feet, every so often glancing back malevolently at Seph, whose fault this all was, for not having a father.

When she finally arrived home, Darshini took a bath, submerging her head under the water, wondering what it would feel like to drown. She imagined it would be rather peaceful. She stuck her big toe in the tap and moved her heel rhythmically, creating waves which lapped against her chin. And just as Aaron had turned the waters of the Nile into blood, Darshini turned the water red, and the relief she felt before turned to regret.

In her condition, Darshini had forgotten to lock the bathroom door. So whilst she soaked in the bloody water, her eyes closed, Mousumi walked in, armed with her jug and towel. As soon as she saw the colour of the water, she dropped the jug and screamed. Darshini sat bolt upright and turned to face Mousumi.

'What happen?' Mousumi asked quickly, nervously. 'You hurt? I call Tuhina aunty?'

'No,' said Darshini, slowly and firmly. 'Don't say anything to anyone. I'm fine. You understand?'

Mousumi nodded.

'No,' said Darshini. 'Say "I understand."'

'I understand,' said Mousumi, quaking.

'Good,' replied Darshini. 'I'll be finished in the

bath in a few minutes and then you can use it. All right?'

'All right,' Mousumi said, desperate to leave the bathroom.

'And don't worry,' Darshini called after her, 'I'll clean the bath before you use it.'

Mousumi pretended not to hear and ran to her room, her towel dragging behind her.

Telling her parents she had tummy ache – she decided that at least that way she wasn't really lying – and therefore didn't want to eat dinner, Darshini went to bed early and curled up in the foetal position. When she finally stopped crying, she propped one pillow up against her back, pulled another to her chest, and dreamed that she, Seph, and their baby were all lying together, facing the same way, a serving spoon, a dessert spoon, a tea-spoon. And they fitted together perfectly.

Whilst Darshini was trying to untangle the knot in her head, Seph was trying to unravel the one in his stomach. He had come home to a thick cream envelope. The address was handwritten in black, in small, annoyingly tidy writing, sloping up slightly – an optimist's scribble. He found his paper-knife and opened it. He had been cordially invited to the marriage of one of his ex-girlfriends on the

314

twenty-first of December. He didn't bother reading any further. He didn't even know she was engaged. No one told him anything any more. Behind the card, another: a wedding list at a well-known and not too expensive department store. One minute, he thought wryly, you're fucking on the kitchen counter, not caring about the broken plates, and the next you're asking people to buy you matching crockery.

In the way you remember words from a song which you haven't heard for years, Seph saw the RSVP number on the bottom of the card and immediately recognized it as her home line; he couldn't remember the last time he had dialled it. Without thinking what he was going to say, he phoned. Luckily, she wasn't in, so he left a message thanking her for the invitation and saying he would be delighted to go, even though his tone belied his real thoughts. Then he read the invitation a little more closely and saw 'Seph & *Partner*'. He wondered who he could take. Sitting down on his bed, he opened his bedside drawer and took from it a small paper bag, containing a box of condoms. Putting the contents back in the drawer, he straightened out the creases in the bag and then with an old fountain pen wrote her name in capital letters – GISELA – evenly spaced across the crumpled paper. Not a sexy name, he thought.

315

Though when he had been with her he had thought it a beautiful name. Three years ago. Then underneath he started to write the names of all the women he'd slept with since her. There were more than he had thought there would be, and he started to decrease the space between them so that he wouldn't have to turn the bag over. There wasn't one name he wanted to take.

He sighed and thought about Gisela, speculating what she might look like now. He had no regrets about her. He didn't suddenly think that he had missed his chance or that it could have been him. Even if it could have been, he didn't want it to be. Girls came, girls went; Seph might occasionally casually imagine what they were doing with their lives, but he didn't pine to have them back in his life or to be back in theirs. His bridges were no more than charred embers. How easily people who once took up all the pages of our lives become nothing more than footnotes.

Yet there was one girl he refused to consign to the pages of history. No, not refused, *couldn't*. He thought about the places where he had touched her, *their* places: in between her toes, inside her bellybutton, behind her ears, deep under her arms, her perineum, the soft corrugated flesh around her anus, marking his territory. He thought about whether anyone else had touched those places, *was* touching those places, and his stomach contorted in pain.

Her face flashed before him like a subliminal message when he least expected it – when giving a presentation, or when at lunch with clients – and left him unsettled for the rest of the day. Every night he thought of the first time she had told him that she loved him. He had been working at home and had told her not to disturb him, so she had occupied herself with her colouring book (she said it was relaxing) for more than an hour, but then, momentarily tired of filling in the outlined blanks, she had stood up and declared like a proud statesman, 'I . . .' pausing for effect, 'I . . .', another pause, 'am in love . . .' pause, 'with you!' As she said 'you', she had pointed at him with the index finger of her right hand, looking satisfied, giving him a coy movie-star smile, then tilting her head down and gazing at him for a short moment, before returning to her colouring-in. She had neither required nor requested a response. She hadn't needed his permission to be in love with him, nor did she have any fear of rejection. Her love for him stood alone, without needing acceptance or reciprocation – Ciara may have dipped him in the river Styx, but Darshini had found his heel.

One night, a month on, when he looked in the mirror, instead of seeing his own face he saw the face of someone else, darker, with a heart-shaped

317

face and a Cupid's bow mouth. He reached out to touch it, but before he could the image disappeared. And then it came, like the first spit of rain before a hailstorm, a lone tear crawling down his cheek, wiped away with the back of his hand, and then a sniffle, and then another silent tear from the other side. He told himself to take deep breaths but it didn't help, and he cried out loud, his body wracked with sobs, a thin string of saliva dripping out of his mouth, his whole face hot and wet. He couldn't stop. His stomach muscles started to ache from convulsing. And still he couldn't stop. It is always much more painful to lose something that could have been than something that was.

CHAPTER FIFTEEN

Cuckoo in the Nest

Darshini's Regret shed its old skin like a snake, rubbing itself against nearly made telephone calls, lonely nights and silence until it was all scraped off, and it emerged as simmering Bitterness.

For the first time since they had collected Mousumi from the airport, they were all in the car together. Tuhina went to get in the driver's seat but Prakash took the keys from her hand and said flippantly, 'I'll drive.'

Prakash never drove on family trips. His inconsistency and lack of anticipation irritated the other two immensely. Nothing was ever said, but it was acknowledged by the fact that Tuhina had insisted on driving to the point where it had become routine. Sometimes Prakash would wait for what seemed like hours for a gap in the traffic before pulling out, and even then it was only after being prompted – 'I think you can go now,' said through gritted teeth. At other times he would rush into a turn, the car careering around the bend at such speed that they would have to hold on to the arm rests, or be harassed by a line of beeping cars which had been forced to brake suddenly. Prakash would always ask ingenuously, 'What are they all beeping at?' He speeded up when coming to a roundabout; slowed down when joining a motorway.

Tuhina raised her eyebrows at Darshini; Darshini raised hers back and shrugged. Mousumi waited patiently by the door, waiting for it to be unlocked.

'It's central locking,' said Tuhina, looking over.

Mousumi looked blank. Tuhina's skin prickled with irritation. Silly, silly girl – how many times had Mousumi been in the car already; she should have learned by now. 'The door – it's unlocked. You can open it,' she explained, indicating with her hand. Mousumi still looked blank. Tuhina took a deep breath. Then she walked around swiftly, jostling Mousumi out of the way and opening the front passenger door forcefully. 'Here you go!' she said with a strained smile, her face dropping as soon as she turned away.

Mousumi got into the car gingerly and sat down, her body tense. She could feel Darshini's knee in the small of her back, pushing through the seat, but she didn't dare say anything.

'All right, Mou?' Prakash asked, giving her leg an affectionate little rub as he went over the directions. She nodded nervously. 'Hmm?' he asked, looking up, not having seen her gesture.

'Very fine, thank you,' she said quickly, glancing over her shoulder to see Tuhina staring at her.

The temperature in the car was just right to cook the simmering animosity to perfection. They all brought their own ingredients.

'What do you want to listen to?' Prakash asked Mousumi.

She selected a pirate radio station, which had once been picked up inadvertently by the extra sensitive aerial, and was now number two in the pre-programmed stations (the stations were pro-grammed strictly in order of preference). It was run by a modern Indian granny from Hounslow, whose play list consisted of movie songs from both new Bollywood blockbusters and classics like *Bobby* and *Meera Nam Joker*. Darshini didn't mind at all; she thought a lot of the tunes were rather catchy. What she did mind was that Choice FM 96.9, which was pre-set station number two and belonged to her, was no longer there. Mousumi should have been assigned another pre-set number – she was temporary; Darshini was permanent, and so should her station have been, she thought. Choice FM had been ousted by Ganesha Greatest Hits.

'Where's my station?' she asked.

No one said anything, because no one knew who she was addressing the question to, or what she actually meant. So she said again, 'Where's my station?'

'What do you mean, darling?' quizzed Tuhina.

'Choice FM. 96.9,' she said, nodding towards the stereo display.

'Prakash,' said Tuhina, 'do you know what she's talking about?'

'I'm talking about my radio station,' interrupted Darshini, '*that's* what I'm talking about!'

'Well, what do you mean, where is it?' questioned Prakash. He was a Man of Science, and as far as he knew the sound coming from the stereo was made by airwaves.

'I mean,' continued Darshini, getting exasperated, '*my* radio station – Choice FM!'

Mousumi instinctively knew that she had done something wrong, but she wasn't quite sure what – Darshini was speaking too quickly for her to understand.

'I suppose, as always, you've let *her* have her way?'

'*What*?' Prakash questioned, looking over his shoulder for a moment.

Faced with her father's direct eye contact, Darshini thought about backing down, but this was

322

too important an issue. 'You've given *my* radio station to her – channel two is mine. You know that,' she stated, exhaling loudly.

'It is not your radio station. It is *my* radio station in *my* car and you should stop acting like such a spoilt brat!'

'Prakash,' Tuhina intervened, 'it's not your car, it's a family car.'

'Family? *Family!* Since when have we been a family? It's always you two together. So funny, and so clever. Laughing always at me. Only family when it suits you!'

Tuhina and Darshini looked at each other in astonishment, and raised their perfect eyebrows.

'Don't give each other that look!' Prakash exclaimed, without turning around. The two-headed tigress didn't know where to turn.

'Prakash, be careful!' screamed Tuhina, as in his rage he accelerated towards another car.

'Don't bloody you tell me how to drive!' he yelled.

The two-headed tigress was caught on the back foot by this unprecedented show of hostility and didn't know how to react. It was as if a deer had just bitten her on the nose – it didn't hurt, it was just unexpected. After the initial shock, a light, playful little smirk pirouetted on her lips; aggression without authority engendered little respect.

323

So when they finally arrived at Hampton Court Palace – the journey having been accompanied by the most unsuitable soundtrack of upbeat and giddy pop songs, which Mousumi hadn't dared turn off, as she hadn't dared move at all for the entire ride – they breathed a collective sigh of relief. Prakash, sensing that he would have to make the first move, capitulated and asked cheerily, 'So what should we do first, then?'

'Whatever you like, Prakash,' said Tuhina pointedly.

'Yeah, Dad, whatever you like,' Darshini repeated, her tone at once both indulgent and flippant.

He was being humoured again. There was nothing he could do. Mousumi smiled; she was too nervous to do anything else. This wasn't the kind of argument she had seen her parents have; it was more akin to a game of chess than a wrestling match.

They walked across to the garden entrance in pairs – Prakash and Mousumi took the lead, and Tuhina and Darshini followed behind. They stopped in the garden shop and Mousumi hovered near a pot of begonias.

'You want?' Prakash asked cheerily. 'They'd look nice in your bedroom.'

Mousumi nodded shyly.

'Well, that's decided, then!' Prakash said, puffing his chest out and picking up the pot. Walking past

Tuhina and Darshini, his face obscured by flowers, he asked, 'Either of you want anything nice for your bedrooms?'

'No, thank you,' they said politely in unison.

After that, they continued around the estate, through the walled flower garden with its colourful borders and avenues lined with interlacing vines. Mousumi stopped to sniff the flowers and touch their velvety petals. Prakash did the same and commented loudly that they were nice, but not as nice as the ones in his own garden. Mousumi agreed with him. The other two hung back and said nothing.

But it was the wisteria arch that delighted Mousumi the most. It had featured in one of her favourite films – the hero and heroine had skipped through it, holding hands and singing. Unable to contain her excitement, she ran down, twirling around and humming.

Prakash grinned and, turning to Darshini and Tuhina, exclaimed, 'Look how much fun we're all having!'

'Yes, Dad!' exclaimed Darshini. 'Aren't we just!'

Tuhina tried to stop herself from smirking.

Whilst Darshini had been cocooning herself in her own thoughts, Mousumi had taken the opportunity, like a cuckoo, to lay her eggs in Prakash's nest. It was now Mousumi that Prakash cooked his favourite dishes for, Mousumi who accompanied him on his grocery trips, Mousumi who sat and watched cricket with him, Mousumi whom he lavished his attention on. The realization that her position as empress had been usurped made Darshini furious. Once she had been the only one. Now she saw reminders of her cousin's influence everywhere: in the long black hairs which were caught in the bath plug-hole, in the piles of children's books (which Prakash had bought to help Mousumi learn English) cluttering the coffee table, in the boxes of soft shandesh (which Prakash had to make a special trip to Euston to buy) in the fridge, in the lightweight waterproof pink jacket (which Prakash had bought to protect Mousumi from English summer showers) hanging on the coat rack. And she didn't like it one bit.

Tuhina, on the other hand, was mystified rather than enraged. She too had noticed the rapport developing between her husband and her niece, but told herself that it was good for her, as it kept Prakash occupied and out of her hair, although she did wonder what on earth he saw in a fat teenager with bad skin and no personality. 'No personality' was Tuhina's biggest insult. It was just so effortlessly derogatory. But despite her cool exterior, it still riled her that Prakash should take such interest in someone who was so, well, unworthy – just because Tuhina didn't want Prakash's attention, it didn't mean that she wanted him to give it to someone else, although as a forty-five-year-old mature woman, this was not something she could confess even to herself.

Prakash was the happiest he'd been for years. He smiled a lot. He hummed Bengali film tunes to himself whilst cooking. He took extra time and care choosing his tie and shirt every morning. He had lost weight, his skin had become brighter and his eyes sparkled. At last he felt appreciated and valued. At last he felt like a man. His role was now that of provider, carer, protector. Equality in law can never vanquish inequality of the heart and soul. Women may need to be cherished, but men need approbation.

Prakash had only felt powerful once in his life before Mousumi had come along. And that was when he had first met Tuhina.

Being the kind of woman to disregard the customary courting conventions of the time, she had fallen pregnant. She didn't tell anyone else; not because she was ashamed, but what would be the point? She only asked for an opinion if she required one. She believed that people are rarely unable to make decisions. Deep inside, there is no umming

and aahing. Even before you know it yourself, a conclusion has been reached somewhere in the recesses
of your stomach, solid and unalterable, and
the questions which you ask of others are pretences,
an attempt to surround yourself in the shrubbery of
moral complexity, to appear to be a better, more
thoughtful person. Seeking moral confirmation was
a deceit too far for her.

So she sat with the others and waited, watched by
a receptionist whose distaste resided in her brown,
down-turned mouth, like a woodlouse in a piece of
bark. And she wasn't the only one. Some of the
nurses acted like Pharisees in the company of
prostitutes, protected from infection only by the
strength of their virtue and righteousness. It didn't
bother Tuhina at all. She was a great believer in
sticks and stones. And after twenty minutes of dirty
looks and accusing stares, the doctor walked in to
lead her to the slaughterhouse.

Prakash wasn't sure whether it was right or
wrong, because he had never really thought about it;
mused, yes, but *thought*, no. His opinions on most
things were young and unsure, as fragile as a daddy-
long-legs' spindly limbs. They changed constantly,
dependent on which paper he had read, which
news programme he had watched, which person he
had talked to. Like a lump of plasticine which can
be moulded into any shape but has no intrinsic

form, Prakash, by having every opinion, had none at all.

So when he saw Tuhina, he didn't pass judgement. Well, not of that sort, and not straight away, anyway. What he did think was how wonderful she was to look at. Although he was quite aware that his profession required cool neutrality, he wasn't blind. No one is immune to the charms of a beautiful young woman, least of all a virile young man.

So when she came round from the anaesthetic, his bedside manner was impeccable. The drug gave her eyes a heavy-lidded drowsy sensuality and her mouth seemed especially puffy. He helped her into a sitting position and held a glass of water to her lips. When he had gone to lift her up, he had inadvertently touched her back through the parting in the gown, and had kept his hand there for a moment more than was necessary. She seemed vulnerable, in need of his help. He felt strong, powerful, needed. Was he not now her saviour and protector? What would she have done without him? Imposing neediness on Tuhina was how Prakash made himself feel like a man. So in the years to come, when the gratitude failed to appear, Prakash felt he had been cheated, like dry land when the rains did not arrive after seasons of drought. He failed to realize it was his own doing, and that the only person who had conned him had been himself. And all he had ever wanted was a *thank you*!

Darshini noticed the difference. Once he had sought her love and approval; now he didn't seem to care. She tried all sorts of tactics to win her place back in her father's affections, but nothing seemed to work. She was extra sweet to him, but he received her niceness as a pop-star would receive a teddy-bear from a teenage girl, with distant gratitude. She was extra rude to him, but he seemed impervious to her hostility, failing to rise to the bait. There was only one other way to get through to him, and that was through *her*. Darshini's mouth turned into a sulky pout and her eyes darkened as she started plotting.

Darshini wasn't generally one for scheming, and at first wasn't sure where to start. She wished that a toss of the coin could sort the problem out, but the difficulty was that the solution wasn't binomial. What she did know was that any successful plan of action must incorporate an accurate prediction of how the other player will behave. So what Darshini tried to work out as she sat in Hyde Park, feeding the ducks and swans with some Almond Thins which she had found in the bottom of her bag, was how formidable an opponent Mousumi would be. Perhaps she should just physically muscle her way back into her father's affections, raising her hand

and shouting 'Me, me, *me!*' But that didn't seem a very elegant solution. Darshini looked up at the cloudless cerulean sky. The sunlight defined every leaf, branch and blade of grass with the kind of clarity that only a late summer day can bring, every colour as true to itself as it would ever be. Darshini wished that people could be understood with such clearness.

Darshini had learned to read on her fourth birthday. She had shown absolutely no interest in words until then, to the consternation of her parents, who would sit her on their knee, *The Very Hungry Caterpillar* in hand, and try to make her follow the story, but she would neither turn the page nor ask any questions. Her nursery-school teacher didn't seem overly concerned, but what did one expect from the state sector, Tuhina grumbled. So it was a great surprise to them when on her fourth birthday Darshini brought home her tin of words and, holding each slip of paper in her hand, read the words out loud and clear, and then promptly started to read the title on the cover of one of Tuhina's books – *Decisions, Strategies and New Ventures* – which was lying on the coffee table.

Mousumi's English reading progress wasn't as abrupt. She seemed to learn in fits and starts, like an old banger with a clogged oil filter. So Darshini thought she would help her along. Tuhina knew

Darshini's generosity was a Trojan Horse, but couldn't see what was inside it, so waited, patient but curious.

Mousumi felt she had been granted a reprieve. After the magazine episode, she had been uneasy around Darshini, ashamed. So when Darshini offered her an olive branch, she grabbed it with both hands, and Darshini reeled her right in. They started simply enough with the children's books which Prakash had bought. They began with *Once upon a time there were four little Rabbits, and their names were Flopsy, Mopsy, Cotton-tail and Peter* and moved, with Darshini trying to hide her smile and Mousumi trying to hide her blushes, to Margaret's refrain of *I must, I must, I must increase my bust.*

The tin itself was innocuous enough – an old tobacco container, slightly rusty at the hinges. But what it contained was far more vicious. It had at one time been filled with *Cat*, *Mat*, *Hat*. And at another, *Cake*, *Bake*, *Make*. Nice little words to be practised at home and read out in class, then remembered. But when Mousumi opened it one night to do her homework, she pulled out the following: *Dad*, *Stay*, *From*, *Away*, *Fucking*, *My*. At first she was confused; she knew it was bad and her lower lip started to tremble with fear. Then, with shaking hands, she tried to put the words in order. What she came up with was: *Stay Away From Fucking My Dad.* She could hear Tuhina in the kitchen with Prakash; they seemed to be having a row. (They weren't; they were talking extra loudly to be heard above the television.) Did Tuhina think that, too? But she hadn't; Prakash knew it! But she knew that lies can be just as damaging as the truth, and as her father would no doubt have said, there's no smoke without fire. So, despite being guilty of nothing, she felt blameworthy – to her, the fact that Darshini thought it was enough. She wanted to run away, but to where? She was in a foreign country, knew no one, had nothing. She wanted her mummy.

Placement was what tipped the scale. It was meant to have been read: Fucking Stay Away From My Dad. The positioning was the difference between distress and devastation. Mousumi's honour and integrity were now in doubt. And she hadn't even done anything. What would her family at home say if they heard? She would be disowned. Wiping the first trickle of water from her eyes, she ran up to her bedroom.

Her crying was so loud it could be heard from the kitchen. Prakash heard the caterwauling, and looked out of the window to see if he could spot the ginger tom who patrolled the area, but the garden was empty. Tuhina turned the television off, ssshed Prakash, and cocked her head to one side.

'It's coming from upstairs,' she said definitively.

Darshini loitered in the door of the den, listening both to her parents and to the bodiless wailing above her. When she heard her parents climb the stairs, she tiptoed into the sitting room and went over to the coffee table. Looking down at the pieces of paper, she rolled her eyes and thought, The idiot girl even put the *fucking* in the wrong place. When she realized what all the bawling was about, she gave an exasperated sigh. Scooping up the accusation in her hand, she tore it into little pieces and threw them into the bin – your word against mine. Then she went upstairs to watch events unfurl.

Mousumi was absolutely unintelligible. Strands of dribble hung from her mouth like strings of glue, her bloodshot eyes had nearly disappeared into the swollen flesh of her cheeks, and her whole body shook as she tried to catch her breath. There were damp patches on her trousers where the tears had cascaded down her face and dripped off, and her skin was blotchy and red. Prakash went to sit down next to her and comfort her, but the moment he approached her she yelped as if in pain and started shaking.

'You have to tell us what's wrong,' he begged, but all they could make out was a garbled sorry and a repetitive strain of 'I want to go home,' like a voodoo chant.

'But *why* do you want to go back home?' Prakash pleaded with her.

In the far corner of the room, Darshini narrowed her eyes at her dad's concern and anxiety – once again, it was Mousumi who was the centre of his attention. Tuhina knew that this was Darshini's doing, and tried to visualize what had happened, but all she pictured was a dictionary and, strangely enough, a pornographic magazine. She peered at her daughter, looking closely at her face to see whether she could glean any information from the angle of her eyes or the setting of her mouth, but she wore the same expression as when she had got into trouble as a child. It was a look that said, 'You may think I'm wrong, but I have my reasons.' Certainly not apologetic, but not antagonistic either, just a statement of the facts.

After sedating Mousumi with a new drug which had been recommended to him just a few days earlier, and which he was therefore pleased to have the chance to try out, Prakash sat down with a large whisky and asked Tuhina what was to be done, not because he wanted a discussion but because he could never make an important decision on his own. The responsibility for the consequences was too onerous a burden. For him an accusation of indecision was preferable to being blamed for making the wrong decision.

335

* * *

Hariprasad was having other Mousumi troubles to deal with. The third response to Rekha's advert, from a government clerk, had only come in yesterday, but after the first two no-shows Rekha had insisted that Hariprasad phone the prospective husband as a matter of urgency, and arrange a rendezvous for her and the clerk, in order to show as much enthusiasm as possible – no treat 'em mean, keep 'em keen strategy at this delicate stage of the operation.

And now the clerk was proving to be difficult. He didn't seem to have any buttons to press. As they wandered around the zoo, he nodded at what Hariprasad had to say, but he had an agenda of his own, and that was to meet Mousumi. He liked what he had read in the advertisement and so had his parents. She seemed ideal. And now he had the bit between his teeth, he wasn't about to let go without a struggle. 'So when can I meet her?' was his constant refrain. Hariprasad tried reverse psychology, acting so keen to marry off Mousumi, like a second-hand car salesman trying to flog a lemon, that most buyers would have thought the goods faulty, but the clerk showed no signs of desisting. Hariprasad had no choice. Leading the clerk to the far side of the tigers' enclosure, with one swift move he hung him over the concrete wall and

336

dangled him by his feet. Hariprasad's skinny arms were enraged with strength. The two tigers, sunbathing and flicking away flies with their tails, looked up, semi-interested, and yawned, revealing their sharp incisors. The clerk wriggled frantically, but Hariprasad would not pull him back.

'This is it!' Hariprasad declared. 'If you don't promise to stay away, this is it for you, you bastard sister-fucker!'

'What the hell's the matter with you, man?' the clerk yelled back, the blood rushing to his head. 'Don't you want your niece to get married to a decent, respectable man like me?'

'Nothing's wrong with me!' shouted Hariprasad, indignant. 'You're wrong! And if you don't swear on your own mother's life that I'll never see your sorry face again, I'll drop you right now.' At this, Hariprasad's grip seemed to loosen slightly. The clerk fell closer to the tigers by millimetres.

'OK, OK,' he said, trying to raise his hands in surrender, although the effect was lost as he was still upside-down. 'I'll forget I ever heard about her. And I'll try to forget I ever met you!'

Hariprasad considered the clerk's words – he sounded honest, but Hariprasad needed to make sure. 'You promise?' he asked slowly.

'I promise, I promise!' said the clerk quickly. 'On my mother's life!'

Hariprasad was satisfied with this answer. He pulled the clerk back over the rail and dumped him unceremoniously on the ground.

After the clerk had straightened out his clothes and combed his hair Elvis-style, Hariprasad grabbed his hand, shook it vigorously and said, his voice once again calm, 'Well, it was very nice to meet you, young man!'

The clerk pulled his hand back, muttered 'banchut' under his breath and then hurried off, looking back every so often to see Hariprasad grinning at him, his eyes still ablaze with purpose.

Rekha was making her way to the tiger enclosure, where she was to meet the clerk. She had made good time on the journey over, so ambled through the zoo at her leisure, stopping to feed monkey-nuts to the chipmunks and laugh at the bottom-flashing baboons. She had managed to keep her outfit clean and her face made-up; leaning on the wall of the tiger enclosure, she looked almost elegant. But there was no one to appreciate her efforts.

Rekha was utterly disheartened. She couldn't imagine why none of the prospective sons-in-law had turned up. She asked herself if it was some sort of cruel joke. Would she never wear a cream raw-silk sari embroidered with seed pearls? Would she never feed her son-in-law with her special cardamom-scented pilau rice, full of almonds, cashews and raisins? Would she never be a grand-mother, and give her grandson his first spoon of aromatic rice-pudding? Would she lie on her deathbed with only her spinster daughter and a lowly servant to see her into the next world? Rekha's problem was not that she had put all of her eggs in one basket, but that she could only conceive of there *being* one basket. And the quality of her eggs was decided by Fate. Her eyes watered a little, but her mouth remained stoically upturned. As with the death of her husband, she would accept what was written on her forehead with good grace. What is meant to be is meant to be!

It was Tuhina who made the phone call; Prakash didn't like being the bearer of bad news. It was four in the morning in London, half past eight in Calcutta, and Rekha was still in bed when she heard the phone ring.

Rekha had never received a phone call at that time in the morning. In fact, she didn't receive many phone calls at all. When she had married she had lost touch with all of her childhood friends, and Sachi hadn't encouraged her to make any more – why let women indulge in idle gossip and complain about their husbands, when they could put their time to far better use doing the domestic chores? So her first instinct was that it was a death call. But then she remembered that both her parents and Sachi's were dead, and there wasn't anyone else in the right age group or suffering from a terminal illness. Her apprehension then turned to a more childlike curiosity. When she heard Tuhina's voice, though, her stomach lurched – it had to be serious.

Tuhina used the kind of voice she employed when she had to explain to someone why they had been overlooked for promotion. It was firm – no blubbering, now – but sympathetic – it's a real shame. She tried to put a positive spin on the story: Mousumi had been a wonderful person to live with, they had all had a lot of fun together, and her English had definitely improved, but it really was very difficult living so far away from home, and the real lump-in-your-throat job – she missed her mother.

Rekha didn't say much. She wasn't sure what to think – her thoughts were like prairie dogs, popping out of their burrows and then scurrying back in before she had a chance to catch one. She mmmed a lot, and said 'I understand' a few times, even though she didn't.

When she put the phone down, she felt that she had failed. The umbilical cord may have been physically cut, but Rekha still felt every disappointment, every frustration, every letdown, as her own. (If Mousumi had ever had any successes, she would have felt those, too.) It wasn't a tangible failure, but like poison gas, although it could not be seen its effects could be felt. A lethargy descended upon her, her eyes lost their shine and her limbs felt heavy. She stood by the phone for more than half an hour, swaying slightly, like a fat piece of seaweed caught in the current, until Hariprasad burst through the door.

Hariprasad had become an early and enthusiastic riser. By the time Rekha had woken up, he had already been for a run, drunk his first cup of milky coffee accompanied by a piece of toast with honey, read through *The Statesman* and had a shower; now he was all ready to prepare Rekha's breakfast. So when he saw her out of bed, staring absent-mindedly into space, he was worried. But before asking what was wrong, he led her, like a guide-dog, to a chair, nudged her into it, then went to put the kettle on. Conversation on an empty stomach was fruitless, he thought; sugar and fat fed the brain. So it was only after he had fed Rekha two sweet samosas, a piece of buttered toast and two cups of extra-sugary cha that he asked her what was the matter.

Lottery Winner was the only phrase which could describe his expression. Mousumi was coming back home! Rekha wondered what all his excitement was about. But she was perplexed, not suspicious, and tried to seem as excited as him – she didn't want to seem unfeeling. For a mother to have her maternal welcome upstaged was more than just hurtful; it was shameful, too, and to be avoided at any cost. But Hariprasad's enthusiasm was infectious, and soon Rekha had gone from being disappointed to thinking how wonderful it was that her one and only daughter was coming back home. Hariprasad planned what they should cook for her welcome-home dinner and what gift they should take to greet her at the airport – he was the quarterback, Rekha was merely a cheerleader.

Is any action ever truly altruistic? Who cares. Certainly Hariprasad didn't. And neither did the recipients of his generosity and affection. What of the fact that he might himself be a beneficiary of his actions? Surely pleasure was a public good – one person's share of it didn't mean that there was less in the world for someone else, or that someone else's happiness was diluted. He did of course understand the concept of schadenfreude, but that's what it was to him, a concept – he could never imagine taking delight in another's misery. He was simply so blinkered by his devotion that he never thought of those on the periphery of his designs. He didn't think about the unhappiness of the owner of the cat that he had semi-blinded, or the mother of the shy doctor who would now never be a grandmother. In fact, so focused was he on the main prize that he even forgot about Rekha, or rather, the issue of what to do with her.

Everyone was in a bad mood with everyone. Darshini was in a bad mood with Prakash because he was helping Mousumi pack, tucking into her suitcase little affectionate keepsakes to remind her of England, amongst them a Union Jack umbrella to be used in the monsoon season, the official *Illustrated History of the Tower of London*, a tin of Assam tea from Jacksons of Piccadilly (yes, the irony was lost on him), and a jar of Sir Nigel's Vintage Marmalade (like Sir Nigel, Mousumi had found the other varieties a little too sweet). So this was how Prakash's England was bundled into the historical suitcase, which was now filled with nostalgia and affection.

Tuhina was in a bad mood with the airline company, because due to her secretary's inefficiency she was listening, for the fourteenth time, to the first twenty bars of Vivaldi's Spring from the Four Seasons as she tried to confirm Mousumi's return flight. And when she finally heard a human voice, she realized that she had been transferred to a call centre in India (no, the irony *wasn't* lost on her) and was speaking to a woman who pronounced Heathrow *Heat Row*.

343

Prakash was in a bad mood with both Tuhina and Darshini because of their indifference to Mousumi's imminent departure. He expected, well, he wasn't sure *what* he expected, but it was certainly more than an apathetic OK and let's get back to business. 'She's family,' he thought, 'and yet they're treating her as if she was a stranger.' Prakash's idea of family was simple, concrete, and based on blood. The two-headed tigress's was far more mercurial and complex. Western, even, Sachi might have said!

Mousumi was in a bad mood with herself. She had let herself down. A couple of days ago she had wanted to go home, and now she didn't. What was there for her back home? There, she had no father, and even when she had he had been oppressive and unaffectionate. Here she had Prakash, who was warm and gave her the attention she craved. There she stood out as odd; here she blended in as average. There she slept in the same room as her mother; here she had her own turret in the tower. Like an old piece of origami, Mousumi had come unfolded, and she liked herself more without creases. But it was too late.

Seph was in a bad mood, too. For him, tomorrow had become a concept instead of a reality. It never actually happened; each time it was nearly in his grasp, it slipped away, looking over its shoulder, gently laughing at him. It used to breathe down his neck, pushing him harder, come on, *come on*, but now he could barely feel its presence. His procrastination had once had a languid countenance, an elegant two fingers to the world – I'll do this when I'm ready and not a second sooner – but now it had lost all of its seductive arrogance. Instead it had started to garrotte him like a mafia assassin. He wished he could stop thinking and start doing. He thought about buying himself a motivational book – he had spotted *The Ten Questions* on a few desks at work, hidden under piles of paper – and then the ridiculousness of the notion struck him and this cheered him up, but only briefly. What bothered him most was that he had always been someone who was in control, always *chose* what to do, but now he couldn't even work out what he was meant to do with himself. Introspection had hobbled him.

CHAPTER SIXTEEN

Ciara

Ciara was forty-five but looked far older, in an ethereal, unchanging way. She had never paid any attention to herself, and when she finally looked in the mirror and saw her true reflection, it was too late. Always one to look forward, she now looked back, and when she did there was no smile on her thinning lips. It was at that point that her hope stopped triumphing over her experience, and she saw herself as others did. But loss of hope is not the same as despair – it is taking life for what it is, not what it could be. Finally, she stopped dreaming.

She made her way around Cushendall and realized that it had never really loved her, not in the way that she had loved it. It had protected her out of duty and decency, not affection. The people had always held her at arm's length. Not Seph, though; no, they had welcomed him, he was one of their own. And now he had turned his back on them. There was a sense of justice about it, she thought.

She started at Tavnaghan Cottage, at the foot of Tiveragh, the fairy hill. She had believed in fairies once, thought that if she wished hard enough she would see one. Summer was coming to an end, and the tourists were turning their backs on the clean, blue sky and bright sunlight for the thick, grimy air of the city and the artificial strip-lighting of their offices. She stood at the red gate between the stone walls and looked at the white building. There were no cars parked in the courtyard – It seemed deserted. There was no padlock on the gate and she opened it slowly, then walked round to the back of the cottage. She wasn't worried about getting caught; she knew that even if someone saw her, they wouldn't say anything – everyone in the village trusted her, she seemed incapable of malice. And she didn't do anything spiteful; she simply stood looking out over the golden field, which was gradually turning russet from the setting sun, and over at the hills in the distance, and thought about what lay beyond them. Then she left, carefully closing the gate behind her.

Walking past the Sailing and Boating Club, which Seph had been a member of, she took a seat on one of the patio benches. She remembered the summer barbecue which she had gone to a couple of years back. The charcoal smell of smoking sausages and the sweet aroma of blackened corn-on-the-cob filled her nose. Looking out to sea, she saw a few sailing dinghies, the colourful sails bending one way, then another. From the shore the actions seemed choreographed, graceful. She thought about how she too had congregated with the other women, talking about their sons and daughters, helping dish out the potato salad, telling the little ones to behave and stop messing about. She talked like them, she dressed like them. But still they didn't take her in. They didn't include her in the gossip about how the commodore (married) was having an affair with the social secretary (fifteen years younger than him), or how it was well known, but keep it to yourself, that the treasurer was fond of funding his soft spot for a glass of fine malt with pennies from the coffer. But their rejection didn't hurt her any more. She slowly rose to her feet and continued on her way.

Stopping outside the Old School House on Mill Street, she remembered when Seph had encouraged her to join the Cushendall Development Group. She had been on the environment team, and had helped brighten up the village by placing flower tubs around the place. They had allowed her to pick the flowers – amongst her selection had been crowd-pleasing sweet peas, as well as the more fashionable scabious (a rather outré choice, some had

348

commented with eyebrows raised), and she had taken her responsibility seriously. At that time, she had taken pride in her work, and they had congratulated her, told her what a wonderful job she had done. Now she saw their gratitude as something less than praise and more akin to charity. But their pity didn't bother her any more.

She walked a little further down the street and came to a stop across the street from Johnny Joe's. She looked at the building thoughtfully, admiring the pale-pink walls and red doors and window sills – she had never noticed the colours before. By now it was evening, and she could hear the chatter of the crowd inside and the sound of the musicians warming up. It was the first time that she had ever been late for her shift. But she didn't care about pleasing people any more.

'All right, Ciara?' asked Fat Annie as she walked through the door later that evening.

'Fine, pet,' she answered.

But Fat Annie thought that Ciara looked more tired than usual, and said to her, 'Why don't you take a half-hour break? I'll take care of it here.'

So Ciara wiped her beer-splattered hands on an old tea-towel and walked to the parlour, which was packed with folk listening to the band. She stood at the back and listened to an upbeat number, 'Whiskey in the Jar', tapping her foot with everyone

349

else. When the song came to an end, Brian, who played both the violin and the cittern (multi-talented, he liked to think), said jokingly, 'They've let you out, have they, Ciara? Well, this next song's for you, then,' and the band started to play a love song, 'I Know My Love', and everyone smiled as Jim sang the chorus, 'I know my love by her way of walking, And I know my love by her way of talking, And I know my love by her suit of blue, But if my love leaves me, what will I do?' Throughout the song, Brian kept looking up and half-smiling at Ciara; and instead of looking away in shyness, she half-smiled back.

At closing time, as everyone else filed out, Brian kept his place, nursing an empty glass.

'You finished with that?' Fat Annie asked, going to remove the glass from the table.

'No,' Brian said, wrapping his fingers tighter around it.

'Suit yourself.' Fat Annie shrugged. She'd always thought Brian was a funny one.

Ciara followed in Fat Annie's wake, wiping down the tables. When she came to Brian's table, she didn't say anything about the empty glass, but instead wiped around it.

'I'm finished with it, you know,' he said, trying to make eye-contact with her.

'Oh, I wasn't sure,' she replied, glancing at him,

shy again, then going to remove the glass. But as she did, he caught the edge of her cardigan, causing her hand to knock the glass over. He had been meaning to deliberately touch her hand. Both of them flushed red.

'Sorry,' they both said at the same time, slightly embarrassed.

'I'm not very good at this,' he said cautiously, 'but I'd quite like to take you out for a drink some time – I mean, if you want to, that is. But if you don't want to, that's fine.'

'I'd love to,' Ciara interrupted him, placing her free hand on his shoulder. She could feel the muscle under it, tense, nervous. It felt unfamiliar to her. But good. Warm.

'Oh,' Brian replied. He hadn't known what to expect, but he hadn't been expecting it to be so easy. 'Oh,' he said again. Ciara quickly removed her hand from his shoulder – maybe he had changed his mind. Then he overcame his surprise and asked, 'What about tomorrow?'

'Tomorrow?'

'Oh, well if you're busy tomorrow, then another time.'

'No, no, tomorrow's fine,' she reassured him.

'What about lunch, then?'

'Lunch?' Ciara repeated.

'Or if you're too busy for lunch, we could have a

coffee?' There were no coffee-houses in Cushendall, but that's what was said on all the American cop dramas that Brian was addicted to.

'No, lunch is fine for me,' she replied.

'Right,' said Brian.

'Right,' said Ciara.

'So, I'll pick you up at about noon?'

'OK,' she said, and picked up the empty glass and walked away. But then she suddenly turned around and said, 'Brian?'

Putting on his jacket, Brian heard her call his name, and his body froze. He looked up at her and said as calmly as he could, 'Yeah?'

'You don't know where I live, do you?'

'Oh, right,' he said, laughing nervously. 'Good job one of us is using our brain!'

It wasn't the smoothest of operations, but it achieved its aim. Fat Annie, who had been surreptitiously watching the gauche display, asked Ciara, in as offhand a voice as she could muster, 'Got yourself a date, then?'

'A date?' Ciara asked, a little startled. 'No, no, pet, nothing like that. Just a little bit of lunch.'

Fat Annie was unconvinced. 'Well, 'night,' she said, her eyebrows slightly raised.

''Night, love,' Ciara said, hoping that Fat Annie hadn't noticed her blushes in the darkness. Ciara couldn't date – she was a mother! With a grown-up son! The thought of it was ridiculous. As far as she was concerned, only young women with cantilevered bottoms, pneumatic breasts and pillowy lips went on dates. In all their fancy finery. To bars where they drank funny-coloured drinks from funny-shaped glasses, and made funny conversation. She had seen these women on the American TV serials that she treated herself to in the evening, along with a cup of tea and a piece of Victoria sponge. *They* went on dates. Not middle-aged women with hollow cheeks and breasts like pocket-flaps. But Brian had seen past that, or rather through it, to someone docile and weak. Someone who might need him.

That night, Ciara couldn't get to sleep. She may have decided that she wasn't going on a date, but she couldn't lie still as thoughts of what to wear and how to fix her hair filled her mind. She turned one way, then another. She wanted to look pretty. If only for once in her life. So she prayed to God for it. She prefaced her prayer with an acknowledgement of both her selfishness (*Lord, I know that there are others in the world with needs far more important than mine*) and her frivolity (*Please forgive me for asking for something so superficial*). Then, palms pressed together, she finally fell asleep.

In the morning, when she got up and looked in the mirror, she was sure there was a change – her eyes seemed brighter and her cheeks rosier. Happy, she opened the bottom drawer of her dressing table, where she stored all of Seph's gifts, unopened, unused, and picked up a bottle of bubble bath. Ciara wasn't one for bubble bath. She felt that bubbles were excessive. But then this, she reasoned, was a special occasion.

After her bath, she sat in front of her dressing table and carefully applied her make-up. She put on the face that she wore for Seph's visits: over-applied pink lipstick and furiously flushed cheeks.

But when she opened the door and Brian saw her, he said, 'You look beautiful.'

He had been taught to say that.

Brian did his utmost to show a keen interest in Ciara and what she had to say – he wanted to show that he wasn't just after one thing. He wanted to know her likes and dislikes. Her favourite colour. What kind of music she liked listening to. Textbook stuff. And then he asked her about Seph.

Brian had known Seph since he was a little boy. Very casually, of course, just a 'Hey' here and an 'All right?' there, but well enough to be interested in how he was getting along. He asked Ciara where Seph worked. She wasn't sure – East London, she said. Or maybe Central. Or maybe North. He asked her what he did. Something to do with business, and money, she said; sorry she couldn't be more precise. He asked whether he had a girlfriend; she didn't know, he never talked to her about that kind of thing. He asked how often she visited him; she never had. Brian was embarrassed and his cheeks burned red. His was meant to have been a friendly inquiry; now he felt as if he was prying. So he changed the topic of conversation and made a mental note never to bring Seph up again.

Since she had moved to Cushendall, no one had ever shown an interest in Ciara, never asked her about herself, never really cared. But now, in Brian, Ciara had found someone who did. When he asked her how she was, he meant it. When he asked her whether she'd had a good day, he meant it. Theirs wasn't a romance of grand gestures: no flowers or fancy dinners or expensive gifts, but it was one of ease and comfort: home-made chicken-and-leek pie, walking the dog holding hands, sitting by the fire watching TV. And Ciara wondered how she'd lived so many years without. She thought about telling Seph over the phone, but then decided that such important news should be imparted face to face. She couldn't wait until next time he came home! He'll be so pleased for me, she thought.

Seph wanted to go home. London had very little time or sympathy for someone who didn't know in which direction they were heading. It didn't indulge unhappiness or sorrow; no time for it, no time for it at all! It offered a father's brusque speech – Come on, boy, pick your chin off the floor and get on with it – not a mother's warm non-judgemental embrace. At least at home he could slow down, have the time to do what he wanted, not what had to be done. He was tired of waking up every morning fantasizing about just fifteen minutes more sleep, his head aching; there were only so many times he could drown his sorrows. He was tired of sitting in meetings where people said, 'I'm not *comfortable* with that suggestion,' when they thought he was wrong. He was tired of thinking about his career plans, and his skill set, and his developmental needs. He was tired of eating a sandwich at his desk every lunchtime, whilst filtering data on a spreadsheet; ordering in Basque chicken and buttered green beans at eight thirty, still working on the same spreadsheet; drinking an extra-strong coffee from the vending machine at midnight, still the same spreadsheet. His life hadn't changed, but he had.

He called Tuhina to say he was sick again. 'I'm really sorry,' he said. He meant it. 'Take your time,' Tuhina said firmly. 'And don't come back in until you're better.' She meant it, too.

He took the first flight home. He had forgotten how, just a few weeks back, he had thought he would never return. Those people he thought he was better than, those people he was no longer one of, those were the people he now wanted to see, who would pat him on the back, offer him sympathy, take care of him. And there was, of course, his mother, whose love and attention was once stifling, suffocating, but who was now the only thing which might get rid of the empty feeling in his belly. And this time, when he arrived at the airport, instead of feeling drained, he felt hopeful.

Ciara didn't open the door. He speculated where she might be on a Thursday morning, but couldn't come up with anything likely, apart from maybe the grocery store. He went to the back of the house and lifted up the flower pot on the kitchen window ledge, where the spare key was kept. 'You'd never keep a spare key outside the house in London!' he thought, trying to fall in love again with the place that had raised him.

But when he went inside, his brow furrowed. Something was different. Something was wrong, although he couldn't work out quite what. He looked around, but he didn't know what he was looking for. Everything looked the same, but something was missing. And then he realized what it was: the smell of his mother's cooking. The smell of home and devotion. He reasoned that he hadn't told Ciara he was coming home, so she wouldn't have known to cook for him as she usually did. Never mind, he thought – as soon as she saw him, he was sure she'd prepare a feast.

In the meantime, he would unpack and then take the dog for a walk; he missed having the dog around. As he climbed the stairs, he called out, 'Meg? Meg?' but there was no bark or familiar pant to indicate she was around. His forehead still creased, he hooked his fingers in his mouth and whistled, and then listened out for the gentle thud of her padded paws hitting the wooden floorboards, but there was no sound. Walking into Ciara's room, he scanned the room for Meg, but she wasn't there. He was about to leave when curiosity got the better of him, and he decided to take a better look. He couldn't justify it, but he convinced himself that what his mother didn't know couldn't hurt her, and besides, what could she possibly have that was secret?

He started in her wardrobe, flipping through the hangers; there seemed to be a few new additions to her sparse collection, which smelled of lavender and treated wood. He wondered what had inspired his mother, who hadn't bought anything new in ten years, to suddenly invest in flippy skirts and beaded sweaters, and decided that she must have finally decided to upgrade her image to match all the expensive creams and perfumes he had bought her.

This conclusion pleased him and a little smile crept on to his face. Next he went to her dressing table. Kneeling on the floor, he opened each drawer; they all contained uninteresting knick-knacks until he came to the last one. In it were all the gifts that he had ever bought for her, lined up neatly, unopened, unused, apart from one bottle of bubble bath. He picked it up, opened it and took a sniff. He hadn't smelled it before he had bought it; the fragrance was intensely floral and seductive. Unsuitable for his mother, he thought, screwing the top back on. Never mind; at least he knew for next time. As he put the bottle back, he felt the corner of something. Pulling out the drawer further, he found three photographs: one of a puppy, one of a family, one of a striking man with an arrogant freckled nose and broad shoulders. He stared at the people in the photograph; he knew them, yet he didn't. They looked like family, but he didn't have any apart from his mother. His belly felt hollow; he didn't want to know this but now he had found out, and he couldn't unknow it.

That's how Ciara found him. Cross-legged and hunched over like a child, not staring *at* the photographs but *into* them. She stood there for a while; so absorbed was he that he didn't notice her, until at last she said quietly, 'Seph?'

He looked up at her, first surprised, then angry.

'Seph,' she pleaded, seeing his expression. But he stormed past her, still clutching the photos, and raced downstairs. Entering the sitting room, he stopped still in his tracks.

'Seph!' said Brian brightly. 'How are you, son?' The over-familiarity made Seph even angrier, and he thrust his hands into his pockets and hunched his shoulders. As soon as he saw him, he knew what Brian was doing to his mother. The thought made him sick to his stomach. And Meg was sitting near Brian's feet, which angered him even more.

Seph didn't reply. He turned around and glared at Ciara. 'What's he doing here?'

Ciara shook. This wasn't how she'd imagined it to be; how it was on the soaps she watched. In them, there would be soft-focus tears, followed by understanding and hugs and redemption. Not rage and bitterness.

When Ciara didn't answer, Brian said, 'I was just helping your mother with some shopping bags . . .'

Seph glanced into the kitchen. He could not see any shopping bags. Now the man was a liar, too. That meant he was scared of Seph – if he wasn't, he wouldn't have lied. This realization calmed Seph down a little – he was the man of the house again.

'I didn't ask you. I asked her,' said Seph clearly, without emotion.

Hearing herself referred to as *her* by her son made Ciara shake even more.

'Please don't be like this, Seph,' she pleaded.

Brian wanted to help her, but he didn't know how. He wasn't sure what would make it better for her – leaving or staying – so he stood still. 'Let me explain. Please.'

'I don't want to know,' Seph said. It wasn't a knee-jerk reaction; he simply didn't see the point.

'But I need to tell you,' she replied.

'Why?' He shrugged. 'Why now?' He didn't seem angry any more. He seemed unconcerned.

Ciara looked at Brian. All he could offer her was a sympathetic look. He felt powerless to say anything; Seph was not his son, nor was he a child.

Then, very calmly, Seph ripped up the photos one by one and dropped the pieces on the floor. 'That's what I think,' he said. He wanted nothing to do with the past any more. He couldn't make himself love her. They were too different, too far apart. He needed someone who understood him. Ciara never would.

Ciara stood in the same spot for a very long time. She didn't sob. She didn't say anything. She just absorbed it all. Brian stood next to her for a very long time, too, although it hurt his rheumatic knees. He didn't say anything either, because he didn't know what to say. But he held her hand very tightly and didn't let go.

CHAPTER SEVENTEEN

Another Case of the What-Ifs?

The crisp cool of autumn came; the sun still shone but every so often there was a gust of wind which chilled to the bone. People started to walk with their heads slightly down, protecting their faces from the occasional bluster, instead of lifting them up to catch the sun; sunflowers turning into frailejon. Scratchy leaves blew across the street like discarded sweet wrappers. Seph watched them from his office window and rubbed his arms. He had given himself a schedule to stick to: wake up at quarter to seven, ten minutes in the shower, a pretzel and a large coffee on the way to work, an hour's run at lunchtime, an hour's swim in the evening. Routine was a brace for his mind.

But on Sundays, the most melancholy day of the week, a March moth compared to Saturday's Emperor butterfly, he couldn't help but let his mind break free, and the man who had always been worshipped and adored felt lonely. Memories of his mother were already fading. They had started to change from widescreen movies in vivid Technicolor to scratchy home cinefilms.

He took it in turns to feel sorry for, then angry with himself. He looked back and realized that his pride had turned into arrogance, his indifference into callousness, and his confidence into vanity. Everyone's weaknesses are manifestations of their strengths.

And then there was *her*. It was now Seph's turn to suffer from a case of the what-ifs. First of all he tried to argue himself out of it. He remembered something that Father O'Neill had once told him about worrying – 'Think to yourself, in ten years' time will this really matter? Will I wonder why I cared at all? Will I laugh at myself for having worried so much?' He had said it in a voice which implied experience and erudition; at the time, Seph had thought it profound. Now he realized it was trite. But he wondered whether there was any truth in it, all the same.

He tried to convince himself that it wasn't Darshini he missed, but the things she did. The way she went to sleep with her face pushed between his shoulder blades; the way she knew when he wanted a cigarette before he did, and lit one for him; the way she buttoned up his shirt. But his emotions had context. He didn't simply miss intimacy in the abstract, he missed intimacy with *her*. He didn't miss being loved; he missed being loved by *her*. And when he finally allowed himself to come to that realization, he knew what he had to do.

Seph, who had fought against the irrationality of faith all his life, had nowhere else to turn. Pulling his Saint Joseph locket from the shoe box, he made his way north across the city to the church of St Mary Magdalen. By the time he arrived he was late for the six-thirty mass, and the choir had already started to sing the Kyrie. Seph stole into the back row, hoping that no one would notice him. He didn't want to be seen in church. He didn't want to have anything in common with the other bowed heads; surely he could sort his own problems out? But then why was he here? He blew on his hands to keep them warm. He hadn't been to church for so long that he was a split-second behind the rest of the congregation. When they rose elegantly, he scrambled to his feet; when they kneeled gracefully, he dropped untidily to his knees. Surely someone would peg him as an impostor? So concerned was he with keeping up appearances that he forgot why he was actually there. So worried was he about being noticed that he forgot that the others were not there for him but for Him. It was only after the priest and the altar boys had filed out to the sombre sound of Mozart's B Minor Adagio, and the people had left, after bowing to the altar and fervently crossing themselves, that Seph found himself in the church alone with God. And, boy, did he have a lot of explaining to do.

He started off with peripheral topics: how he'd been, what he'd been up to; he thought it would be rude to make a request at the outset. The conversation was awkward and one-sided at first, but then the two started chatting as if they were old friends. And when Seph finally told Him about what he'd done, instead of feeling judged he felt relieved; at last he had shared his burden.

An hour later, as Seph left the solitude of the church for the tumult of the darkening streets, still clutching the Saint Joseph locket tightly, he said to himself silently, over and over again, *Peace be with me, Peace be with me.*

Prakash moped around the house rather like a fading sports star whose glory days were behind him, looking at photographs of himself when he was younger. What was there to look forward to now? The one member of his fan club had left. Not that he was prone to histrionics; but now there was no one for him to fret over and nothing for him to busy himself with. The two-headed tigress didn't need him in the same way. Mousumi had gone, and he once again felt alone; his day was longer, more elastic, more empty. He felt his age. Mousumi hadn't fooled him into feeling younger, in the way of an Eastern European blonde hanging off the arm of a balding middle-aged man in a gold-buttoned blazer; what she had done (albeit inadvertently) was to make him not care about getting old, not wish he had a different life, had made different choices, but to live for the moment, to *stop worrying*.

But now, ambling around the empty house (where *was* the two-headed tigress?), he started thinking again. What had he been working so hard for all these years? *This?* Why, for a start, did they need so many rooms? They didn't use them; they hardly ever went into them, forgodssake.

Whenever Prakash was in a bad mood, he would reject materialism. He liked taking on the role of an ascetic upon whom the corporeal world had been forced, a position he thought to be beyond reproach. He went into his favourite room – the kitchen – and appraised all the fancy gadgets – the juicer, the coffee machine which hissed like an angry cat, the blender with its four-speed setting, the stainless-steel hob with eight plates and a special contraption for cooking in a wok. It all seemed clinical and superfluous to him now. Had his own mother not crouched in a corner grinding spices in a stone mortar, frying them in mustard oil on a kerosene-fuelled burner? And the dishwasher – Tuhina didn't even allow its use! Prakash puffed out his chest indignantly and marched into the silent garden. 'Call this a garden!' he said out loud. There was no response, no calming cacophony of crickets; English insects were far too polite to make a noise!

He went back inside and made his way into the den. In the corner stood a forty-two-inch plasma-screen television which had been accessorized with the complete cable sports package – a Christmas gift from Tuhina to him, so he could watch all the cricket matches he liked. Presents were his favourite target; his ingratitude was always ex post facto. It was just showing off, he thought to himself, as he ran his hand over the smooth screen. Hadn't he survived in India with only a transistor radio? (His family, being reasonably wealthy, had had one even before the transistor-radio-in-exchange-for-sterilization programme – something he was quite proud of.) Prakash could always do without when there was no chance of *being* without.

What had been Mousumi's reaction when she had seen Hariprasad at the airport with her mother? She had barely registered, she was so morose. They had approached her with wide smiles and open arms, and she had responded with a polite nod of her head. When Rekha had asked her whether anything was wrong, she had replied, in a sterner tone than she had ever used before, 'I'm tired.' Surprise had flashed across her mother's face. In the airport loos, she had scowled at the beggar-woman crouching in the corner, offering a jug of water with which to wash her hands. When Hariprasad had suggested he carry her suitcase, she had shrugged him off. And when she had got outside, she had complained about the heat and dust and the too many people. Rekha had felt embarrassed; she had told Hariprasad what a mild-mannered and respectful daughter she had. And instead he had been confronted by a right little madam. Sachi had been right about Western influences.

Hariprasad himself had been perplexed. At dinner that night, Mousumi had toyed around with her meal, chewing sulkily where she would have once wolfed it down. By virtue of her size, he had imagined that Mousumi would have been a girl who liked her food, but she had displayed little interest in the dishes that he and Rekha had painstakingly prepared for her welcome-home meal. And she had said nothing, apart from asking Rekha to pass the salt, which she had done with an unnecessary amount of formality and with a very English *please* on the end. As they had munched away in silence, he had wondered to himself: Where was the uncertain dreamer? She didn't look so unsure now, with her mouth set in a defiant sulk, and her once wistful eyes hard and cold. The girl who had once pored over movie-star magazines had now turned into a diva herself. She had even gone to bed without eating dessert.

In fact, she was just miserable. Mousumi hadn't missed the boat, she had jumped off it, landing in a murky river. What irked her the most was that she hadn't been pushed; she had taken the step herself. As she sat on her mattress a couple of weeks later, and heard the clang of metal as her mother washed the pots, she felt her extravagant stories rotting in her stomach – who would listen to them now? Instead of being surrounded by an appreciative audience of gentle geriatrics, she would have to face the haughty indifference of teenage girls, who would contradict her tales with a sneering 'Yeah, *right*,' so why bother at all? Seeking criticism, not praise, may be conducive to self-improvement, but it is hardly balm for an already frail ego. She remembered sitting in Prakash's car, in the front passenger seat generally reserved for grown-ups, deciding which radio channel to listen to (Prakash always let her choose unless there was cricket commentary on). At home, she had usually taken the bus, and the few times that she had been in a taxi she had been seated in the back, whilst her father lounged in the front telling the driver exactly which route to take. The sound of whining dogs, once the beginning of a lullaby, was now fingernails scratched against a blackboard; she longed for the night-time silence of her English room. Her blood was nectar to the nocturnal mosquitoes which settled on her bare legs; in England, the only bugs she had seen were fuzzy bumble-bees making their rounds of the flowerbeds, and a delicate garden-spider spinning its web between the branches of a bay tree. Cruel nostalgia, which turns the future grey and bathes the past in blushing shades of rose and lilac, had begun its insidious attack as soon as she had boarded the plane.

After fourteen days of Sulkiness, Rekha wanted 'words' with her errant daughter. It wasn't a job she relished – that had been under Sachi's jurisdiction – but she had to fulfil her duty. She wondered where to begin. She had to be firm without being confrontational, she decided as she wiped her hands with purpose. But she also had another problem, which was how to introduce Hariprasad. For the last two weeks, she had been sneaking out like a teenager to meet him, telling Mousumi that she was going shopping. Hariprasad, in his endeavours to see Mousumi again, had tried to convince Rekha that the best thing would be for him to visit the house so that Mousumi would have the opportunity to acclimatize to him, but Rekha was having none of it. But then she had realized that she couldn't keep sneaking around for ever. She tried out some lines, looking at herself in the bathroom mirror, putting on the face of a calm and understanding mother.

'Hariprasad has been very good to me since your father died, and from now on I want you to accept him as family.' No; too authoritative.

'Hariprasad is a friend of ours. He'll be spending some time with us from now on, so I hope you'll make an effort to get along with him.' No; too casual.

'You know the nice gentleman who met you at the airport a couple of weeks ago? Well, he's become a good friend of mine since your father died, and been very kind to me.' No; too vague.

'What do you think of Hariprasad?' No; too open-ended.

Rekha pursed her lips. The task was turning out to be more difficult than she had anticipated. The problem, of course, was that she was trying to retain her respectability by not revealing too much, putting clothes on the naked fact to cover its modesty.

But as is often the case, all her preparation was wasted and the matter was taken out of her hands when a familiar persistent knocking on the door was heard. Rekha, wrapped in a towel, tried to pull on her clothes – it would be inconceivable to open the door in a state of undress, even for her lover – but as she pulled the chemise, which rumpled and clung as it touched her damp skin, over her head, she heard Mousumi say, 'Ma, I'll see who it is.'

She heard the door creaking open (the hinges still hadn't been oiled – Hariprasad was a Romantic and not one for DIY) and put her ear up against the wall to see if she could hear what was being said. There was definitely a conversation going on, but the voices and words collided to produce an indistinct wave of noise. Then it stopped. She heard footsteps approach the bathroom, and hastily struggled to pull her top over her breasts, even though the door was bolted shut. The skin on her lower back came out in goosebumps as droplets from her hair dripped on to it. What had been said? Had the truth been revealed? Rekha felt naked.

'Ma?' Mousumi called through the door.

'Hmmm?'

'I'm just going to the shop with Hariprasad to buy some sweet samosas for breakfast.' The lack of *Uncle* in front of his name made Rekha wince. Where had the girl's manners gone?

'OK,' she replied, her voice rising slightly as she started to panic.

'How are you settling back in, then?' Hariprasad asked Mousumi as they walked along Park Street.

His tone was jolly, upbeat. Walking side by side, she stared straight ahead as he looked at her profile, anticipating that she would turn around to answer him.

'Fine,' she replied simply, turning the other way to look at two scrawny dogs fornicating on the street – although they didn't look as if they had enough strength – as an irate shopkeeper tried to separate them with a stick. Then she turned her head to face him, equally indifferently, and gave him an 'And?' look. He wasn't prepared for that. Her shy vulnerability had been replaced by succinct frankness. Once a Lamb's Ear, she was now a thistle. He stuttered, searching for the right thing to say, the sentences that would soften her, massage her back into the luscious fat dreamer.

'You must be pleased to be back home,' he suggested. Mousumi didn't say anything. Hariprasad decided to change tack. 'Do you remember me?' he said, comic in tone, almost like a whooping chimpanzee, as if there wasn't the possibility that she didn't.

'Yes,' she said, unimpressed by his clowning around. When Prakash had fooled around, Mousumi reminisced, by telling her rude jokes about his patients' bits and pieces, and mimicking them, it was funny. This man wasn't Prakash and he certainly wasn't funny. He was too try-hard. She wished he'd shut up and leave her in peace. She'd never had that wish before.

'Remember the magazines I used to let you read in my shop?' he continued. He said the 'I' lightly, but lingered on it long enough to make sure that she was reminded that he had done something for her; not for it to be seen as a favour, of course, but rather a gift.

'Yes,' she said, not with any antagonism but certainly without gratitude. Again, Hariprasad was stumped. Again, he found himself rummaging around for something to say. Again, he tried to remind her of her link to him.

'Do you still like those sweets I used to give to you? Creamy Kisses? We can go and get some now, if you like.'

'No, thank you,' she replied. She didn't like Creamy Kisses any more. She liked Galaxy chocolate, wrapped in golden foil and chilled in the fridge for precisely an hour and a half (any more than that, Prakash had said, and you'd break your teeth).

Hariprasad's was a schoolboy error. Quite simply, he had focussed his attention on himself and not on her. He may have been asking her questions, but they were all about him. He hadn't even asked her whether she had enjoyed her trip to England. For one so considerate, how careless!

In the sweet shop (one of his, of course), he

noticed her looking at the tray of soft shandesh.

'I bet you haven't had any of that in a while!' He smiled. Maybe that was the key: soft shandesh. The way to a fat girl's heart is surely through her stomach.

'Actually, Prakash used to buy it for me when I was in England. It's nicer than the stuff here,' she said, rather melancholically. Mousumi's un-intentional double offence hit Hariprasad hard; his face burned as if it had been scratched by a kunoichi's neko-te.

'Nicer?' he trembled. 'Or just different?'

'Nicer,' she confirmed.

Hariprasad bit his lip. 'And who's Prakash?' he asked, even though he had already been told by Rekha.

'My uncle.' There was a certain yearning in her voice.

'Oh,' said Hariprasad.

No fear; one so devoted would not give up so easily, but Hariprasad realized that he had to retreat and regroup. He *would* win back her affections; it was just a matter of devotion. And time.

When they arrived back at the house, Rekha was ready to be confronted, but nothing happened. And although Mousumi was vaguely curious as to how her mother had met Hariprasad, she certainly wasn't about to ask. They weren't friends, they were mother and daughter. And children should respect their parents; to question her mother in any way would, she felt, be questioning her authority. So they all ate their sweet samosas in silence.

Since returning to India, Mousumi had refused to go back to school. At first, Rekha had just thought that she needed a period of readjustment, time to get back into her daily routine. But Mousumi was still showing no sign of wanting to go back. Ever. And although Rekha didn't think education was that important, it wasn't as if Mousumi was helping with the cooking or cleaning either. Neither did she show any interest in finding a husband – the one time Rekha had mentioned it, Mousumi had said casually, with no feeling, 'I don't want to get married.'

Rekha had gone to the kitchen and sobbed silently. 'It's just a phase she's going through,' she told herself. 'God will give me good things in the end; I just have to have faith.' But all Mousumi seemed to do was watch makeover shows on television and read fashion magazines. And since her father's death, she didn't even try to hide the fact that she did these things. Going to England was supposed to have increased her worth on the husband market, but it had done just the opposite.

Neither was Hariprasad proving to be any help. Rekha thought that he may have been able to show

376

some fatherly authority and tell Mousumi to get her act together, but each time Rekha complained about her behaviour, all he said was, 'Oh, let her be, let her be . . .'

In fact, Mousumi's crabbiness was turning out to Hariprasad's advantage – by defending her, he hoped that she would see him as her ally. And although he had been surprised by the change in her manner when she had first returned, after a few days he had quite warmed to her – there was something quite loin-stirring about her un-responsiveness; there was nothing he liked more than a challenge. The best way to warm her up, he thought, was to show an interest in the same things as her. So Hariprasad became her TV-watching companion and provider of fashion magazines. He learned all about skin types (after a quick appraisal, he thought Mousumi was probably a combination type); body shapes (Mousumi's shape wasn't clear, but he generously termed it hourglass) and how to dress each kind; the importance of a base coat; and how to tone that tricky area at the top of your thighs. And each day, he sat a little closer to her on the sofa, making sure that whenever he passed her the plate of onion bhajis, their fingers touched. And she smiled at him. And started to laugh at his jokes. She was giving him all the right signals. He knew what she wanted.

In truth, Mousumi was beginning to warm to Hariprasad, but not in the way he thought. She thought he was funny, a bit like a court jester. And he didn't nag her, like her mother. But that was about it. Nothing less, but certainly nothing more.

Rekha had decided enough was enough and had gone to have her palm read by Babaji. He would tell her what was what. Babaji looked at Rekha's expression carefully. She looked both down-in-the-dumps and fed-up. What do middle-aged women usually get depressed about? he pondered. Children, he thought, maybe husbands. And as she was one of his favourite customers, he decided to give her good news on the family front, something that would cheer her up.

Meanwhile, Hariprasad decided to seize his chance. Sitting on the couch with Mousumi, watching an infomercial on covering grey (All you have to do is spray it on! So simple and easy to use! And it won't come off on you or anyone else!), he made his move. Sidling up to her slowly, he watched for her reaction. She seemed absorbed in watching the TV. She's playing hard to get, the little minx, he thought. When he was inches away, he launched himself at her, his tongue down her ear and his hand up her skirt. Mousumi screamed and leapt up.

'What the fuck do you think you're doing, you cunt?' she yelled. She spoke in Bengali, apart from the 'cunt' – obviously she had learned bad language in England, too, Hariprasad noted.

'But I thought . . .'

'But you thought what?' she screeched.

'Sssh, sssh,' he whispered, trying to calm her down; he was worried that the neighbours might hear the racket she was making.

'Why?' she asked, a crease appearing between her eyebrows. 'Are you worried that the neighbours will hear? And tell my mum?'

At the second sentence, Hariprasad felt as if he had been shot in the belly. His face lost all its colour and his eyes widened. 'You wouldn't!' he pleaded. He hadn't accounted for that possibility. Indeed, he hadn't accounted for anything other than success.

'Wouldn't I?' Mousumi said slowly, a little plan starting to formulate in her mind.

'Please don't,' Hariprasad begged.

'What's it worth?' she asked, raising her eyebrows.

Hariprasad was confused. 'What do you mean?' he said.

'I mean, how much money do I get to keep my mouth shut?'

'A thousand rupees?' he enquired tentatively.

'A thousand rupees!' she spat. Just *one* of Darshini's lipsticks would cost more than a thousand rupees – she had worked that out a long time ago. She wasn't going that cheaply. All those fancy pots of creams and lotions that Darshini had, all those lovely clothes – she would have them too. Why shouldn't she?

'Twenty thousand rupees,' she announced, as if the amount were of no significance.

'Twenty?' Hariprasad gulped. But he knew he had no choice.

They went to the ATM together, where Mousumi leaned over his shoulder, taking delight in watching him punch in 2 0 0 0 0. And as soon as the notes emerged, she presented her hand and Hariprasad placed them squarely in her palm.

'Thank you!' she said. 'I'll see you at home, later.'

Rekha nearly dropped dead when she saw Mousumi that evening. Her mouth lolled open like a gummy Great Dane's, and she squinted at her daughter as if she had the sun in her eyes. Gone was the long, oily hair, replaced by a glossy, angular bob. The bushy eyebrows had been shaped into perfect arches. The grubby nails had been manicured into smooth ovals and varnished a deep blood red. Her ill-fitting and dowdy clothes had been replaced by a pair of jeans and a T-shirt. She resembles someone I know, thought Rekha, but I can't quite put my finger on who. The only thing she could manage to say was, 'Where did you get the money to do all of that?'

'Uncle was very generous to me,' said Mousumi,

smiling sweetly at her mother first, then Hariprasad.

'Is that true?' Rekha asked him, shocked.

Hariprasad simply nodded. Rekha was overcome with emotion – he was already treating Mousumi like his own daughter – and her already tremulous body trembled even more. 'Have you said "thank you" to Uncle?' she asked, dabbing at her eyes.

'Of course I have,' Mousumi said happily, adding carefully, 'and I've also decided to go back to school next week. I think I'm ready now.'

At this, the tears started to flow freely from Rekha's eyes. All that worry for nothing. Dabaji had said as much.

God hasn't given me a bad hand, she thought as she went to sleep that night, still sniffling a little.

CHAPTER EIGHTEEN

It Ain't Over 'Til the Fat Lady Sings

Tuhina sat at her desk, feeling pleased. She had eaten two rocket and crayfish salads, a lemon torte and some fruit-vegetable-herb concoction made by a company which her bank had financed (It was green. She felt relieved that it wasn't *her* who had made the deal), and her belly felt satisfied. In fact, after all that food she felt rather snoozy and content.

She got up from her desk and closed the door to her office, standing against it and looking over her room. Although not one to admire her own achievements, there was nothing wrong with taking stock. She had had her own office for fifteen years; that was something, wasn't it? The rubber plant which had been there from the beginning (of Management Level) was starting to lose its shine, but it had aged gracefully. The maroon Chesterfield leather sofa was looking worn on the seats, although not on the back (people always leaned forward when talking to Tuhina); but it looked distinguished, not tattered. A little smile crept on to her lips.

She walked to the glass panelling at the front of her office, and saw a rumba of rattling women standing around Penelope's screen (Looking at what? she thought. Shoes maybe, or a picture of a film star?). Tuhina liked shoes and film stars, too, but she had no inclination to look at them with the other women. She wondered briefly whether she wasn't sociable enough, but then decided that even if she wasn't – and who was the judge? – that was how she preferred it. Every so often, Tuhina would question herself, just to make sure there was no room for improvement, and then accept herself – no, there wasn't!

Turning her back to the wall, she stood in front of her desk and looked at the photograph of her and Darshini (taken by Prakash) on the wall. She cocked her head and looked closely at Darshini's swimming costume with the double frill on the hip. A happy, carefree type of frill. Only the very young can get away with frills, she mused. And then she looked at Darshini's face staring at her, expectant, entirely dependent. It made her smile. Those were good days, she thought. Not that she was sentimental. Of course not. But then she corrected herself: *these* are good days. Only those who don't appreciate what they have wallow in the past.

She suddenly wondered whether Rekha had a similar photograph, of Rekha holding Mousumi as a child. She didn't think so. She couldn't imagine Sachi taking such a photo. Although when they had been children, in the time when having your photograph taken was a special occasion, he had wanted to be in every one. Once, as her mother Joya was trying to take a portrait of her in a pink silk dress with a lace underskirt, in the shade of a flowering sandalwood tree which matched her outfit, Sachi had interrupted. At first, he had merely tried to distract Joya, but as his efforts proved to no avail, he insisted that he too would be in the photo.

'Let me take one of your sister, and then I'll take one of you,' Joya had said, trying to appease him. But he was having none of it. *He* would either be in the photograph or it would not be taken at all. Afterwards, when Joya gently asked whether he might in return take a photograph of herself and Tuhina, he refused, and walked off even as she tried to hand the camera to him. It incensed Tuhina just thinking about it. And looking at the photo again, she felt lucky. Not that she was a believer in Luck. She had always considered her position in life to be the product of hard work and determination (a surprisingly Protestant view for someone raised a Hindu), but there is a gap which only Luck can fill. This thought made her feel sad. The afternoon was turning out to be an emotional trampoline, and Tuhina wasn't one to get emotional at work. Or ever, if it could be helped. Maybe there was something funny in the green drink. She took a deep breath to clear her mind, saw a pile of paper on her desk and decided to get back to work. Enough was enough.

Prakash decided to call Tuhina at work. He usually only called when there was a domestic problem – a leaking washing machine, a bust boiler, a burst pipe. Those kind of problems flustered him, and he relied on Tuhina to deal with them. But this time he was calling because he was at a loose end . . . well, lonely. Tuhina looked at the caller ID and wondered what had broken this time.

'Hello,' she said pleasantly. 'What's gone wrong, then?'

'Nothing,' Prakash replied.

'Then why are you calling me?' Tuhina asked, slightly perplexed, slightly brusque.

'Just for chat.'

Just for chat; the phrase disorientated Tuhina. Prakash never called just for a chat. She looked at her watch: three o'clock. Far too early for him to have taken any pills or drunk any alcohol. 'Oh,' she said. Awkward silence. 'So are you having a good day at work?'

'Yes. Are you?'

'Yes,' she said. The pile of paper wasn't getting any smaller.

'So, what would you like for dinner tonight?'

'Anything you like.' She fiddled with her pen, and began to tap it rhythmically on her desk.

'OK. I'll think of something nice for you.'

'Thank you,' she replied, the beating becoming faster. There was more silence, but still he didn't put the phone down.

'What time you think you will be home?'

'About eight, I should think.'

'OK, see you then. Bye.'

Tuhina rolled her eyes. 'Bye,' she said as she dropped the pen and put the phone down promptly.

Having made the call, Prakash felt better. Tuhina felt better once it had ended. But the conversation had acted as a painkiller for Prakash, treating the symptoms but not the cause.

First of all, he called in sick for afternoon surgery.

'Rose Mary,' he said slowly.

'Yes, Dr Majumdar?' She replied even more slowly.

'I'm not very well,' he said firmly.

'Oh dear, Doctor!' Rosemary said, not overly concerned. 'What's wrong?'

'I'm not sure,' he replied, stalling for time. He hadn't thought through his made-up illness very carefully. 'I think I have a problem in my head . . . in my throat, more specifically.' He did a little cough-cough to demonstrate, then continued, 'Throat *and* nose,' and sniffed loudly.

'Well,' Rosemary announced drily, 'you sound absolutely *terrible*. You must go straight to bed!'

'Yes, I think you're right.' Prakash sounded stoical, forgetting for a moment that he wasn't actually sick. 'I think I will probably have afternoon off and take some rest.' Then he added as an afterthought, 'You will be able to find a locum?'

'Of course.' Rosemary had flipped open her Rolodex to the locum agency's number the moment she had heard Prakash's opening gambit. 'Don't worry yourself with that,' she soothed.

'Thank you.' Prakash suddenly felt a little sheepish.

'Oh, you're quite welcome, Doctor,' Rosemary said, a knowing smile on her face.

After putting the phone down, he fixed himself a stiff drink. Well, stiff for just past three in the afternoon. If only it was seven, he mused, he could have justified a stronger aperitif – he needed to steady himself for what was about to happen. He was going to teach that two-headed tigress! He was going to show what he was made of! Sterner stuff than he had ever been given credit for, that was for sure! And then she would miss him, and realize how much she needed him and how much she loved him . . . Absence was guaranteed to make her heart grow fonder!

First of all, he made a list, headed IMPORTANT THINGS:

1. Money (cash for general use, credit card for plane ticket to India, debit card for alcohol & other miscellaneous goods from Duty Free)
2. Keys (both house and car)
3. Change of underpants (toothbrush & paste usually provided)
4. Lucky handkerchief.

He was proud of his list – it showed his organization and foresight. He wondered whether he should write a note to inform her of his grand plan. No, he decided; she thought she was so clever – she should be able to work it out. And perhaps he should call Mousumi? No, it would be even better as a surprise, he decided.

After all his effort, Prakash decided to take a little nap and bounced up the stairs to his bedroom; he felt he deserved a snooze. Unfortunately, his celebratory drink had been a little stronger than he thought, and he fell into a deep sleep where he dreamed of his teeth falling out.

He woke up to the sound of canned laughter.

Bleary-eyed, he could see that the television was on. Tuhina hadn't wanted a television in their bedroom but she had grudgingly allowed him one. He didn't remember turning it on. He looked across at Tuhina's side of the bed – there was a bowl of tortilla chips and a small jar of salsa on the bedside cabinet. He ran his tongue across his teeth and down the insides of his cheeks – he couldn't taste salsa and tortilla chips, only slightly alcoholic bad breath. On his bedside cabinet was his list. Instinctively, he reached out for it and put it under his pillow, and then drew the covers up to his chin. He needed to get out of bed, but he felt groggy.

'You're awake!' Darshini exclaimed as she walked in. 'You were fast asleep! You didn't budge even when I pushed you, and not even when I turned the TV on!' She jumped back on to the bed next to her father, and put her hand on his forehead. 'Are you OK?' she asked, concerned. 'Mum called and said that Rosemary had phoned her to say you'd called in sick or something. What's wrong with you?' She was peering at him carefully, looking for a clue to his complaint.

'I just don't feel very well.'

'Well, don't worry, Dad,' she said, giving him a kiss on the cheek. 'I'll look after you. I'll make you some chicken soup. And toast. That will make you feel better.' And then she nestled up to him and

389

continued watching TV. Prakash's Grand Plan had ended as quickly as it had started.

Tuhina didn't need to see the note to know what Prakash had been planning. When she went to bed that night, carefully removing the empty soup bowl from his bedside table, she sat by him and stroked his back gently before getting ready for bed. It was only a small gesture, but she wanted to make it.

Darshini decided to skip school. In fact, she had been skipping school for the past week. She had attended the first day of term, where her class had been told that this was the year where their futures were decided (no one was sure whether this was a scare tactic or encouragement) and that they had to think hard about what they wanted to achieve and then work even harder for it! But she wasn't interested. How could she care about maths and chemistry and economics when she was so miserable? How were equations and graphs and formulae going to help her? So the next day she wrote, on her dad's headed paper from the surgery, that tests were being conducted on one Miss Darshini Majumdar; she thought that sounded ominous enough. Her teachers would be updated as soon as the results came through – the good doctor didn't want to speculate in the meantime, although the prognosis wasn't promising (well, there's nothing wrong with a little melodrama from time to time).

Tuhina knew exactly what she was up to, but she didn't say anything. She wondered how long it would go on for. She was concerned, but not overly anxious; she decided to keep a close eye on the proceedings.

What amazed Darshini was how easy it was to do absolutely nothing. Contrary to first appearances, the unflappable demeanour which belongs to an unlined brow, she was actually a bit of a fidget. She especially couldn't stop moving her hands. Seph would often take both of hers in one of his and squeeze so hard that she couldn't move them again for half an hour. 'That'll stop you from fidgeting – it's not ladylike!' he used to say. But now she discovered that her hands were happy to do absolutely nothing, along with the rest of her. Nothing, apart from breathe and stare into the mid-distance. That was all she wanted to do, and *could* do: nothing. Either that, or sleep. Minutes turn into hours turn into days turn into weeks turn into a whole fucking lifetime, Darshini thought. Maybe she could spend the rest of her life doing nothing.

Then after two weeks, sitting on the sofa one morning, staring out of the window at nothing in particular, Darshini felt something digging into the underside of her right thigh. Getting up slowly, she looked down to find a ten-pence coin. She hadn't tossed a coin since – well, *since*. She picked it up and ran over the raised image of the lion with her thumb. It felt familiar, reassuring. Maybe just once more, she thought, just once more.

She sat with the coin in her hand for three hours. Prakash came home for lunch to find her sitting on the sofa, staring blankly ahead.

'Why aren't you at school again?' he asked.

'I'm not very well,' she said in a voice which implied she was perfectly fine.

'What's the wrong?'

'Just general illness.'

He put the palm of his hand on her forehead; it was a nice temperature, moist but not clammy, a very healthy forehead, in fact.

'Take rest,' he said, and then went to the kitchen to make her some chicken soup, just in case.

After Prakash left for his afternoon surgery, Darshini went up to her bedroom. She started rooting around in the drawers of her bureau looking for something, she wasn't sure what, but she knew that as soon as she came across it all would become clear.

It was a photograph taken of them, in Seph's bed, just before they went to sleep. Seph had held his camera at arm's length, the other arm around Darshini's shoulder, and taken the picture. The top of her right nipple showed, not covered by the duvet. 'Like a Cadbury's Chocolate Button!' Seph had said when the photo had been developed. Darshini had rolled her eyes but it had made her smile anyway. She looked carefully at his face, the lean, muscular arm around her shoulder, the creases in the skin which covered his stomach. It gave her bellyache. She flipped the coin.

Seph returned home, agitated. He had been rummaging through his desk at work, looking for a pencil sharpener (for a propelling pencil – that's how distracted he was), when he had come across a wallet of photographs. There was a Quality Street assortment: friends with their arms around each other and unfocussed, half-shut eyes; some blurred shots of blurred things; one of the photocopier (question mark); one of the team assistant's over-sized bottom (question mark, exclamation mark); and some of random people he didn't quite recognize but who weren't entirely unfamiliar either. Seph asked himself why on earth he would take such an incoherent bunch of photographs in the first place. He wasn't usually one for either taking photographs or appearing in them. He flicked through them again. Something seemed to be missing. Then he recalled that it wasn't his camera which had been used to take the photographs, but a disposable one which had been left at an office drinks night. But why had the photographs ended up with him? He counted them – there was one missing. It took him a few minutes to recall who the last photo had been of. His stomach lurched. 'Just to finish the film off' he had said to quieten her protestations.

As soon as he returned home, he started looking for it. There wasn't much to search through; he wasn't a hoarder. Suddenly the photograph meant everything to him; it was concrete evidence, proof that she wasn't just a figment of his imagination, proof that *they* had not been imaginary. Then he remembered that he had given it to her. It was her possession; and it was her decision whether or not to destroy it.

Darshini hadn't been out of the house for days. She ventured out huddled in a coat and scarf, even though the weather didn't really warrant them. In her coat pocket was the photograph. It was already dark.

She wondered what to say if she saw him, but she wasn't one to plan. Although she then ingenuously planned to say whatever came into her head. By the time she arrived at the door to his apartment block, she had convinced herself that he wouldn't be there, and then she would know and another chapter would be closed. She pressed on the buzzer, but there was no response. She agonized over whether to press it again, and rubbed the coin, which was still in her hand. And then she heard a voice behind her.

'Hey,' it said quietly. It was the kind of voice which would be used to summon a cat – *Here, kitty kitty*. She turned around and saw him standing a few feet away. If there had been anything in her head she would have said it, but all she could do was pull a face, at once both self-conscious and aloof. She was unable to look him in the eye, and her gaze darted from his nose to his lips to his hands to his lovely, lovely feet.

'Are you going to say anything?' he coaxed.

'I can't think of anything to say,' she said sheepishly.

'Neither can I,' he admitted.

He moved towards her and cupped a hand gently around her neck; his thumb ran over the lump in her throat. Leaning down, he kissed her. She didn't respond, but neither did she pull away. Her face and mouth were warm, but her nose was cold. He rubbed it a little with his fingers.

'Your nose is cold, but the rest of you is warm. It's funny.' He smiled.

'I know,' she said, scrunching up her nose. 'I think I have bad circulation in my nose.'

So he kissed it to warm it up. And then they went inside.

Mousumi stood in front of the mirror and admired her new shell. She held up her freshly painted nails and rested her palm underneath her chin and her fingers on her cheek, as if someone had asked her a very interesting question and she was deep in thought. Then she slowly rocked her head, so that she could watch her short shiny hair swing from side to side. She pressed her glossed lips together and pouted. She fluttered her mascara-loaded eye-lashes and coyly touched her throat. Then she picked up the hairbrush from the dressing table and held it to her lips. She smiled coyly, as if she were teasing her audience over which song she might choose. And then she sang and sang and sang. And she didn't care who heard.

THE END

Acknowledgements

I'd like to thank, in no particular order:

My family: JB, AKB and Ali McFunz for your love and patience.

Alex, for constantly administering love, affection and understanding in large doses.

Ann-Margret and Katie, for being the best friends a lady could possibly have or wish for.

Lucinda (Her Majesty) Hicks, for calming me down when I'm screaming and shouting.

Peter, for all the help, thoughtful comments and *constructive* criticism!

Victoria Darling, for being patient, when I'm not.

Sarah (Radio) F-M, for listening to me go on and on and on. And on.

Jo, for providing much-needed support and understanding.

Clare, for indulging my love of otiose conversation.

Tom, for the highest-quality banter and blarney!

Gerry, for telling me to get on with it . . . (You are a gentleman, sir.)

Ayesha Karim, without whose encouragement I wouldn't and couldn't have persevered.

My editor Jane, for believing in me . . .

You're all stars.

Q & A
Vikas Swarup

'THIS BRILLIANT STORY, AS COLOSSAL, VIBRANT
AND CHAOTIC AS INDIA ITSELF . . . IS NOT
TO BE MISSED'
Observer

How a penniless waiter from Mumbai became the
biggest quiz-show winner in history . . .

Eighteen-year-old Ram Mohammad Thomas is in prison
after answering twelve questions correctly on a TV quiz
show to win one billion rupees. The producers have
arrested him, convinced that he has cheated his way
to victory. Twelve extraordinary events in street-kid
Ram's life – how he was found in a dustbin by a priest;
came to have three names; fooled a professional hitman;
even fell in love – give him the crucial answers. In his
warm-hearted tale lies all the comedy, tragedy, joy
and pathos of modern India.

'A ROLLICKING READ AS WELL AS BEING A
POLISHED, VARNISHED, FINISHED WORK OF
IMPRESSIVE CRAFTSMANSHIP'
Hindustan Times

'*Q &A* IS A POIGNANT, FUNNY, RICH, BEAUTIFULLY
WRITTEN NOVEL WITH AN UTTERLY ORIGINAL AND
BRILLIANT STRUCTURE AT ITS HEART. A RARE JOY'
Meg Rosoff, author of *How I Live Now*

'SWARUP IS AN ACCOMPLISHED STORYTELLER'
Daily Mail

0 552 77250 X

BLACK SWAN

A SELECTED LIST OF FINE WRITING
AVAILABLE FROM BLACK SWAN

77115 5	BRICK LANE	*Monica Ali*	£7.99
99313 1	OF LOVE AND SHADOWS	*Isabel Allende*	£7.99
77243 7	CASE HISTORIES	*Kate Atkinson*	£7.99
77240 2	SAYONARA BAR	*Susan Barker*	£6.99
77386 7	ONE NIGHT AT THE CALL CENTRE	*Chetan Bhagat*	£6.99
77269 0	THE FAMILY TREE	*Carole Cadwalladr*	£7.99
77358 1	THE PRINCE OF TIDES	*Pat Conroy*	£7.99
99767 6	SISTER OF MY HEART	*Chitra Banerjee Divakaruni*	£6.99
99954 7	SWIFT AS DESIRE	*Laura Esquivel*	£6.99
77182 1	THE TIGER BY THE RIVER	*Ravi Shankar Etteth*	£6.99
77285 2	RAKING THE ASHES	*Anne Fine*	£6.99
99890 7	DISOBEDIENCE	*Jane Hamilton*	£6.99
77179 1	JIGS & REELS	*Joanne Harris*	£6.99
77312 3	UNTIL I FIND YOU	*John Irving*	£8.99
77154 6	SWIMMING UNDERWATER	*Sheena Joughin*	£6.99
77139 2	THE GOOD NEIGHBOUR	*William Kowalski*	£6.99
77104 X	BY BREAD ALONE	*Sarah-Kate Lynch*	£6.99
77190 2	A GIRL COULD STAND UP	*Leslie Marshall*	£6.99
77284 4	THE ALMOND	*Nedjma*	£6.99
77181 3	BETWEEN TWO RIVERS	*Nicholas Rinaldi*	£6.99
77145 7	GHOST HEART	*Cecilia Samartin*	£6.99
77287 9	PORTOFINO	*Frank Schaeffer*	£6.99
77167 8	THE APOTHECARY'S DAUGHTER	*Patricia Schonstein*	£6.99
99960 1	WHAT THE BODY REMEMBERS	*Shauna Singh-Baldwin*	£7.99
77250 X	Q & A	*Vikas Swarup*	£6.99
77187 2	LIFE ISN'T ALL HA HA HEE HEE	*Meera Syal*	£6.99
77309 3	A SAUCERFUL OF SECRETS	*Jane Yardley*	£6.99